# Hero for the Holidays

For more books by Maisey Yates,
visit maiseyyates.com.

# MAISEY YATES

## Hero for the Holidays

CANARY STREET PRESS

CANARY
STREET
PRESS™

Recycling programs
for this product may
not exist in your area.

ISBN-13: 978-1-335-00629-5

Hero for the Holidays

Canary Street Press
22 Adelaide St. West, 41st Floor
Toronto, Ontario M5H 4E3, Canada
CanaryStPress.com

**Printed in U.S.A.**

To all the readers who have been patiently waiting
for this story—Fia and Landry's happy ending
is your present from me this year.

# CHAPTER ONE

LANDRY KING DIDN'T believe in love at first sight. Hell, for years he hadn't believed in love at all. But when he looked down at the girl sitting in the blue plastic chair, picking black fingernail polish off her thumbnail, swinging her black boot-clad feet back and forth in rhythm, and determinedly not looking up at him, he felt his world shift.

And he understood.

Broken hearts, audacious hope and the concept of being turned inside out by a feeling.

"Lila?" He'd said her name quite a lot over the past few weeks. Getting used to it. Praying it. It still felt new now.

Their surroundings were entirely bland. Government offices tended to be. He couldn't quite believe this was happening, and it seemed like far too commonplace of a setting for this moment to be taking place. But he supposed this was commonplace enough.

Kids getting shuffled through a system. Moving through different homes.

It was the details of this particular situation that made it extraordinary.

It was the fact that, for the first time, he was looking at his daughter.

That made it extraordinary.

"I'm Landry King," he said when she didn't say anything.

She looked up at him. And the fiery expression on her face stopped him cold.

She was the most miraculous, incredible thing he'd ever seen.

"I know who you are. All the information was in that packet."

"Well, I hope you like what you saw."

"I don't know about that. It looks like you live in the ass crack of nowhere."

"That is true," he said, thinking of Four Corners Ranch. "It is basically that."

"I'm not going call you *dad*. I had a dad."

He felt like he'd been stabbed through the heart, clean. It wasn't the first time, though. So there was that.

"You don't have to," he said. "Though, the truth is, biologically I am your dad." He'd even done a test to make absolutely sure they'd found the right kid. Because it hadn't seemed real. It hadn't seemed possible.

"Yeah. But I had a dad who *chose* me. He didn't give me away. And didn't choose to die."

"I know that," said Landry, his voice rough. "For what it's worth, I know this doesn't take away from who your dad was to you. Or that your parents chose you, and loved you. That they were your mom and dad. But, I didn't *choose* to give you up."

She frowned. "You didn't?"

"No. It was out of my hands." He shoved aside his anger. He shoved aside the painful memories. Lila didn't need to have his stuff projected onto her. She'd been through enough.

He'd done his swearing and yelling these past few

weeks. The past had been an open wound for a long time. And this had made it bleed. But this little girl had been through enough and she didn't need a father mired in his own pain, his own anger.

She needed someone to take care of her.

She needed someone to love her.

And thank God they'd found him.

He'd sent his information over to the adoption agency several years ago, when he'd finally tracked the agency down. He'd had his information placed in the file so that someday, if his daughter ever wanted to contact him, she could. It was a closed adoption, and that meant that he was just going to have to wait for the day she reached out. If it ever came.

But some kids liked that information. They wanted to have the option. And so he made sure that it would be available to her.

What he hadn't expected was the phone call he'd gotten six weeks earlier.

That Lila's parents had been killed in a car accident eleven months ago. That she'd been in care ever since, because there was no family on either side. And that eventually someone had discovered that she had been adopted at birth, and had thought to look through information with the agency. That was where they'd found his name, along with his stated desire to be put in contact with his child if she ever wanted to find him.

It was irregular, they'd said. A miracle.

But if he could pass a home inspection, and a background check and other things required for fostering to adopt, he was first in line.

He hadn't hesitated.

It had been like the sun had come out from behind

the clouds for the first time in almost fourteen years. It had been like a sea change. It really had been a miracle.

A damned miracle wrapped in a shitty tragedy. Right then, he questioned himself a little bit. Because he wasn't just taking on a kid, he was taking on a traumatized one.

But she was his. *She was his*. And now she was finally with him.

And he knew what love at first sight was.

There were a lot of other things he didn't know. Like how to have a functional family, how to be a decent dad. His own dad was a narcissist straight from the depths of hell, his brothers were cagey assholes and he wasn't any better. His sister... Well, thank God Arizona had a fifteen-year-old stepson, so probably had a little bit of wisdom on what to do when you ended up with a kid who was already a teenager. His brother-in-law, Micah, certainly knew a thing or two about being a good dad.

The King family was notoriously isolated in the context of the Four Corners Ranch family. The McClouds and the Garretts had always been thick as thieves, made closer still by marriage. And then, Alaina Sullivan had gone and married Gus McCloud and created an alliance there too.

The Kings didn't have bridges, they had barricades.

"Did you like the pictures of the bedroom? I know it's not decorated. It's plain. Because I wanted to take you out shopping for whatever you wanted. I figured we'd do it while we were here. Because there are more places to shop in Portland than there are back in Pyrite Falls. I'm not going to lie to you, kid. There's pretty much no shopping over there."

"You're really selling it."

"I get it. It's not like you were given a choice. I know what that's like. Being a kid, the adults around you making all these decisions on your behalf."

"Let me stay here, then." She looked up at him, angling her head. "They think they're going to find me a family. But they're not. Jack and Melissa Gates were my parents. You're just some guy. I don't need another family. I had one."

"Here's the deal," he said, fighting against a host of emotions he didn't quite know how to sort through. He wasn't idiot enough to think that a thirteen-year-old was going to fall to her knees and thank him for showing up to adopt her. He knew too much about thirteen-year-olds. He remembered being one too keenly. But hell, maybe part of him thought that she would see it for what it was. A damned *miracle* that her biological father at least was able to reunite with her when she needed him.

Hell, it wasn't even a reunion. This was his first time ever laying eyes on her.

He felt the connection. Like his heart had been ripped right through the front of his chest and was now…sitting right in front of him in a blue plastic chair. She didn't feel anything. And that hurt a little more than he thought it would.

"Okay. You never have to think of me as family, then. But the thing is, I think of you as mine. I've been wanting to find you," he said. "I didn't want to disrupt your life, but the truth is, the way that they got in touch with me was that I contacted the adoption agency to give them my info. So that someday if you wanted to you could look me up."

She tilted her chin up, looking stubborn as hell. "I never would have."

"Good. I guess I'm glad of that. Because that means at least that you've been happy all this time." He sighed and took his cowboy hat off. "This is where you were going to be raised. If I'd had my way. Four Corners Ranch. It's a good place. Full of good people."

"Like you said. I don't really have a choice. They keep moving me around. From house to house. I can run away. I could live on the street. But what good would that do? I'm not really looking to go down the meth track. I don't have anywhere to go, and I don't have anyone in this world who loves me."

*I do.*

He wanted to say it. But he had a feeling she wouldn't be able to believe it now.

"You have someone who wants to take care of you. Very, very badly. And I'll buy you whatever you want for your room. It's your room. You can do whatever the hell you want with it. I will buy you fuchsia paint. And I will paint the walls my damn self."

He'd refreshed a cabin on the property to be ready for them to move in. In six weeks, he had done a hell of a job. There was still more work to be done, but he knew he could no longer live in the main house. The rub was, he hadn't really explained what was going on to his family. In fact, he'd just kind of done it. There would be some explaining to do when he got back. This was a chapter of his life that he never talked to anybody about.

Hell, only one other person on the planet knew about Lila.

"You're trying to bribe me with *stuff*? Really?"

"Yeah," he said. "I don't really have anything else."

"It's better than nothing I guess."

He really felt for the kid. She had nothing but a host of bad options, from her perspective. She could keep getting bounced around foster homes for the next five years. She could run away, like she'd said. He wasn't Jack and Melissa. He wasn't going to be.

But he wasn't the system either.

"On the ranch you're going to have tons of room to run around. I've got horses and—"

"Horses?"

"Yeah." He thought he might've found a little bit of an in there. "Lots of horses. You can have one. Just for you."

"Do you have Wi-Fi?"

"Hell yeah. We aren't animals." He figured he should probably watch his language a little bit around a kid. "Sorry."

"So what happens after this?"

"Well, they tell me they're going to send a caseworker out to check on you in two weeks. I've already passed all kinds of checks. I'm approved like any of the foster families you stayed with before. My house is approved. And if you hate it, you can tell them that. And maybe they'll take you away. But I hope you won't."

"I guess I just don't understand what you're doing." She frowned. "Why you showed up. Why you... You're really young."

"Yeah," he said. "Lila, I was seventeen when you were born."

She looked shocked by that. "You were?"

"Yeah. We were too young. Okay? It wasn't... It wasn't that I didn't want you. It was never that. The choice got taken away from me. But… I'm your father. And it doesn't matter whether you think of me that way or not, I think of you as my daughter. I have this whole time. So whether or not you ever feel it, I do. I do."

Her social worker had given them some space to meet alone, but right after that, the woman, Angela Carter, came into the room. "What do you think, Lila?"

"I don't have a choice, do I?"

"Not entirely. But Mr. King passes muster for me, if that helps. If he didn't, you wouldn't be leaving this office."

"I guess it doesn't really matter," she said. "Because wherever I go my parents are dead."

"That's true," said Landry. "But you know, I have brothers. And a sister. So you will have uncles and an aunt. And a cousin."

"A cousin?" she asked.

"Yeah. My sister, Arizona, has a stepson. He's just a little older than you. And she's expecting a baby, actually. So more cousins."

And he'd found it. He knew. Something that got underneath that armor she was wearing. Family. She might not be able to see him as her dad. But he had more family than just himself. He had quite a lot of family, in fact.

"I didn't have any uncles or aunts."

He'd known that. Because no one who was part of her adoptive family had taken her, so he'd assumed there was an estrangement, or no one. In that sense, he was offering her something totally new. Horses and aunts and uncles.

"I got a vacation rental in the city tonight," he said. "You'll have your own room. I figure we can go shopping for some stuff and get some dinner. And then we'll head back to Four Corners."

She didn't say anything. She didn't even nod. But Angela Carter handed him a case file. "We'll see you in two weeks, Mr. King. I hope everything goes well. She's a good kid."

"I already know that."

They went from there to the mall, where he had a feeling that he'd had been soundly taken advantage of. Because he bought that little girl every single thing she asked for.

He hadn't known what to expect, but apparently stuffed animals that looked like their skeletons were showing were big with the teenage girl set.

He bought countless bottles of nail polish shaped like skulls, a bed set that was black with mushrooms and frogs. He learned what boba tea was, and they both had some with cotton candy on the top. He was deeply suspicious of the entire thing.

They amassed shopping bag after shopping bag. A giant fuzzy beanbag that looked like someone had skinned a Muppet and repurposed it, string lights, and the pièce de résistance was that he had been roped into buying the kid a *gecko*, which included a terrarium, heat lights, a spray bottle for moisture, and crickets. A box full of crickets.

So when he drove back to Four Corners the next day, he had about twenty bags full of merchandise in the back of his truck, and had a lizard in the back seat. And a kid in the front.

Well, one thing was for certain. His family was sure as hell going to be surprised.

He and Lila took the drive in relative silence. He let

her have the aux cable and choose the music, which made her less full of hate and gave him a headache, but he felt like he was trying at least.

It wasn't the nice getting-to-know-you ride he'd wanted. But he wasn't sure if he knew how to get to know another person. It was a hell of a bad time to realize that.

But thankfully, they made it back quickly enough, and when they turned onto the long dirt road that would take them to King's Crest, the King family ranch, Lila straightened a little, looked out the window.

"This is it," he said.

The King house was full as usual.

Landry could fully admit that they were an unconventional family. He'd heard of something once called a trauma bond, and he thought that maybe they might all have it. Their mom had left when they were young—because their father had been difficult at best, and a gaslighting narcissist on days ending in *y*.

He had been cold and distant. And cruel. Unless he was love-bombing them and making them question their sanity. Good times.

When his sister, Arizona, had gotten in a terrible car accident, their dad had blamed her. He'd shamed her. Made her feel worthless. He'd seen her pain as weakness, and he'd exploited it.

But the thing about their dad was that he had four sons. And there was a point where Denver had had enough.

His oldest brother was a mean son of a bitch when he had to be. But he was straight up. He didn't go in for any of the manipulation tactics of the senior King, and Landry had always strived to emulate Denver.

He felt like Daughtry and Justice did the same. They worked the land together. Hell, until recently they'd all still shared a house. But Landry would be moving into his own place now.

Even with all that, he didn't feel like they were especially close. They worked alongside each other; they were that kind of close. They had common goals. But they didn't share things about their lives.

But Denver always seemed to be trying to outrun their father's legacy. And when it came to doing good, his brother did his best.

He had a hard time softening. A hard time showing any kind of caring, but the doing was there.

Justice seemed connected largely to his friend Rue, who put up with him in spite of the fact that he was... Well. One of *them*.

And Daughtry was impenetrable. He kept his cards close to his vest, and always seemed prepared to burn the whole hand if anyone got too close. And again, Landry knew he wasn't any better. He was the one showing up to dinner with a secret kid.

Nothing like family secrets.

But then, they all had their secrets, he supposed. Denver had done his part to bring the family together, and they all got along great. The way they'd been raised had made it hard for them to talk to each other. To talk to anyone, really.

Their dad had liked to foster rivalry between the boys to make them tougher. Which mainly meant telling Denver and Daughtry they were his right-hand men, while making Landry and Justice feel like they didn't measure up.

Landry hadn't even understood the extent of the

damage his dad had done in the community until the
man ~~had gotten~~ arrested and sent to prison for his in-
volvement in a debt collection gone wrong that had
ended in the death of one of his employees.

That was when Denver and Daughtry had gotten
wise to it.

Justice had never seemed surprised. But he'd never
said much about it.

Denver's response to it all had been to take control
of King's Crest and aggressively turn it around. Daughtry's had been joining the police force in an effort to
make things right in the broader community. Arizona,
who was one year older than Landry was, had hated
their dad already and she hadn't made any bones about
it. She'd coped with it by getting meaner.

Landry had been young still, and nursing a broken heart. Maybe part of why he'd decided to improve
things here on the ranch had been to prove that he
could. That he was good.

But then, they all shared that complex.

The truth was, this place was founded on pain and
dishonesty.

"So, the whole ranch is run by four families," he
said, as they turned onto the long road that carried
them off the main highway. "Technically, it's four in-
dividual ranches, but we share profits and finances,
vote on new initiatives and have big meetings once a
month to make sure everyone—down to the newest
ranch hand—feels involved. We have a teacher, kids
go to school here in the one-room schoolhouse. There's
a…a farm store on the property with fresh produce and
baked goods people can buy. King's Crest is our piece.
We have cattle."

"Meat is murder," Lila said.

"I watched you eat a bacon cheeseburger yesterday."

She shrugged. "It's tasty murder."

He was maybe in over his head.

"Right. Okay. So my brothers and sister live here on this chunk of land. I already told you about all of them. We're renovating this barn up here, turning it into an event space. We have a lot of buildings on the property. My great-great-great-grandfather used to run a saloon on the property. Lot of gambling and…" He realized he couldn't finish that sentence.

If one thing was true about his family, it was that lawlessness ran in their blood.

He was trying to be the change he wanted to see. Or something.

"All right, kid. You have two choices. Our place, which is just up the dirt road apiece, or we go straight in to meet the whole clan. How do you want to do this?"

"You're leaving it up to me?" she asked.

"Yeah. If you're not ready to meet everyone, then we won't."

"Where do they think you've been the last few days?"

"Just taking care of some business. We don't really police each other."

"But you all live on the same ranch."

"It's complicated. Listen. I never said that I was getting you a *perfect* family. Just a family."

She looked at him. "I don't really look like you."

His stomach tightened. "No, you don't."

"Do I look like any of them?"

"Not especially."

"Oh. You know I never really cared about being adopted. So I never dreamed about meeting my biological family. But you'd think there'd be something cool about it, like that we'd look alike."

Damn. That was complicated. He looked in her eyes and he could see that it was for her too. That there were questions she didn't want to ask, and ones he didn't know how to answer. His throat worked.

He gritted his teeth. "Sorry."

"I want to meet everyone. Let's just do it. This is heinous. But my life has been like a fever dream for the last year. I'm kind of over it. If it sucks, we can dip."

"Do all kids your age talk like this?"

"I'm on the internet."

"Okay," he said. She said that like it explained something. He wasn't entirely sure that he understood what.

He killed the engine on the truck, and they got out. He stood in front of the farmhouse, which he had called home for the last thirty years. And he looked at it with new eyes. Because this was the first time Lila was seeing it.

"This is…home base. For the King family. For whatever it's worth."

"It's…something," she said.

It was two stories, with a wide porch. A big enough house to accommodate everybody. If there was one thing their dad had been big on, it had been public appearance. That was all part and parcel to his narcissism. He'd also been an unscrupulous business partner to the other families on the ranch, and had taken advantage of many people in town. Their reputation was basically shit. They'd done their best to redeem it. But people's memories were long. Especially in small towns.

Also, he and his brothers were still half-feral. They

might mean well, but they just hadn't had a great example of how to manage…anything.

"Come on," he said. "Let's go. They'll all be having dinner. I bet steak."

"Great. I can't wait to eat a baby cow."

"I didn't say it was veal, Lila."

She rolled her eyes. That felt like a triumph. Teenagers were supposed to roll their eyes at their dads. Maybe that meant he was doing a good job.

They walked up the front steps, his feet heavy, hers much lighter, even in those clodhopper boots of hers. And he pushed open the front door. "Hey," he shouted. "I'm back."

He could smell garlic bread baking, and his stomach growled. Rue must be in residence. His brother Justice's best friend. Denver was great at grilling, and he could throw together a mean potato or macaroni salad, but he was not a baker. Rue, on the other hand, was organized, neat and an excellent baker. Landry had no idea what she saw in Justice. But they were attached at the hip, now and ever.

"Smells good," he called.

Rue stuck her head out from the kitchen. "Landry," she said. "Welcome back." Her eyes landed on Lila. "Oh. Who's…"

Just then the back door swung open and slammed shut. And he heard heavy footsteps and men's voices. And then through the doorway came Denver and Daughtry. Each man was holding a plate of steaks, and they stopped when they saw him in the entry. "Hey," said Denver.

The footsteps on the stairs meant that Justice was headed in too. He was only going to say this once. Jus-

tice stopped on the landing. And then he heard footsteps behind him. The whole gang was just about here.
Right on time.

He got out of the doorway and turned just in time
for Arizona, Micah and Daniel to come in.

"Great," said Landry. "I'm only going to say this
once. This is Lila," he said, gesturing to the girl at his
side. "She's my daughter."

That earned him a rousing round of loud questions
and swearing. "Hey," he said. "There's a fucking kid
here, watch your language."

Lila, for her part, looked torn between amusement
and horror. He could imagine that meeting a whole
room full of strangers wasn't really ideal when you
were thirteen. But he also knew that she had met a lot
of strangers over the last year.

"Like, she's your *actual* daughter," said Denver.

"Yes," he said.

"How long have you known about her?" Denver
asked.

"Let's see," said Landry, pretending to do math.
"Thirteen years."

*"Thirteen years,"* Justice exploded from his place
on the stairs. "And you've never mentioned it. Never
once."

"Nope."

Now Lila just looked entertained. He could imagine it was kind of enjoyable to be the bomb that got
thrown into someone else's life when you had nothing
but bombs thrown at you.

"Why now? Why is she here now?"

"I'm adopting her."

"If I let you," said Lila.

He turned to her. "Okay. Yeah. If she lets me."

"You said she was your daughter. What do you mean you're adopting her?" Justice asked.

"Well," said Landry. "I don't have parental rights. She was adopted when she was born and…and last year her parents died." He shot her a quick apologetic glance for saying that so bluntly, but he just wanted to get this part out of the way. "And so now it's me. I'm doing this. For her."

"But only if I decide I don't hate it here," said Lila. She looked around at everybody. "This was fun, though."

Nobody seemed to have any idea what to say to that. Though he knew they'd have questions later. Questions he wasn't intending to answer.

"All right, you all look like idiots standing there staring like that," said Landry. "Let's eat."

# CHAPTER TWO

Fɪᴀ Sᴜʟʟɪᴠᴀɴ ꜰᴇʟᴛ like life was finally going her way. Her sisters were all in love and having lives. Which, when you were the responsible one left behind to take care of everybody, was kind of a big deal. She had the weight of the world on her shoulders for years.

From having to take care of the ranch when her parents had bailed, to joining forces with the other families, the youngest one in the group, the only woman in that group, to make decisions about the ranch being a collective. How they were going to support each other, and how they were going to strengthen things. And they'd done it. Then she had to fight for the improvements to Sullivan's Point. For the gardens, the farm store. Everything.

And now it just finally felt like she could finally rest a little bit.

Everything with the store was going wonderfully. Sales were booming and the store was bringing more business to everyone, just like she'd thought it would. They were able to sell meat and produce direct, in addition to continuing with the bigger beef sales the Garretts and Kings made. Other local ranchers, farmers and artisans were benefiting too.

It had become a well-known stop along the highway to Oregon's coast. Thanks to her.

And for once, it was a town hall meeting night and she wasn't going to be the one bringing up a big item of business. It was really kind of awesome. They had town hall meetings once a month, and for the past couple of years, she felt like she'd been at the center of them. Pushing for more money. Pushing to make improvements. But finally everything was moving smoothly at Sullivan's Point, and she didn't need to do that. She smiled as she drove over to the barn area. They always hosted the town hall. They provided a lot of the food. Everybody brought something, but she and her sisters were accomplished bakers, and they provided pies and jams, pastries. Bread.

This was another thing Fia was so proud she'd built. She'd overseen restoring the old Sullivan barn into a meeting space, and now the front was grassy and well tended, with a big weeping willow tree, a firepit and an area for dancing. There were picnic tables and benches, and she knew a lot of the staff on the ranch ate lunch there during the day.

It was a safe space. Comforting and happy. Cheerful.

She'd known she was never going to be able to build a massive cattle empire like the Kings and Garretts, and she hadn't had the interest in horses the McClouds did. It had been bold to follow her own instincts. To follow her heart.

But Sullivan's Point was a labor of love for her. It was everything. She'd known at sixteen this was going to be all on her. Their father had been having an affair, and Fia had found out. She'd been desperate to try and deal with it, to try and keep it secret to hold everything together, even while knowing it would fall apart.

But she'd determined then that Sullivan's Point, her family, her sisters…they'd be hers. Her responsibility. And she'd kept that promise she'd made as a desperate, angry teenager.

She could only be proud. This was her legacy.

She was the only one living in the house these days. Which was strange. She wouldn't let herself think that it was lonely.

It was *normal*.

She was twenty-nine. Being on her own was a completely fine thing. She didn't really envy her sisters; they were living lives she'd known she'd never have. She was just happy for them. But she hadn't thought through the flipside of all this, which was that success as she'd defined it meant…being alone.

She wasn't alone, though. She reminded herself of that as she surveyed the meeting space. She had Four Corners, and everyone in it.

Well. Almost everyone. Some of them could disappear without a trace and she'd be happier for it.

A cheering thought, really. One she used to fuel her actions.

She hummed as she started to get pies and cakes out of the back of her car and position them on the table that was already set up for the meeting. She loved this part. The calm before the storm. Before all the families, the ranch hands and some townspeople descended on Sullivan's Point to have a conversation about the goings-on at the ranch, and then have a big bonfire party. Complete with live music.

The first person to show up was Alaina, along with her adorable, pudgy baby Cameron, and her husband, Gus.

She was really happy for Alaina. That everything

had turned out okay, even with all the drama from her unexpected pregnancy. But she'd found the support she needed. She'd found the man she needed. After Cameron's biological father had left Alaina pregnant and alone, Gus had stepped up and offered to marry her. It had become so much deeper than convenience. They were really, truly in love now.

Rory and Quinn arrived next, with their significant others. And again, Fia really didn't feel isolated. Or rather, she *tried* not to. She didn't want any of that. Didn't need any of that. She had the ranch. It was her life.

Her family.

Well, and so were her sisters. She'd chosen them. She'd chosen to shape her life around theirs. Very definitively.

They got everything set up like it was a well-choreographed dance. It was one of her favorite things. The way that they worked together like a team. Even with them living on their own now, it was like that.

Quinn and Rory still worked on the ranch, so it wasn't like it was entirely different. Alaina mostly focused her efforts at McCloud's Landing, because she was passionate about horses. Plus she had a child to care for. Fia understood that.

By the time the others arrived, and the barn started to fill up, Fia and Rory were having an in-depth conversation about a TV show they were both watching, interspersed with Quinn's commentary on the most popular products of the farm store, while she looked over some spreadsheet on her phone. Which was just very Quinn.

She felt him arrive before she saw him. She always

did. You would think that after all this time he wouldn't impact her the way he did. But it was always like that. Always a prickling on the back of her neck, a jolt at the base of her spine. Always her stomach plummeting down into her pelvic bone.

The bastard Landry King had made an appearance.

"What?" Rory asked. She looked over quickly. "It's Landry, right? I mean…just go bang him, Fia. My God."

It was a frequent refrain. If she had a reaction to Landry, a reaction of any sort, then her sisters would laugh about the sexual tension between them. Joke about the fact that they needed to get it out of their systems. And Fia was great at playing that off at this point. Laughing along. Or scowling if it felt like an angry or more annoyed response would seem like the right thing to do. The truth was, no one actually knew what happened between her and Landry. If they did, they wouldn't joke about it. That was for damn sure. Because it wasn't funny. Not a damn thing about her relationship with Landry King was amusing. Nor was it fodder for whatever *enemies to lovers tee-hee* romantic fantasy her sisters had about them.

They had no idea.

They were all in love, and married. They had functional romances. They had no idea what it was like to have experienced being mired in the most intense, beautiful, sharp, toxic, painful relationship a person could ever imagine. They had no idea.

And she was going to make sure that they stayed completely in the dark.

Because God love them all, they'd escaped this.

They had gone and fallen in love without being tangled in the barbed wire of a broken heart.

"Can't," she said, trying to sound breezy. "I decided I was going to find some bar himbo and bang it out with him this weekend. Landry is going to have to wait."

She opted for light today. Because things were fine. Because she didn't need to look at him and feel a jolt go through her body. Because she definitely never needed to remember what it had been like when he touched her.

Because that kind of memory led to all sorts of other memories, and she had given those up for both lent and sanity.

"Sounds fun. Bring back his panties as a souvenir so that I believe you," said Alaina.

"I don't have anything to prove to you," said Fia.

It was true. She didn't. She had Sullivan's Point. And the successful farm store. It was all the proof she needed. Everything that she had worked so hard for was paying off.

She was finding new ways of making Sullivan profitable all the time. Thanks to Landry King, as it happened. He had been part of the primary opposition to them getting the money to open the store. Sometimes she had wanted to scream at him. Really yell at him. But they didn't do that. She sniped at him. Sometimes she snapped. Lost her temper. But she more or less tried to keep it on lock. For his part...

Sometimes she wished that he would get angry at her. But every time she looked at him, he looked back with a kind of cool indifference. Honestly, it was the thing that made her want to lash out the most. Much more than hating him, it was a tangle. And he seemed completely unflappable in the face of her. In the face of all their memories. In the face of the ghosts from the past.

And right now, not only did he look unflappable, he looked sexy.

That was really the most annoying thing about him. After everything, she still found him hot. He was tall and broad-shouldered, with a jaw so square she could cut herself on that angle point. It was usually covered with rakish, dark stubble. And he had the kind of midnight blue eyes that haunted a woman.

They were a weird thing, blue eyes. Especially on a dark-haired man. There was just something about them. It elevated his looks. It was annoying. And maybe there was something to be said for the fact that he was just her own personal brand of whiskey, or maybe he was universally problematic.

Hard to say.

She preferred to believe the latter, as the former made her feel like she was caught in a net she would never escape. She didn't like that feeling.

So instead, she took her seat in the Sullivan portion of the barn, and did not look as the Kings took their seats in the King quadrant. Even though she knew they had. Because it was all timing. This perfectly choreographed dance of the town hall meeting.

She sneaked a peek, eventually, and frowned. Landry had his phone out of his pocket, and he was... She wasn't mistaken the man was texting. Which was something she had never before seen him do.

Well. Good for him. Maybe he'd joined one of those dating apps. Maybe he'd found one that catered especially to obnoxious, undependable cowboys with big penises.

The thought sent a jolt straight between her thighs.

The truth was, she would join that app. That was the worst part.

She looked away and turned her focus to the front of the room, where Sawyer Garrett, their meeting chair, had taken the stage.

"This should be a pretty quick one," he said. "Only one submitted matter of business. And mostly, I think we're all looking forward to going out and eating. It's a little chilly out, but we got the bonfire going and the heaters fired up. So mostly, tonight it's just going to be a feast."

That brought cheers up from the barn. It was full now. Of the Four Corners families and their employees. All of whom were looking forward to the monthly shindig. It was a well-deserved break. The truth was, there weren't a lot of breaks in ranching.

The days moved on, with the land and animals needing what they needed. They didn't care if it was sunny or rainy, Sunday or Christmas. It moved in a rhythm.

She liked that about it. She got comfort from it.

She got *tired* from it sometimes, but mostly, it was comfort.

And once a month they did this. They gathered together, they ate, they socialized. They played poker. And she did her best not to tangle with Landry.

Once a month. She went through all this once a month.

Sometimes she wondered why she'd committed herself to living here. To dealing with this baptism in her own personal hell. But there was no other option. She refused to be run off her land by a man.

*Fuck those men.*

She refused to have her life turned upside down, a life that she had fought so hard for, just because of them.

Of him.

She was proud of all she'd achieved. And so, she dealt with seeing him. So, she dealt with all this.

"The lone order of business is coming to us from Landry King."

Her shoulders went stiff, a bolt of lightning streaking up her spine.

She held herself steady. She tried not to react.

"Come on up, Landry."

"The first part of this is a petition for an increase in the budget," he said.

And she swore that just for a second, his eyes flicked to her. Rested there. And she was transported back to another meeting nearly a year ago, when he had outright refused to increase the funding for the Sullivans' project. The budget was the budget, he'd said.

And she hadn't managed to keep her cool. No. In that instance, she let the anger she felt for him in the present—and all the burning anger she experienced when she thought of their past—take her over.

*Look who's a fucking accountant.*

She remembered. Because she always remembered when she messed up with him. Always remembered when things got too real. Too intense.

Always.

"I'm sorry," she said, lifting her hand, but only as a formality. "I'm unclear as to how you think that we can redistribute the budget when the budget has already been made for the year."

"I thought you might have a problem with it, Fia," he said. "But believe me when I tell you this is part of a plan that's going to benefit everybody."

"I benefited," she said. "Thanks."

"I took a class," he said. "It was about finding your niche in ranching. And that's the second part of this. I want everyone to be thinking about that."

"I believe that's what my farm store is, Landry. My niche. *Thank you*." She sounded so sugary she wanted to die. But she had to go sugary or she'd get salty real fast.

"It's true," he said. "Sullivan's Point is probably the most advanced when it comes to this. But then, you've had to be."

He made what she considered a triumph sound a lot like an insult, and she marveled at his ability to do that. And to fill her up with hate all the while looking so handsome.

"Is that so?"

"Yes. And that's the kind of thing I want to do with King's Crest. I'm asking for an increase in the budget to renovate the main barn. I want it to serve as a meeting space, and an event space. Eventually, I'd like to do what they did at McCloud's. Put in small cabins, but instead of using it as therapy space, I'd like to use them as guest rooms. We'll be able to host destination weddings, small conferences and the like. It would likely increase business to Sullivan's. Because you could hopefully provide some food. Which I know you're all very good at."

She was beginning to get angrier and angrier. Partly because it wasn't a stupid idea.

But their ranch was already *so* profitable. The Garretts and the Kings had a monopoly on beef in Oregon. They were massive operations. And the two of them together being able to share profits made them unstoppable.

What Landry was proposing now would undoubtedly line the pockets of the Kings even more. But it would benefit all of them.

"Why?" she asked. "I mean, what triggered this?" She tried to regroup. "It's only that we laid our plans out at the beginning of the year and yes, I know that I didn't adhere to that entirely last year, but that was about unexpected expenses related to a project we'd already approved. You're talking about new endeavors and I want to know why now, and not at the new fiscal year?"

Something flickered over his face she couldn't read. Like she'd caught him in a lie. But she wouldn't betray that. That she could read him like that. That she knew him like that.

"Because ranching is a tough business," he said. "It's a tough life. And the whole point of our banding together was to be able to cover the weak spots. The downtimes. Adding more irons to the fire is going to help us do that."

"Thank you for explaining our jobs to us," she said, crossing her arms and staring up at him.

She wasn't just being bitchy. It was November. They would be doing their big Christmas party soon, and they had a budget for that and it was *busy*. His timing was bad. And weird. And stupid.

He ignored her. "I read about a guy who has a giant spread out in Texas. Not only do they have guesthouses and event centers, but they have their own beer. They have a line of jewelry. They have all kinds of stuff associated with the ranch. Think about the kind of brand we have in Four Corners. Think about what we could do if we all banded together. And I mean all of us. Not just the families, but everybody who puts work into this place. Think about what we could do."

Damn him. Damn him for being inspiring.

"The truth is, I've already started work on the barn."

"Without clearing it with us?"

"It's my barn, Fia."

"But the money is going to come out of our general pot."

"I started it with my own," he said. "But if you want to share in the profits, I expect an upfront investment. If they can't come out of the official branch budget... Well, you can all chip in. Invest."

"No one's going to invest," said Fia.

"Hell," said Wolf Garrett. "I will."

She should've known that Wolf Garrett would be an annoying wild card. He seemed to want to invest just to bother her.

"Hell, me too," said Sawyer.

And that wasn't why Sawyer was investing. He was practical, and he'd been one of the founding members of the collective. He would only do it because he believed in it. Which made her want to savage him.

Reflexively, she turned to look at the McClouds. She was burning daggers into the side of her brother-in-law's head.

Gus, for his part, said nothing.

"I'll chip in," said Hunter McCloud.

Tag, Brody and Lachlan all raised their hands in agreement as well, and so did many of the farmhands.

Wisely, Gus kept his mouth shut and his hands in his lap. As did all the Sullivans.

"We're not going to just take you at your word," said Fia. "I need a business plan."

"Really? Did I ask to see a business plan?"

"You kind of did, Landry," she said.

"Well. It looks like I have backing either way. Thank you, everyone. That'll be enough to get us kicked off. More information to come. Now everybody can go eat."

She was fuming. Burning with outrage. The man was a scourge. He was a pain in the ass.

It was just that it wasn't fair, not that it wasn't a good idea. It was that it was such a double standard. The Kings had been obstructionist to her expansion efforts, and now they wanted her to get on board with theirs? Maybe not supporting the expansion when it did seem like a pretty good idea was petty. But God in heaven, wasn't she owed a little bit of petty when it came to Landry King?

*You aren't going to stop him.*

No. And she would potentially be done out of the profits when it was successful and made money.

Dammit.

She was still fuming by the time she went outside and linked up with everybody else. And she got outside just in time to see Landry get in his truck.

And pull away.

"Where's he going?"

She realized that she'd broken her cardinal rule of never acting like she gave a shit what he was doing.

"I dunno," said Alaina. "Maybe he also found a himbo down at the bar."

"I don't hate that," said Rory, smiling slightly.

"Go find your man," said Fia. "Both of you. I'm going to have a drink."

"Fia," said Alaina. "Sisters don't let their sisters drink in response to Landry. You'll only end up wasted and sad."

"This is not fair. Because he was so awful about me wanting to open the farm store."

"He was. And you'll notice that none of us jumped in to offer money. None of us. And we all have our own places. Levi could easily invest, and so could Gideon. Gus obviously could, but he didn't put in, because we are all supporting you. Right?"

"And I appreciate it," said Fia. "But you do think I'm being petty."

"Yes," said Quinn. "I do think you're being petty. What he's proposing is a good idea, and there's absolutely no reason in all the world to oppose it. Except for being petty. But, you also know that I am pro doing your due diligence on things like this. I think you're right. I think you should demand a business plan from him. Go by tomorrow and see what exactly he's up to."

"Well, that isn't a terrible idea," she said.

Except that she never darkened the property line of King's Crest. Not ever. It was like it was going to kill her.

Maybe.

"Great," said Rory. "The problem is solved."

"I'm not sure that I could call the problem solved exactly. Because Landry is still here."

"Honestly," said Rory.

And Fia pretended to smile indulgently. While inside she felt acrid.

Because the truth was, she had to coexist with Landry whether she wanted to or not. Their shared past hadn't meant anything for a while now, and it couldn't going forward.

So yeah. She would tell herself she was just being cautious about investing any money right now. And she would go by and look at his plans. Tomorrow.

And tonight, she would forget about him. And have a good time.

HE HAD BEEN uncomfortable leaving Lila back at home, but he hadn't thought that it was a good idea to bring her tonight.

There would be a time and a place. But there were things he needed to talk to Lila about first, and he was still waiting for her to get through this period of adjustment before bringing up anything else.

They'd made it through the first visit from the social worker. Lila hadn't begged to leave. So there was that. He was always trying to find the balance. Between letting her talk about her parents or her grief, between trying to explain his own grief over her birth and letting her live this new life. She'd put a moratorium on the past one night when things had gotten too hard.

He'd been okay with that. It gave him a reprieve. They'd agreed that when she was ready to hear more, he'd tell her whatever she wanted to know.

It was a tightrope walk. Because he couldn't dump his trauma and pain onto her. He'd had enough. He was her father, not her confidant. But there were also things he needed her to know. None of it was simple.

But for now, he was going with…peaceful.

He'd been texting her the whole time he was at the barn, and he had raced right back to the house.

The truth was, this initiative meant more to him than anything ever had, because it was part of his figuring out *how to be a good dad* plan.

Lila was going to need…so much. He wanted to be able to buy her clothes, to give her all the things that she needed and wanted. He wanted to be able to buy her first car, and send her to college.

He wanted to be successful so that he could *give* her something. He wanted there to be jobs at the ranch that she could take if she wanted, and money to take with her if she didn't.

The unbearable weight of responsibility, of caring for another human being was really…something.

But it was what he wanted to do.

So it meant he had to go after this with single-mindedness. It was like all the energy that had been stored up inside him all this time, all this need to be a father, was rushing through him now like a storm.

He wanted to get it right. And some days he didn't know what that looked like. Emotions were hard. He'd certainly never seen them displayed in a healthy way. He knew how people hurt and manipulated the ones they professed to love.

He didn't actually know how love was meant to look.

But he knew hard work. So he was starting there. With work. With endless stuffed animals, a gecko and a new barn.

"How was your meeting, Landry?" she asked, sitting at the table with a bowl of chicken noodle soup.

She had told him that she didn't need him to make her anything. He'd put a lot of ready-made meals in the place so she could help herself when she needed to or just wanted to. Even though most nights they ate at the main house with the whole King crew.

Right now she was homeschooling. She wasn't going to the one-room schoolhouse on the property. She was doing an online course with the middle school she'd been at before.

It was going all right, from what he could see. But he was a little bit worried about her not being around other kids. Eventually it would change. Eventually.

But she and Daniel had grown to have a pretty good rapport, and he enjoyed seeing that.

She also got along well with his family.

Hell, they got along a little better than he'd anticipated. She was a tough nut, kind of an angry little thing sometimes, but that was fair, considering everything she'd been through. And hell, it was fair considering her genetics. The Kings were kind of a sullen group, all-up.

"It was fine. I got backing for my plans with the barn."

"That's good. It's a good idea, TBH," she said.

He felt like that was pretty damned high praise. Coming from a kid who mostly thought he was an idiot. He didn't know what *TBH* meant, but he'd learned not to ask because it always earned him a look that made him feel old and uncool.

He was *thirty*, for heaven's sake.

"Well, thanks for not running away or anything while I was gone."

"That's the worst part about this place," she said.

"In the city there's actually some places to run to. Out here? I'm just going to get eaten by a bobcat."

"A bobcat's not going to eat you," he said.

"It won't?"

"No. It'll just maul you and chew on your knuckle-bones a little bit. Then a bear will probably come and eat you."

She grimaced. "Thanks for that. Next time the social worker asks me how it's going, I'm going to tell them I have nightmares because you told me that I was going to get eaten by wild animals."

"Good. Make sure you get me in trouble."

She wrinkled her nose.

He looked at her, and his heart felt two sizes too big. He liked it when she made this particular sort of stubborn face, and it reminded him of his sister, Arizona, which probably meant it was a King face.

She definitely continued to take advantage of the fact that all he wanted to do was make her happy. Bribed him into ordering her all kinds of shit online. He doubted anyone had ever seen a delivery truck go up the road this many times in a month.

Hell, probably not in a *year*.

But he basically bought the kid whatever she asked for. Her bedroom was packed to the gills with stuffed animals. He wasn't above buying her affection. He didn't really know how else to do it.

"You should come out and do some work on the barn tomorrow," he said. "You know, all this… If you choose to stay with me, to let me adopt you, it's going to be yours."

She blanched. "What am I going to do with the ranch?"

"At least the money that it generates will be yours. I'm doing what I can to make it better for you."

"Oh." She looked down. "I have money. In a trust. From my parents."

"Good. That's good." He tried to feel supported by that, and not undermined.

"It's not a lot or anything. They weren't rich."

"Neither mine. But I'm going to leave you something. I promise you that."

"Don't talk about that," she said, suddenly looking upset.

"What?"

"What you're going to leave me. It's just… I already have an inheritance. And no parents."

He felt like he'd been poleaxed. The kid was letting him know, even if not emphatically, that she didn't want to lose him. His throat went tight. He thought of all the things he had left to say to her. But he just didn't want to disrupt this. This little pocket of happiness that they'd found. Because there would be time for deeper conversations later. He was going to have to hurt her again. He didn't want that.

So he was just going to enjoy this. *For now*, he was just going to enjoy this. He wanted to tell her that he loved her. It was the strangest thing. He couldn't recall ever saying those words in his life. He was sure he had. To his mother, probably. Sometime before she left.

He never said them to his father. He never said them to his brothers, or even to his sister, which made him feel bad a little bit.

But he wanted to say it to Lila. He was also just terrified of breaking this thing they were building.

And he just needed time. Time healed wounds, and

he supposed time was maybe the only thing that built a strong foundation. So he was just going to keep giving it time until he was sure it wasn't going to crumble.

## *CHAPTER THREE*

FIA WAS UP EARLY, and ready to go take on Landry.

*Fucking Landry.*

She told herself that it was not vanity that had her paying a little more attention to her red curls this morning, or putting on some emerald green eye shadow that she knew highlighted the intensity of her eyes. She also told herself that red lipstick in the morning on a ranch was perfectly appropriate.

She tried never to think about the time that she first wore red lipstick, and where she had left it behind on his body.

She gritted her teeth.

No. She didn't need to go there. She didn't know why it was such a struggle sometimes. Why it was so difficult to let all that go.

She felt tangled up in it more than usual right now, and she couldn't explain that. But maybe it was because it had been years since she'd gone to King's Crest. And not by accident.

And *maybe* she wore kind of a short dress over her woolen tights, which was going to make her feel a little bit cold, but she also knew she looked cute.

So whatever.

She drove out to the ranch, and she did feel just a tiny bit bad as she headed toward King territory.

It was funny, to have lived on this ranch her entire life and have deleted this whole portion of the collective from her mind.

She couldn't remember the last time she'd driven up this road, and yet she knew it by heart.

It looked familiar and foreign all at once.

The way that her heart shimmered in her chest was the same.

Like she was fifteen and about to see him, that giddy new love spreading through her, like the first bite of cotton candy. Sweet, fluffy and clinging to her tongue.

But it vanished.

Oh, how she knew that.

But her heart could still feel that same old joy, that same old anticipation. That same old need. It was like loving Landry King had worn grooves into it, so deep and so entrenched she'd have to cut her whole heart out to get rid of them.

And she wouldn't do that. Not for him.

Because she still loved too many other things in her life. Because she still had so many things worth caring for, and Landry King didn't deserve her whole heart. Even if she couldn't do much of anything about the grooves.

So she just had to accept that rolling up on King's Crest would always present as a new wound. Fresh and sharp as it had always been. With little that could be done about it. It was the cost of being human, she supposed.

She drove past the farmhouse. She had never spent much time there. It wasn't like they had openly been in a relationship back then.

Theirs had been secret. A method they'd used to escape their untenable situations. A wild, untamed need that had been theirs, only theirs. They hadn't been helpless teenagers dealing with family drama, they hadn't been two kids living in the middle of nowhere. When they'd been together they'd been king and queen of their own kingdom.

They'd held all this bright, wonderful feeling between them, and they'd found pleasure. Real, adult pleasure, and they'd wielded those dangerous things between themselves, and in the end they'd gotten hurt.

They hadn't known what to do with all that emotion. It had been jealous. And mean. She'd wanted him all to herself. If he talked to another girl, she went feral. He'd once put a dent in the side of his truck with his fist, because she'd been talking to another guy. They'd been mutually, ridiculously horrible.

She had been so obsessed with him. It was all she could think about. She had dreams for a while. Of what she wanted to be when she grew up. And they rotated. She had wanted to do all kinds of things. And then for a while there, she had wanted Landry. And that was it. She dreamed about kissing him. Touching him. When she lost her virginity to him, she'd been more than ready. If she had one secret that she quite enjoyed, it was that Landry King might've taken her virginity, but she'd taken his too.

She supposed in the end of all things she could claim that as a little bit of a perverse victory.

Then her heart sank because the problem was, there was simply no victory to be had in that complicated landscape of her and Landry.

Well. There was going to be one today. She wasn't

going to oppose him for the sake of it, but she was going to make things a little bit difficult for him. And frankly, he deserved it. He'd done more than make things difficult for her when she was trying to expand Sullivan's, after all.

She saw the old barn, and some sawhorses set up outside, power tools and the like.

So he must be at work today. Already.

Well. That was fine. She cleared her throat and tossed her hair, pulling the car up to the front and turning off the engine. She got out and surveyed the place.

And Landry strolled out of the barn. Black hat on his head, tight black T-shirt molded to his muscular body. She knew that body. Except, she also didn't. He had been a kid the last time she'd seen him naked, just as she'd been one. He was a man now. And she might've watched him grow and change every day since then, but it still hit hard, every time. And the way he looked at her, she had to wonder right then if he'd been hit hard too.

Normally, Landry didn't have a reaction to her. But right now, he looked like she'd walked up and punched him.

"What are you doing here?"

"I came to check out your new venture," she said.

"Why?"

"Because. It seemed like the thing to do. I mean, after all, my issue was that I wasn't going to decide to invest on the spur of the moment without actually having a look at the place."

"Was it? Or was it actually that you had some kind of prejudice against me."

"I just wanted to—"

"Listen. I'm busy."

He was acting cagey, standing there with his arms crossed, looking worried.

"You have a woman back there or something?"

She would really rather never think about Landry and his women. Though, she was certain that he must have them.

Still, she couldn't come up with a reason that he was acting this way now if not for that.

"There's no woman."

She narrowed her eyes. "Then why are you being strange?"

"I'm not being strange. Maybe it just seems strange to you, because you crashed the middle of my workday to check up on me."

"I'm not checking up on you. I don't care what you do. But I do care whether or not this is a smart business venture. I don't want to be done out of it because I didn't do my due diligence."

"You were given a chance to invest the same as everybody else. If you're done out of it, it's going to be because of your own stubbornness, Fia. And it wouldn't be the first time."

That was so dangerously close. Dancing so perilously close to the edge of that knife that they pretended hadn't damn near gutted them both.

"Yeah. Whatever. I think you may have issues with how far this is from the main road."

He snorted. "Oh. Little Miss We Just Made a New Road can't figure out how I'll handle my problems?"

"You would have to make a new road through your own pasture. Are you going to do that?"

"Come back later. When I have some time to show you what I'm thinking. I have an appointment soon."

"I may not have time to come back later."

And then, she heard footsteps running toward the barn. A child ran in. Well, not a child, per se. But a young girl. A teenager. With curly red hair and sharp green eyes that Fia had never seen anywhere but on her sisters.

Or in a mirror.

"Hey, Landry," the kid said. "Did you know there's a calf out by the—"

The kid stopped talking and looked at them both. But it was the expression on Landry's face that made something catch low in Fia's stomach and hook tight.

Then she looked back at the child.

She had Fia's coloring. That much was obvious. And the same oval-shaped face. But there was something else, and it was *something else* that actually made her the most unnerved. It was the way she was also quite perfectly a small, female Landry King. The way her shoulders were set, the arrogant jut of her chin.

This combination of her and Landry right in front of her was the most undeniable, terrifying thing she had ever seen in her life.

A come-to-Jesus moment she'd been certain she would never have.

Every word, every thought, everything, evaporated within her, leaving behind nothing. Nothing but this hot insistent feeling, a need almost, to run toward that child and pull her into her arms.

The girl, for her part, didn't seem to be reacting to Fia's presence, except she stopped talking because there was a stranger in the barn. A stranger when she had only been expecting Landry, who clearly was *not* a stranger to her.

"Where's the calf, Lila?"

*Lila.*

It was a punch in the gut. *Lila.*

*Lila.*

That was a name she had never spoken out loud. Like a pearl beyond price she hadn't allowed herself to have. And he was saying it. Like it was nothing. And more than that, she knew who he was.

"Lila," she whispered.

"Fia," he said slowly. "I'd like to talk to you a little later."

"The calf is outside," Lila said, frowning. "I didn't think he was supposed to be out of the pasture."

"He's not. We probably have a little bit of a jailbreak. Is Uncle Denver out there?"

"He went somewhere back by the house."

"Can you grab him, and then he'll get the pickup truck and I'll meet him in about ten minutes?"

"Sure," she said, scampering back out of the barn. And Fia felt a strange panicky sensation in her stomach. This awful fear that she would never see the child again. It was like terror. And she found herself moving out of the barn quickly, her heart pounding hard. And then he had grabbed her arm.

"Wait," he said. "Just wait."

*He* looked panicked. And that only made her that much more so.

"Landry, what... What is this?"

"I can explain it. But the thing is, Fia, I haven't talked to her about you yet. She... It's complicated, the time hasn't been right. I don't want her finding out that you live on the ranch like this."

"You were okay with me finding out that she was here like this?"

She knew who this was. Just like he did.

He had brought *their* daughter back to the ranch.

Her *baby*. The one she'd only held for a moment, because she'd needed to protect herself. The one no one else knew about.

No one but her and Landry.

Their child.

The one that she had very deliberately made not theirs. She had given that child a family. Parents. The most wonderful parents.

Why was she here? Here at Four Corners, where she was never supposed to be?

It didn't make any sense.

"I don't understand..."

"I was going to talk to you," he said. "But only after I talked to her."

His words blended in with the buzzing in her ears. She was...dizzy. Overfull with so many feelings and she didn't have the words for any of them. The anger was easy. It was the...the hope, the panic, the joy, that was what she couldn't sort through. The feeling like she was standing in the center of a miracle, one so fragile it was like dandelion fluff. And if she breathed too hard it would fly away on the breeze.

So she didn't explore those feelings. She clung to anger.

With Landry, anger was always safest.

"Why is she here?"

"Fia," he said. "I don't want her to see us having a

fight about this. I can't...not like this. She isn't in the right space."

"So she can know about you but not...about me? You don't want her to know..."

It was like something grabbed hold of him then, something feral and not quite *him*.

"That you gave her away. I don't want her to know that her mother gave her away."

His words sent her reeling backward, like they were a gunshot that hit her right in her heart. "I... I gave birth to her, and I put her directly into her mother's arms. Because it was the right thing to do. Because I couldn't give her what she needed. I didn't *give her away*. I gave her a *life*. And you dragged her back here? For what reason? Why?"

His gaze was frighteningly flat. "Her parents are dead."

She really couldn't breathe then. "They're dead? Jack and Melissa..."

She watched his expression, watched as he tried to sort through what she was saying. "You know them?"

"Yes, I...*knew* them. I met them."

He put his hands on his head, like he was trying to hold himself to the earth. Then he put them down, dragging them along his face as he went. "Well, that's something I didn't know. Why would I fucking have known? You just came back with no baby. After disappearing for *two fucking months*."

"Stop," she said. It was too much. She couldn't process the pain that was coursing through her body. She couldn't rehash her and Landry's baggage while knowing that their daughter was outside.

She was trying to process this. She had to disappear

into herself. Into a bubble inside her chest that didn't feel anything, not anger or pain or hope.

Her parents were dead. She was here. She didn't know Fia was here too.

"You haven't told her about me?" she asked.

"The truth of the matter is, Fia, you gave her up. At some point I have to have that conversation with her. And then I was going to ask her if she wanted to meet you, try to have a relationship with you. And *then* I was going to talk to you."

"Why not come to me first? Why not come to me with all of this?"

"Because it wasn't your choice to make. It was mine. If you had given your information to the adoption agency, they would've contacted you the same way they did me. But I had already given out my information. I made it known that I wanted the kid, and so I have the kid."

"I'm not sixteen," she said. "I'm not in the middle of trying to hold my family together, I'm not...raising my sisters still. The idea that you wouldn't come to me about taking care of *our daughter*... I can't believe you, Landry. You wonder why I didn't want to raise a child with you? This is the most immature—"

"I'm doing my best," he said. "It's an unwinnable situation. I didn't expect to ever get contacted while she was still a child. I thought maybe she would get in touch with me when she turned eighteen. We would go have dinner or something, and I'd keep all my anger and regret to myself and consider it a blessing I ever got to see her. I didn't expect to end up raising her. When they called me, all I had time to do was get the place ready."

"You didn't have a minute to come and have a conversation with me?"

"No. I didn't. I was thinking about her."

She let out a hard breath. "Were you?"

"There's a reason I was keeping her here. There's a reason she hasn't been introduced to the broader ranching family. My intent was never to ambush you with her."

She didn't believe that. He was being honest about his feelings for Lila, she could see that. She could see he genuinely wanted to do the right thing for their daughter.

Fia could also see that he was still very, very angry about the decision she'd made back then. And whatever he was trying to convince himself of now, he hadn't cared if he hurt Fia. If anything, he wanted to.

"It wasn't?" she asked. "Really?"

She looked out at this moment from the safety of the bubble she'd found. She didn't know how to process this, and she was fairly certain she might be in shock.

But maybe the shock was protecting her. From crumpling to the ground right now. From breaking into pieces.

"Now she's seen you," said Landry. "And we're going to have questions to answer. We need to work this out really quick. You don't get to be half in and half out."

He was acting like this was her mistake. Like she had created this situation when he was the one who had brought their daughter here, and hadn't warned her or Lila.

Anger popped the bubble.

"Don't talk to me like that. Don't *lecture me*. Don't

you dare tell me what I can be when you didn't give me a chance. You let your bitterness drive this choice, not your love."

His face was hard, and not even that accusation broke him. "In or out, Fia?"

There was no question. She'd held that baby in her arms for only a moment, thirteen years ago, and she'd loved her. She'd known she had to give her away. She'd known she'd never see her again.

Now she was here.

She'd survived that once. Living through looking at that beautiful, perfect child and knowing it would be the only time. She couldn't do it again.

Lila was here.

Fia couldn't let her go, never again.

"In," she said. "Let's go talk to her right now."

"No. Let's not ambush the kid in the middle of the day. How about that?"

"No one is suggesting an ambush. But you're the one saying it needs to happen fast, and I'm agreeing with you."

Her heart was pounding. She needed to see Lila. She couldn't stand not having her in her line of sight. Couldn't stand not being with her.

"Let's think about this. She's been here for a few weeks, and I've been trying to help her get adjusted. Hell, Fia, I didn't even know if she would want to stay."

That didn't help. It made her angrier if anything.

"You were going to bring my daughter here, and if she didn't want to stay, you were just going to let her go, and I was never going to know?"

*"You didn't want her."*

The swirl of feelings inside her, the emotional mist, collected like a hurricane then. And exploded.

"*Thirteen years* of living since I had that baby, of growing, aging, seeing more of the world, seeing more of yourself, and that's still how you see it? *Fuck you.*"

She went storming out of the barn and he grabbed her arm. "Meet me. Tonight."

"I don't have anything to say to you. I'll get a lawyer. I'll do—"

"You don't need a lawyer. Come on. I want to do what's best for the kid, Fia. That's it. Maybe I'm doing a shitty job of it… I expected to be able to *meet* the kid someday, I didn't expect to ever be a father. She needs a father. Hell, she could use a mother too."

His words were like poison, and she wanted to spit them back at him. And that was the biggest thing that kept her from running toward Lila now.

That she felt poisonous.

That she felt so angry and wounded.

That she wanted to kill Landry King with her own hands.

They needed to have it out. They needed to have the conversation they had been waiting thirteen years to have. And then they would see what was on the other side of it. But one thing Fia knew, and that was now that she'd found her daughter, she was never going to let her go again.

She hadn't been looking for her. Because she'd made a choice. She had made a choice to give that child the best life she could, and at the time it had felt like that had to be far away from Four Corners. Far away from her, far away from Landry. From their family drama, from their own toxicity.

She *had* wanted her baby.

It was one of the things that had made her hate Landry the very most. That he had offered her a dream. Spun a fairy-tale story where they could run away together and it would work. Make a little home, with their little family. Where they would just be two destitute dysfunctional idiots.

She'd wanted to take it.

She'd known she couldn't. She'd done her best to make the right choice and he'd spent years punishing her for it.

He thought she hadn't *wanted* Lila enough.

She hated him for that. It was the thing she would never forgive him for, of all the things. That he had no idea how much she'd wanted it. And how hard she'd fought to choose the right thing in the face of it.

"Tonight," she said. "Six. We'll make a plan."

But she knew it was more than that. There was so much hard emotion between them, and the truth was, they needed to be able to say it. In the interest of keeping her secret, she'd pushed it down. They'd been civil to each other, even if barely.

Even if barely.

When she drove away from King's Crest this time, she knew she cut her heart out and left it behind.

That was another thing she didn't think she would ever forgive him for.

But maybe most of all, it was something she couldn't forgive herself for.

For giving that man her heart and never managing to get it back.

## CHAPTER FOUR

HE HAD TO have the conversation with Lila sooner than he wanted to. She was out there with Denver, chasing down that rogue calf.

He caught up with them in the north pasture. Lila was smiling and sitting in the back of the truck, and it made his heart squeeze to see her like this. Enjoying the ranch. Enjoying this life. She'd ridden on horseback with him and Denver a few times, and he knew she was itching to get on by herself. She came alive when she was outside. Just like he did.

And yeah, it might still feel kind of theoretical to her, like a vacation that might end. But it was also just damn good to see her happy. And he didn't want to undo that.

But he knew he was going to have to. Because Fia had been definitive. He hadn't meant to cut her out of this forever.

*Didn't you? You bastard. No part of you wanted to hurt her with this?*

Maybe part of him had. Maybe. But it hadn't been his driving motivation. He'd been bound and determined to get Lila settled, to get her happy with everything on the ranch, to make a plan on how he was going to parent.

*Then* he'd planned to talk to her about her biological mother.

She had a hard enough time accepting *him*. She still didn't see him as a father, he didn't know if she ever would. He just hadn't wanted to ambush Lila with all that reality about... About him and Fia. What they had between them was a poisonous wound. One they'd ignored all this time. One they'd never drained.

The truth was, he hated Fia Sullivan.

She could snipe and spit and be generally mean to him, and he just didn't respond. Because he'd shut his feelings down where she was concerned so long ago. Because he'd found the key to take that hate and flip it to indifference.

But now? Now that she wasn't there and yelling at him, now that she was saying she wanted in on this, this thing that he... She didn't even have a right to it. He was the one who had made sure his name was with the agency. He was the one who had made sure that he was going to be able to be there for Lila. And Fia wanted to parent her just the same?

Yeah, hell. Maybe he had an issue with that.

But he had always planned to talk to his kid about her. When the time was right. When it wasn't all so damned new.

Denver got a lasso and caught the calf. Then he ran it down and tied its legs together.

And he could hear Lila expressing sounds of dismay.

"How else was I supposed to catch it?" Denver asked, as his niece hurled accusations at him.

"It just seems so mean," she said.

"So is letting it run off and get eaten by bobcats," Denver pointed out.

"I hear bobcats don't eat you," she said. "They just chew on your knucklebones."

"The thing is," said Denver, "calves don't have knuckles."

"Hey, I…"

And then he just couldn't do it. He couldn't face the idea of wiping that smile off her face. And he realized that while there was definitely some merit in preparing her for what was to come later today, it also wasn't just going to solve everything. He could tell her, but he and Fia didn't have a plan yet.

Having a teenager was way more complicated than he'd given it credit for. And the bottom line was, he'd had a plan, and the plan hadn't been enough.

Words failed him when he needed them, and he could understand why his dad had taken a certain amount of comfort in his narcissism.

Hell, he'd lived out some of his father's narcissism. Was it enough of an excuse to tell himself that it was what he'd seen modeled in his house for all his formative years? Could he relieve his own guilt by reminding himself he'd been formed by a man whose way was the only way?

Dammit. No. Because Lila's own life had been hijacked by loss, and he was fashioning himself as some kind of hero. But his actions weren't heroic.

He'd told himself a lot of stories about why his decisions were good. About why they were right.

He'd been angry.

He was *still* angry.

It killed him to think how much that anger might've blinded him to what was actually right.

His chest still hurt when he thought of Fia. When

he thought of all the pain between them, and he wasn't ready to let that go.

But Lila didn't deserve to take the blowback of anything between him and Fia.

"Denver," he said. "You-all have dinner plans for later?"

"Barbecue," he said. "Per usual."

"I've got a thing. Would you be able to bring Lila up to the house and drop her back home after?"

"Yeah," said Denver. "Sure."

His brother looked easygoing, but he knew there would be questions later. They hadn't asked about Lila's mother, but he knew full well his reprieve was coming to an end. No one knew about him and Fia, not for certain. That, combined with the fact Fia had hidden her pregnancy from everyone here, was the only reason no one had jumped to conclusions. He knew that. He would have to tell them.

But there was a hierarchy of people who were going to find out about this.

Lila was going to come first.

After he and Fia hashed everything out. His family would have to come after that. He didn't know what Fia intended to do with the information. Perhaps she'd already told the Sullivan sisters, which would mean that the McClouds would know, and the Garretts soon after. But he couldn't imagine it.

No. Not that girl. That girl she'd been. Who had come back in a baggy sweater and no baby in her belly. Her hair in a messy ponytail. Her eyes haunted.

He'd known she was in pain, but his own felt so big. He hadn't been able to care about hers. He'd seen it and looked right through it.

"Yeah. Well. I'll talk to you later then. I've got some things to do down at the barn."

"Are you okay, Landry?" Lila asked, frowning.

She favored her mother. It hurt him to think that. He'd been shoving those comparisons aside since the moment he'd first met her and seen that stubborn expression on her face.

He had seen Fia looking back at him in that moment. It was just so…her.

And sometimes he could see whispers of his family. He tried to focus on those times. But a lot of the time, he saw Fia Sullivan, and he felt haunted.

They hadn't said where they were meeting tonight. But he knew. Because he knew her. No matter how much she tried to pretend he didn't. He did.

It was a place that was out of the way. A place that was secluded. Where no one could hear you if you were screaming. Way back then, it had been a particular sort of screaming. Sighs of pleasure, the giddy excitement of discovery, first love and first times. He had a feeling there would be a different kind of screaming going on tonight.

Not that they'd never screamed at each other in anger. They had. They were not emotionally literate back in the day.

Hell, he still wasn't.

His dad…well, his dad had done a number on all of them. And Fia's mom had been at her throat constantly during her teen years. He could remember Fia running to him, red eyed and angry and taking comfort in his arms. But he could also remember well being the source of her anger.

He'd been a shitty boyfriend. He hadn't meant to

be. But he hadn't known what to do with his feelings. He still didn't, to be honest.

His whole family was stunted. They tried. His older brother Denver tried so damned hard. To keep the family together, to make them functional. But they didn't know how to do feelings, really.

Daughtry was endlessly atoning for the sins of their father with his job as a cop. Justice was just trying to bang his way to oblivion.

He was a locked box. Because you couldn't exploit the feelings of locked box.

Seamus McCloud, the patriarch of McCloud's Landing, had been a big fan of using his fists against people.

Their dad wasn't quite so gauche. He preferred emotional torture.

And he was very, very good at it.

"I'm good, kid. Just got some work to do."

He felt bad about lying to her. But parenting, in his limited experience, was a lot of pretending everything was fine and you knew what you were doing so that your kid felt secure in a world that was anything but.

His dad had never done that. His dad was the thing that made the world scary.

In that way, he supposed he was doing better.

Maybe.

"See you around."

And when he did, everything would be different again.

He just prayed he would handle that right.

Because right now, he felt like he was making a mess of things.

Right now, he felt like he'd had his own dark inclinations served up to him on a platter.

He was still angry at Fia. And he could never discount how many decisions he'd made out of anger.

And so he would have to question just what his motive had been here.

Was it really for Lila's benefit? Or had some part of him wanted this?

Well. That was what tonight was for. They had to let the poison out of the wound. Once and for all.

THE CABIN WAS SMALL and dusty. She could remember the last time she'd been here. And she didn't especially want to think about it.

There had been no reason to come anymore. Not after.

She wondered if he'd come up in the years since. If he had ever brought his other girlfriends to the spot. That was the thing. A man could move on from the kind of trauma that had come from their relationship. At least, the consequences that sex had.

She hadn't been able to. It was too hard. She was too afraid.

She looked around the room, surprised by how much smaller it seemed. Back then it seemed like their own world. Something glorious and theirs alone.

She heard him before she saw him. Or maybe she felt him. She turned, and he was standing in the doorway. Wearing that same, heartbreaking outfit from earlier. It still made her stomach go tense. Even now.

She had spent the day in a sort of numb shock. She had spent the day unsure of what she had to say. But knowing she had to be ready to open up a vein and let blood.

She had considered calling her sisters. She had considered asking them to come talk with her. Confessing everything. But something had stopped her. Maybe it was the fact that this wasn't resolved. Maybe it was that she was in shock. That she still couldn't quite accept this version of reality where that baby girl she had given up all those years ago was here now. And worst of all, that the life she had wanted to give her daughter had been so badly destroyed.

Her parents had died.

She must be...grieving. She must be traumatized. And all Fia had ever wanted to do was spare that child trauma. She had wanted to give her the best of everything. She was devastated, and she didn't know what to do with the feelings, because she felt like there was no time to sit in them. Her child was here. Living in Landry's house.

How could she marinate in her own sadness when that was the reality? She didn't have time. It was like the experience of pregnancy and deciding that adoption was the only option in the first place. There had been pain. So much of it. And she'd known that she had to defer it. That she had to put it aside and deal with it later. And she had.

Her parents were too self-involved to notice her depression. Her dad was off having his affair while her mom pretended she didn't know. When Fia was frozen in the most intense postpartum depression. Because it felt like she should be a mother. And there was no baby.

Because she'd felt that child grow inside of her, and she had...

Landry had used that tired language. *You didn't want her. You gave her up.*

There was a difference in how some people said that: she gave up a child.

And how *she* thought it. How she *felt* it. She had given up a child she loved. A child she had carried within her. A child she'd given birth to. And when she thought of those words, she felt them as the deep sacrifice they should convey.

She'd heard people talk about other women who'd done it. They made it sound like giving up a child was the same as taking an unwanted set of dishes to Goodwill.

When she thought of it, she imagined an old newsreel she'd seen of a mother handing her child out a window to firefighters. Helping that baby escape the burning building she was still trapped in.

Yes. She'd given her child up.

Just like that.

She'd continued to burn, and she'd found a way to rise from those ashes, but it had taken years.

She had brought that child into the world. She had grown her and sustained her inside of her body. That child had been *wanted*. And what she had wanted more than anything was to give that child a life that she and Landry couldn't give her.

That made her want to run away even now. Except she wasn't sixteen. She was a woman now. The kind of mother that she could be now was different. The kind of mother that she could be now...

A mother. She was going to be a mother.

But the kid wasn't two pink lines. She was real and vivid. Thirteen and carrying baggage, and Fia felt unequal to the task all over again.

But she wasn't burning anymore.

She had a home of her own.

She met his gaze. "Start explaining."

His eyes flicked away, then back to hers. That blue had been familiar once. Close, hot and intense. It had been years since they'd had a real conversation. Years since they'd been this close.

He was a stranger who could never really be a stranger.

They'd never gotten to excavate their breakup. It had been an explosion after Lila's birth, and it had all centered around Lila—how could it not?—and they were as ever, unfinished business.

They'd never talked about it, but they'd clearly both decided to simply leave it unfinished.

They had to finish it. After thirteen years, they had to finish it. But it started with Lila.

Just like it ended.

Landry nodded slowly. Those blue eyes didn't rest on hers. They were focused on the wall behind her. "A couple of years ago I found the adoption agency that you used. I just wanted to have the info in there so that when…*if* she wanted to find me she could. That's it." Then he looked at her, his eyes level. "A year ago Jack and Melissa Gates were killed in a car accident. Lila was put into foster care. She doesn't have any other family. When CPS discovered she'd been adopted as a baby they contacted the agency for details, and the agency gave them my information. I dealt with a caseworker before they ever notified Lila. I had to go through background checks and inspections, the same thing I would have to do to be a foster parent. That's essentially what I am. Fostering to adopt, but Lila is thirteen, so they wanted to see how she was adjusting before anything was finalized."

"How long has she been here?"

"Three weeks. She's been homeschooling."

She felt like she'd been gut punched. "*Three weeks.* And you've known about her being in care for more than two months. You've known that *she needed us.*"

Her baby had needed her.

She hadn't been there.

It was a nightmare. An echo of the worst, hardest times before and after the adoption.

Those blue eyes looked lost then. And that was a rare sight. At least these days. She'd seen him look like this before, of course. But not in a long time.

"I didn't know what to do," he said. "And I felt like… I had to do what was best for her. I had to care more about what she needed than what you wanted."

And suddenly, she was back in that moment. The last time she was here. And he knew it. He had chosen those words so specifically. So carefully. Because they were words that she had spoken to him then.

It was like that first layer of civility had been removed. Like it had been peeled back. This facade that they had created around themselves. This easy tension that made people think they were attracted to each other, or maybe they had dated once. This game they played that hid the complicated nature of it all.

And it hurt.

They hadn't just burned each other. They had skinned each other alive.

There was first love, and then there was Landry King and Fia Sullivan.

He had been her escape. He had been her everything. And she had been his. They had fought. They had wounded each other. They found solace in each other's arms, and ultimately, they had devastated each other.

Then they had built this scaffolding around themselves. A fake life. A way that they interacted with one another that made it look like they hadn't been each other's deep wound.

Even she came close to believing it sometimes.

But this was it. The wound. They were ripping off the bandages. Exposing it.

It was exhilarating and terrifying, but their secret was here, in the middle of them. This bomb waiting to go off. Everyone would know. *Everyone would know.* They would look at that little girl, who favored Fia so much, and who had Landry's demeanor, and they would know. He had brought this secret that she had kept at great cost to herself right back into the middle of them.

She wanted this child.

At the same time, she was so wildly resentful that he'd done this to them.

It was really like being sixteen all over again.

"Is this a game to you?" she asked. "A chance to get back at me?"

*"No,"* he said, the denial vehement. "This isn't a game. I am not playing with Lila's life. I want to be a father. I always have. You took that from me. I wanted it then, and I want it now. I never stopped wanting it."

She felt her lip curl. "That's what you see me as. This person who stole fatherhood from you." She shook her head. "You should thank me, do you know that? You would've been a terrible father. A terrible husband.

And I wouldn't have been any better. Think about it, Landry. What would we have done? You would've been a ranch hand somewhere else? Or maybe we would've ended up staying *here*. Teenage parents with families that were coming apart at the seams. You would have gone out drinking and other women would have flirted with you, I would have come down to the bar and screamed at you, and where would Lila have been? What kind of life would she have had? Look at what Four Corners is now. It wasn't that then. Don't forget that. Don't forget that this place we've made now is so far removed from everything we had back then. We were…nothing but broken."

"When you told me you were pregnant I was happy, Fia." That hurt. It still hurt so badly. "I wanted to make a life with you, a family. Something better than what we were. I thought you saw things in me, better things than anyone else. I thought you saw more of me than just being my father's son. When I found out you had no faith in me, no faith in us, it was like a death," he said. "You have no idea. You have no idea what it's like to feel like something that precious was taken away from you."

His pain was real. But he'd never tried to understand hers. So why should she try and understand his?

"*How dare you?* Don't tell me what I don't understand. You got me pregnant. I watched those lines change. Those two pink lines. I felt the infinite torture of hope and possibility, and the crushing despair of realizing that there was no way. And you *tormented* me. With this idea that maybe we could run off together. That maybe this dysfunctional version of love we had would be enough. And all the while I knew that

I needed to make a choice. A different choice. The possibility of being a mother was growing inside of me every day. And I had dreams. Visions of what it would be like to hold that baby. To love her. But in the end it was because I did love her that I made that decision. And you wouldn't let me do it. You wouldn't *let me*. So yes. I went behind your back. I went to the adoption agency, and I chose the family myself out of a book."

"How civilized," he said, his expression something like disgust. "To find them in a catalog."

"It was the only thing about it that was civilized. I think you forget how young we were. Lila's thirteen. I was *fifteen* when you first got me pregnant. You were sixteen. And then I was sixteen when the baby was born. It's outrageous. You thought two children could take care of a child… We didn't even know how to be together. We broke up every week."

Agony and ecstasy, that was them. Sometimes the very best and then the very worst.

"We would've gotten it together," he said.

"We wouldn't have. What makes you believe that, Landry? Because my parents had it so together? My family was falling apart, unraveling, while I was facing the reality of this pregnancy. And I looked at my father and I just knew that… It was going to be us. Eventually, it was going to be us. Us getting married young, being each other's only lovers, you getting bored and finding someone else. Sleeping with some other woman behind my back. Deciding to run away and move to California."

"I would never move to California. That's about as likely as me becoming a vegan."

"Fine. Maybe you just would've moved in next door

with her. How about that? I couldn't find a way to have any faith in us when I had to try and think about what we would look like twenty years down the road. Because no one around me ever gave me a reason to hope. Not in us or in anything else. So yes, I chose her parents. And then I ran away. I stayed with them. Because I knew... I knew you weren't going to support me. You wouldn't be there for me in the way that I needed you to be."

"I wanted something different," he said.

"I know," she said. "And I couldn't give it to you."

"Well, look where it landed her. She's back here anyway. And now she's got dead parents on top of it."

"Well, if only I'd had a crystal ball so I would have known I was choosing pain for her," said Fia, her throat getting tight. "Obviously, that isn't what I intended to have happen. Obviously, that wasn't the life I wanted her to have. I couldn't have anticipated that. But you know what, I'm glad that she had them. Because they gave her something. A foundation that we couldn't have given her."

"You couldn't have given it to her," he said. "Maybe I could have."

"I'm twenty-nine, Landry. And I can look back on the kids we were, and I can understand why you believed the way you did. Why you were convinced that at seventeen you were equipped to be a father, that you thought it would work because you really, really wanted it to. But I'm twenty-nine-year-old me looking at thirty-year-old you, and I don't get it. How do you not see it now?"

He looked away from her, and she kept talking.

"You expect this to work? If all you're going to do is

accuse me of taking her from you. If you refuse to see that what I did, I did for *her*. Not for me. Does it make you feel better to pretend that I'm the villain? Does it make you feel better to think that I felt nothing when I handed her to another woman that she was going to call mom for the rest of her life? Would it make you be certain I deserved this pain if I told you I also felt relief, along with sadness?" She shook her head.

"You didn't have to make a complicated choice, Landry. All you had to do was make me the bad guy. And that is the simplest goddamn thing to do. You get to be the victim and the hero all rolled into one. Congratulations. I was the one carrying that baby. I was the one who had to worry about the cost of giving birth. I was the one who had to worry about the shame. I was the one who was never going to be able to dispute whether or not I was the parent. Men can run off. Then can decide they don't want to take responsibility. It is much harder for the woman to do. But you never had to think about that, did you? You weren't the one with something growing *inside of you*."

Her breathing went jagged. "You weren't the one who felt her move. You weren't the one who felt the inevitability of it getting nearer and nearer every day. You weren't the one who was so twisted up with fear and love and hope and despair that you could barely breathe. You just get to stand back and decide what you *think* I felt. And it suits you to make it simple. It suits you to tell yourself that I'm your enemy. As long as you keep doing that, I don't think you're going to be a good father to her. Because you're still the seventeen-year-old boy who looked at me and hated me back then.

That's foolishness. You're thirty years old. Be better or don't bother."

She looked at him, her heart beating so hard she thought it might break out of her chest. Her heart that was so twisted up in all the complicated feelings that Landry King created within her.

She knew that he thought ugly things about her. It was time to have it out. Out in the open, in the broad light of day.

"What if I can't give you what you want?" he asked. "What if I can't tell you that I understand why you did what you did?"

"I don't need your understanding. But I need more than your indifference."

He was looking at the wall, his eyes shadowed now. "You know why I'm indifferent to you?"

"Why?"

"Because that day when you brought me here and told me what you did with the baby, all that love inside of me that I felt for you turned into hate. I had a pregnant girlfriend that I loved, and she disappeared for two months, and when she came back there was no baby and she was done with me. And all I knew was that not only was I *not* going to be a father, but that you didn't love me."

"That is a lie. I *did* love you. But the way that we loved wasn't sustainable. It sure as hell wasn't worth preserving. And it really wasn't worth bringing a child into."

"I thought you saved my life, Fia. You gave me something that got me through being sixteen. I'm not sure I would've lived through it otherwise. I guess for that I'm grateful to you. About the time you dropped me into the despair that I was in after the baby was born, well, I had decided that I was going to live by then anyway."

His words hit her like a slap, and they left her cold. She wasn't sure if she believed them, and that made her feel even worse. But with him... There wasn't any trust. And that was part of the problem. They'd been a refuge for each other back then. In a weird way, even the anger had been a refuge. They'd been angry at their parents, and they'd been able to vent it on each other. But when it had come down to having to deal with adult choices, with a long-term future, they hadn't been able to handle it. They certainly hadn't been able to have this conversation.

They were older now, but would it be any better? They had spent all these years determinedly not dealing with themselves.

At least now they'd started it. At least they'd said some of it.

"We have to make a pact," she said. "Because the truth is, what I did for her then, I thought was the best thing to protect her. You might not agree with me, but it's what I believed. I still believe it. I stand by it. And what you wanted, you believed was going to be the best thing for her. We both loved her then. We both wanted the best for her as we saw it. We couldn't make that our common ground then. For obvious reasons. But now you just have to trust that I wanted what was best for her then, and I want what's best for her now. You have to trust that I..." Her voice broke then. "That I loved her then. And I have loved her every day since."

She had thought of her as a baby. That little baby that she had given to the Gates. She had never let herself imagine Lila growing older. Because it had been too painful.

She had done her best to not think of it.

Now she was here. A whole thirteen-year-old. Something she hadn't let herself imagine.

"I love her. Every day since then I've loved her. I want us to present a united front. I want us to be better than we were when we were teenagers. Because we have a chance to make this better. We have a chance to do better. And we have to, for her."

"You didn't have any confidence we could do it then," he said.

"I didn't think we were what she needed then. I think we might be what she needs now. Because you're right. She's been through too much. You asked what the point of it was, and I don't really know. I don't. But we're here, and we are adults. And we can certainly put aside our—"

"You want me to put aside feeling robbed for the last thirteen years?"

"Did *she* feel robbed?"

Landry took a step back, and he stopped. His face was a mask of pain. And she realized he didn't have an answer to that. Not one that was smart. Not one that was fair.

"Did she like her life?" she pressed.

"Yeah," he said. "It's why... She calls me Landry because she told me she had a dad. A great one."

She closed her eyes. "It's all I wanted. That's all I wanted for her."

"I want what's best for her," he said, his voice raw. "Fia, I know I messed some of this up, and I know my anger is tangled in it. But I haven't told anyone, because I felt like we needed to talk first, and I felt like she needed to know before anyone in my family did."

"I didn't tell anyone either." She breathed out, hard. Long. "Even if you can't understand me, I need you to trust that I want the best for her."

He nodded. "Yes. If you trust it's what I want too."

It was like the anger was siphoned from the room. Maybe not from them, but it didn't pulse between them like a monster anymore. At least not now. Could they do this? Could they actually call a truce and do this?

They needed to. They had to.

"Here we are. Split up and parenting a kid together. This was one of the things I wanted to avoid."

"Yes, same. Also, everyone being in our business, I suppose."

That was like a swift kick. "Yeah. Because everyone will be," she said.

"Yeah. Great. So. Let's go talk to Lila."

She nodded slowly. "Let's go talk to Lila."

## CHAPTER FIVE

THEY DROVE SEPARATELY. He was all for presenting a united front with her, and he wasn't going to take cheap shots at her in front of their kid. The truth was, they were going to have to figure out how to co-parent, and that meant dealing with each other. And it meant dealing with this long-held bitterness.

He had to admit that letting her tear into him, and him spitting back some of his own venom had felt good.

But now they had to actually go and see the kid. And they needed to hold it together.

And he would. For Lila. He had practice with that.

He gritted his teeth and pulled his truck up to the small house, and Fia did the same. They got out, and with a healthy distance between them, they walked into the house.

Only to discover that Lila wasn't back yet.

He shot a text to Denver.

Are you guys almost done with dinner?

Soon. Leaving in ten.

Great.

Now Denver was going to see Fia's car. Oh well. It was all going to come out; maybe it was going to be a little bit messy. There was nothing he could do about it. He had been deluding himself into thinking that it was all going to go according to some sort of plan. That it was all going to follow on easily. He had really hoped for that. But when had life ever been accommodating enough to do that?

Fia looked around the space. It was clean. Mostly. There were some dishes in the sink. And he wondered if she judged him for that.

But hell. She'd never had a kid before.

Not that he had tons of experience with it.

"This is…nice. You moved out of the main house."

"Yes. Moved out of the main house to give Lila her own space. She's eating dinner with the family right now. I expected that Denver was going to have her back."

"It's good that she gets along with everybody."

"Yeah. It's been good. Whatever you think about my family, about my dad, my siblings are good people."

"I've never really gotten to know them."

There were a lot of reasons for that. They'd kept their relationship so secret, she never messed with his family. He had never wanted Fia to get too close to his dad. That was the thing. Because his dad was a horrible bastard, and he had never wanted to expose her to him. Maybe he just hadn't wanted his dad to know how much Landry cared about her. Because then he could use her to manipulate him. Then afterward it had been over.

This was just weird. Having her in his house. Acting like civilized adults.

Being close to each other by choice.

When not naked.

He didn't need to think the word *naked* right now.

He cleared his throat. "They're not half as messed up as they should be. All things considered."

"I like to think that's actually true about all of us. Look at the McClouds. They've even managed to work things out."

"Yeah. Even Gus," said Landry.

The room suddenly felt a bit small. It was the strangest thing, looking at Fia now. What she'd said to him had nearly knocked him on his ass. How did Lila feel? He could honestly say he didn't think Lila felt robbed. She had loved her parents. Unreservedly. She had never felt like her life was less.

Being raised by a couple of teenagers…

He looked at Fia with this weird, tempered anger that he now had. He saw the girl she'd been. And for maybe the first time he looked at the woman she was now.

Really saw her. Not overlaid with his own hurt, his own issues. But just her. As she was.

He was struck by how pretty she was. Nothing had ever meant to him the way she had. It was a sad thing, growing up, growing older, realizing that time had sanded the edges off your feelings so much that you would just never be able to feel pleasure or joy or anticipation the way that you once had.

Because nothing had ever been as amazing as knowing that he was going to see Fia at the end of the day. Nothing had ever felt half so amazing as discovering sex with her.

There had never been another lover, another thrill, to match what he'd had with her.

He knew that was age. Age and wisdom, and the magnitude of suffering they'd experienced in the time since they'd been together.

But looking at her now reminded him of it. And it mingled with the present, and created some sort of potent alchemy that left him shaken.

And just then, he heard the slam of the truck door.

"That would be Denver."

He felt his phone vibrate. He took it out of his pocket. Sending the kid in. I assume we'll talk later.

And he didn't know how to pull that apart. Didn't know quite how to decode it. If it meant that Denver suspected that Fia was there for a reason, or maybe he didn't even realize it was her.

But either way, he didn't come in, and then Lila was scampering through the front door.

She stopped in front of them. Looking between them. "Hi," she said.

"Hi," said Fia.

He looked at her and saw that her eyes were filling with tears. And he realized he was going to have to say something, so that Lila wasn't kept in suspense, and Fia wasn't kept on this knife's edge. He wondered when the hell he developed any sympathy for Fia.

"Lila, this wasn't exactly how I wanted to do this. I wanted to give you a heads-up that…that your biological mother lived on the property, but when we talked about the past it hurt you and I didn't want to make you confront things you weren't ready for. But things went out of order today. And so… This is Fia. She's the woman who gave birth to you."

Lila's face went white, and it was like his whole view shifted.

It wasn't Fia in the spotlight, highlighted as a villain, not now.

It was him.

He hadn't known how to do this, and he'd put both Lila and Fia in a terrible position. He'd fucked up. Because he hadn't been able to see this from any perspective but his own, and Fia's words hit him hard now.

He was thirty.

If he didn't stop seeing this like a seventeen-year-old, he wouldn't be able to do it right.

But that was so tangled up in his own issues. His need to believe he could have done it all right back then made it hard for him to have any new perspective on it now.

Or maybe he resisted it because he didn't want to change. Since change would be a lot like admitting he was wrong.

"Lila," said Fia, and a tear slid down her cheek. "I didn't know that you were here. Until today."

Lila looked at Landry. "She didn't know I was here?"

"It's complicated," said Landry.

He'd messed up. Big time. And he could see it, clearly. On Lila's face. On Fia's.

"How is it *that* complicated?" Lila asked.

"Landry and I don't have a relationship," said Fia. "Not... Not now. So, his information was at the adoption agency, but mine wasn't. I wasn't informed about what happened with you. He acted independently."

"I realized I needed to talk to you about it sooner rather than later, but then Fia came by today..."

"Which actually was not entirely unusual."

He rounded on her. "It was *wholly* unusual. You never come over here."

"Whatever," said Fia. "It's just… This is how it happened. And we decided… I… Lila," Fia said, "I want to be in your life too. And I can understand that Landry was trying to introduce new things to you slowly. Even if I do wish that he had told me in the beginning."

Lila looked between them. "I… I don't know what to say."

"I'm sorry," Landry said.

"It's not like I didn't know I had a bio mom out there. I've always known I was adopted. My parents were really honest with me about that. But I never dreamed about meeting you."

It was that same matter-of-fact, cutting honesty that had gotten him right at first. But it didn't seem like it cut Fia.

"I am so grateful to Jack and Melissa. For the way they parented you. I am so grateful that you didn't want to find me. Because all I wanted for you was to give you the best life. All I wanted for you was for you to have the best parents. I didn't want you to feel like you were missing anything. I didn't want you to feel like you were missing me."

That right there was one of the most unselfish things he'd ever heard anyone say, and it just about knocked him over. He really preferred his self-righteous anger.

She was right. It was simple. It allowed him to feel justified. It allowed him to channel all of this pain into something pure and easily digestible. Easy to understand.

When all of these things seemed more nuanced now.

When he was faced with the fact that what was on Fia's face right now was not indifference. Not even close.

It was love. The kind of love that had made a hard decision.

His own ego had been bruised when his daughter had told him she hadn't felt the lack of him in her life.

The evidence of Fia's honesty was in this moment. That what she wanted really was for Lila. And not for herself.

That she was relieved, *happy*, to know that her child had never wanted in any way.

That she wasn't challenged or harmed or bruised by the assertion.

"I knew your mom and dad," she said slowly. "They were such good people. And they wanted you so much. And that was exactly what I wanted for you. Parents who were ready. We wanted you. But we weren't ready."

Part of him wanted to fight against that. To say that he'd been ready. But he was caught up short by what she'd said. About how much she had wanted Lila. And that much was true. They hadn't planned on having Lila, but she was wanted. Loved. They had disagreed about what was best, and it had been a stark disagreement. One that had created a rift that had carried them both forward until this moment.

And he wondered if he could find a way to hold two truths in his hands at the same time.

To still feel justified in thinking he could've taken care of his daughter. And to recognize that even though it hadn't been what he wanted, Fia's decision had given Lila a good life.

He needed to figure something out. Because if he

couldn't... What Fia said echoed in his mind. About him being no more mature now than he'd been then. About her feeling like she still didn't want to raise a kid with him.

And maybe she was right to say that it was easy to retrofit his memories. To hold on to that feeling of being justified and wounded.

*Maybe you can be hurt without being justified.*

He didn't quite know what to do with that, so instead he focused on those two big things. The obvious love on Fia's face now, and the pain that still existed in his chest. And he allowed himself to imagine holding one in his left hand and the other in his right. He held them both carefully, and with equal weight.

And that was maybe the best thing he had ever done for Lila.

"I didn't know that you knew them," Lila said.

Lila looked bemused, and Fia did look slightly hurt then.

But he could understand that. She might've thought that Jack and Melissa would share with Lila that they had known her birth mother. But maybe not. By the time Lila would be able to understand, that story would have faded from memory. It wouldn't be the most important part of all of it. And maybe they needed to forget Fia a little bit in order to make their family feel a certain way. He didn't know.

One thing he did know was that they'd been a family. Because Lila was a wonderful kid, with her own opinions, her own sense of style and a deep sense of security. All those things had come from Jack and Melissa Gates. And maybe that was another thing he needed to figure out how to hold in his hand. That though she was his daughter biologically, the fact that they'd raised her meant more than he'd been giving them credit for.

They had shaped her spirit.

In the same way that Fia had shaped that stubborn chin.

Just as indelibly.

"I stayed with them for two months," Fia said. "After I chose them. I told them I was afraid at home and I didn't have anywhere else to go. They took me in." Lila looked at Fia with an expression that sat somewhere between shock and deep sadness. "They took care of me. While they waited for you. I knew what they were going to name you, and I got to see your room. They were so excited."

It was like something had shifted inside of him. Because suddenly he could see what Fia had seen. This warm, beautiful welcome that Lila was going to be receiving. These people who opened their home and their arms to her, with the love they were going to extend to their baby.

But he hadn't gotten to see it.

*Because she couldn't trust you. Because you wouldn't listen.*

"I knew that you were going to be in great hands," Fia said. "I'm so glad that you were. I'm so sorry that you lost them."

"Thank you," said Lila softly.

"Landry and I are going to do our best. To be there for you. I know it might be hard to believe. But we both always thought of you. It's okay if you didn't think of us. You were never supposed to have a hole in your life. But we had one in ours. I don't really know how to explain it, but it was one I was happy to have. Because sometimes when you love something really fiercely, the empty space it leaves behind when you can't hold that person hurts, but you're kind of glad it's there too. Because it gives you a chance to think of them. I always thought of you as a baby. I never liked to think of the passage of time. Here you are. And you're *you*. If…if I can be part of this, then I want to be."

Lila looked at him.

"Fia and I want to co-parent," he said. "We are not a… We're not *a thing*."

Fia shook her head. "No. We are not a thing. We're also not sixteen and seventeen anymore. So we have our stuff together, and can get along just fine."

He had a feeling that was for his benefit as much as Lila's. A reminder to behave.

"I don't really get it. Are you guys… Am I going to go between your houses or… Like shared custody?"

"We'll figure it out. Something that works. How about if we start with me spending some time over here. And that way you're not moving things around. You can come and visit me at my house at Sullivan's Point. But you don't have to move your things or officially leave for the weekend or anything. I'm really just a couple of minutes away."

"And you didn't tell her," she said to Landry.

"I said it was complicated," he said.

"That sounds like bullshit, Landry," Lila said. "Just being honest."

"It's…it's *not*. I didn't want to hurt you, I didn't want to hurt her."

The look that Fia gave him was sharp. Because the

truth was, there was part of him that hadn't minded hurting Fia. At least a little bit.

Landry sighed. "I'm glad Fia got to tell her story. I'm glad I didn't try. Because the bottom line is, I haven't been... We have trouble communicating."

"Oh *do* we?" Fia asked.

Lila looked between them.

"We're not exactly *friends*," said Landry.

Fia lifted a brow. "Wow. Way to sell the arrangement, bud."

"Fia..."

Fia turned to Lila and smiled. "Landry made a mistake. But Landry is human. And this is a situation I don't think either of us ever thought we would find ourselves in. But neither of us is unhappy to be in the situation. We're just sad that you had to go through what you did to get here."

"I don't know how I'm supposed to feel about anything," said Lila. "Because this wouldn't have happened if..."

"You don't have to know how you feel about it," said Landry. "You're thirteen. You're not supposed to know what you think about anything yet. You're supposed to have a lot of strong opinions and then change them. Get irrationally mad at things and then feel bad about it. And then figure out how to handle it differently next time. Fia and I are the ones who figure out how to be mature. You don't."

And for once, Fia looked marginally happy with him.

So there. He supposed he'd said the right thing.

"Would you be all right... Tomorrow, it would be

great if you could come over to my farmhouse at Sullivan's Point. I can show you the ranch, and the operation. The farm store."

"You have a store?" Lila looked interested in that.

"Yes. That's one of the primary things I do. I bake, I garden and I run a store that sells all the products that we make on the different ranches."

"That's cool," she said.

"It is. And now that Landry doesn't have to keep hiding you…"

"I wasn't hiding her," said Landry. "I was taking things slow."

"Sure. I…"

He could see Fia struggling with the same thing he did. The desire to hug when it might not be welcome. The desire to say *love*, when you didn't want to put too much on the kid.

"I'll see you tomorrow."

"You too, Landry."

And then Fia walked out, leaving him there with Lila, who fixed him with those green eyes. And it might've been Fia pinning him to the spot.

"Were you just not going to tell her about me? Were you not going to tell me about her?"

He'd considered that when he'd first found out about Lila. When he hadn't been thinking. When he'd been all feelings. But he'd known once the rush of it all had passed, he couldn't do that.

"No. I just didn't know how to do it. Or… I wanted you to feel a little bit more settled. The whole thing was different for her than it was for me. Okay? We had a disagreement. About the whole thing. And we had hard feelings about it."

"Why?" Lila pressed.

"I… I didn't want to give you up. She thought it would be better if we did. And…" To his great shock he wanted to defend Fia. Because it would hurt both Fia and Lila to cast Fia's decision in a negative light. But it forced him to take it and turn it over. To look at it for what it was. It forced him to stop oversimplifying this thing that he let drive him, keep him angry, sustain him all this time.

He let out a breath. "It was out of love. Both of us. You have to understand that. But we were kids. And so it was dramatic and messy and immature. So the more persistent I was the less she wanted to deal with me. And I was listening. She told me very clearly that she just couldn't imagine us trying to raise a baby. I thought… fine then you don't have to. I will. But she didn't want that for you either. She wanted you to have a mom and a dad and a real house. She wanted you to get away from here. Today she reminded me that the ranch wasn't always what it is now. My dad… Listen, I have a pretty crappy dad. Okay? He made living here miserable. Fia's family was kind of a mess at the time, there wasn't a lot of money. Not a lot of resources. We were kids trapped in the middle of it. I thought that if I wanted you badly enough that I could just make it fine. That I could make it work. Fia didn't believe that. Or rather, she didn't think…" He looked at the wall, a bleak kind of understanding expanding inside of him. "She didn't think you should have to be an experiment. To see if we sank or swam. Because it could've gone either way."

Lila's stare cut right through him. "So you've been mad at her all this time?"

"Yes. But with this also… I felt like she didn't give me a choice. So I didn't give her one. And I'm sorry. Because that was a game that I put you in the middle of. I guess that kind of proves Fia's point. In some ways I'm still not ready to be a dad."

"You've been doing okay," said Lila.

"You're handling this well," Landry said.

"What did you think I was going to do? Freak out? I mean, it's surprising, but at the same time I always knew that I was adopted. I knew that you guys were out there. You were just theoretical. Because I didn't need you."

He tried to remember what Lila had said about that. He tried to remember the way she had accepted it, the way that it hadn't offended her. It still made his chest burn a bit.

"I think maybe if I hadn't known that I was adopted I would feel shocked and overemotional to meet my birth mother. But mostly, this is all just kind of surreal. But I…" He knew. She didn't need to say it.

The shock had been finding out that both of her parents were dead. The shock had been going from the stable life she had to cycling through foster care. And on some level, some of this must still feel to her like she was just rotating through foster homes. What was Fia but yet one more woman offering to take care of her for a time? It was going to take time for her to really feel like this was permanent. It was going to take time for all of this to really sink in.

Maybe they would be able to become some kind of family. Maybe they wouldn't. It was really hard to know. What he knew was that he was committed. And after tonight he knew Fia was too. So they just had to figure this out. And not kill each other in the process. For Lila's sake.

# CHAPTER SIX

FIA HAD TO talk to her sisters and it couldn't wait.

She was… She was still in a state of shock. Her entire body felt raw and hollowed out. She'd done her crying. At least for today. She'd managed to go and talk to Lila, and say all the things that she turned over inside of herself for all of these years. When she had imagined explaining to her child exactly why she had made the choice she did, those were the words. *I wasn't looking for you.*

It was both healing and wounding to hear that.

But that, in her experience, was adoption.

Knowing that she had been able to give her baby a better life had made her feel good. She'd been so anxious about how she was going to care for a child, about what she was going to do, and once she'd made the decision to find a couple who really wanted her, and were ready, all of it had gone away. But there was still a part of herself that was missing. And that she carried. She hadn't talked to other women about their experiences, because she had kept it a secret. She had decided that reading about experiences or trying to find out what other people thought on message boards online and things like that was probably a futile exercise.

The truth was, she had figured out a way to carry around the love that she felt for Lila without feeling

sad all the time. At first, Lila's birthday had been difficult. And at a certain point, it had been a day that she
marked within herself in the morning when she woke
up, but it didn't create sadness.

The thought of it now did, though, because Lila
had turned thirteen in foster care. Without her parents.

She had become a teenager in this weird space
where she had no place to call home, and no one to
call a caregiver in a permanent sense.

She and Landry should fix that.

*She and Landry.*

It really was unavoidable. They were linked now.
Inextricably. There was quite literally no way out of
this. She texted each of her sisters, and asked if they
could meet her at the farmhouse. They all lived within
minutes of the place. Gideon and Rory were the far-
thest afield, about fifteen minutes off the ranch and
down the road.

But she signed the text off urgent, and they came.
Quickly.

"What's going on?" Quinn asked as soon as they
were seated in the living room.

"I have... I have something to tell you. And I don't
know how any of you are going to react to it. I... I don't
how to say this."

"The suspense is quite literally killing us," said
Alaina.

"It's not *literally* killing you, Alaina," said Rory.
"Or you would be quieter."

"Sorry. I hate that. I hate when people do that. I'm
really not trying to preface this with a lot of words, but
is just... Well, you always wanted to know what happened between me and Landry."

"Oh my gosh," said Quinn. *"Did you bang him?"*

"Fourteen years ago. Yes."

"Holy shit," said Alaina. "That's… You were *babies*."

Fia's face felt hot and her throat was scratchy.

"There's nothing to do here," said Fia. "We made our own fun." That was minimizing. They'd rescued each other. That was how she'd felt at the time. She'd felt so oppressed by her house back then. Like she was going to burst out of her skin, and there was no one to listen to her, no one to care. She'd had to listen to her mother's woes, bear the brunt of her anger. She'd had to keep her father's secrets.

Landry had felt like an escape from all that. They'd created their own world together. Even the anger had been exhilarating in a way. He'd been hers. She'd hoarded him like he was a shiny gem only she knew about. At home she'd worried about her parents, worried about her sisters. With him…they'd been the only thing.

And then it had become clear the real world could break in. Could collapse what they were.

That they were still teenagers. Still human. Still frail.

And the idea that she was going to be a mother. A *mother*. It had filled her with dread.

"So you've been mad at him this whole time because you guys had sex when you were teenagers?" Alaina asked.

"No. I have not," she snapped. "Regrettably for Landry, not even *his* penis is *that* great." She wished that she hadn't said it that way. She regretted it deeply.

It made her think about things that didn't belong in this moment.

Landry King's penis. Good. Lord.

No.

Restart.

"Okay," said Quinn.

"It's…" She had just faced her child down. Why was this so hard?

Well. Because it was going to take the way her sisters saw her and change it forever. Lila already knew that she was adopted. Landry already knew that she had given her baby up. Everyone that knew so far, had already known.

Her sisters thought of her as a certain person. She could already see the way that they were shaken by the revelation that she'd lost her virginity at fifteen. The rest of this was going to be…difficult.

So she just decided to jump in. To rip off the Band-Aid. Some other cliché. It just needed to be done. Needed to be said.

"I got pregnant. Because that's the problem with being a kid having sex. You don't always behave responsibly."

"Fia," said Alaina. "Oh my gosh."

"I know. And… Do you remember when Mom and I had that fight, and then I left? I was gone for a long time."

"Yeah." Quinn frowned. "Mom downplayed it. She said you just going to stay with a friend for a while. Did you fight about being pregnant?"

"No. She never knew."

They'd fought. Fia had yelled at her for being a terrible mother who didn't care about her children. Because she'd just felt failed. Profoundly. Seven months pregnant and terrified. She'd needed Landry because her mother wasn't there for her, and then she'd felt like she'd had no one. Because Landry didn't support her decision. Because her father was sneaking around with another woman, and Fia had known, and her mother had been stressed and suspicious.

And Fia had…

Well, she'd broken the world.

*He doesn't love you, you know? Because you're such a bitch.*

*Don't speak to me like that.*

*Why not? He's cheating. You know that, don't you? Maybe we'd all rather have her than you.*

Her mother had grabbed her by the hair. *I hope you never have children because you have no idea how hard it is. You'd be a terrible mother.*

*Good thing I never plan on being one.*

"I couldn't hide the pregnancy anymore, and the fight was a great…reason. I ran away. For two months. When I came back, I wouldn't tell Mom where I was. But you know, she didn't really care."

All she knew about mother-daughter relationships were distant at best, sharp at worst. Her sisters had made peace with their mother in some capacity over the years. But Fia never had. Fia was the one who'd had to hold everything together when she'd imploded.

She could never forgive either of her parents for their behavior. They behaved more like toxic teenagers than she and Landry. And that was saying something.

Just remembering that reminded her how it had felt for the world to seem like it was crumbling beneath her feet.

"Fia, I can't believe you went through that by yourself," said Rory.

Quinn frowned. "Where was Landry?"

"That's the kind of complicated thing. He and I had a difference of opinion about what to do. So I decided… I decided that I was going to follow through with what I felt was right. So that's what happened between us. I ran away, I gave up our baby. He…he couldn't forgive me and I couldn't look at him. That's the story."

"Wow," said Alaina. They all just stared at her. And the thing was, there was more, and it didn't get easier to digest. But at least it got…hopeful. Was this hopeful? This incredible tragedy that had happened to this child?

It was like another impossible thing to sort through. Except it wasn't a choice. Not for anybody. The adoption, as difficult as it had been, had been a choice. A real, well thought through choice. An accident was simply an accident. No one got to choose whether or not her parents were still here. The only choice that Lila and Fia had at this point was how they moved forward.

"Landry is adopting her. Our daughter."

And that earned her three open-mouthed, shocked looks.

"Her parents died." Her throat went tight. "I just found out. I just found out today. He has her. At his house."

"Fia!" Rory shouted. "Oh my gosh. You have a *child*. And we have a niece."

Yes," said Fia. "And I don't have any idea how this is going to look or how Landry and I are going to manage this, because we have no practice being civil to one another. Absolutely none at all. But we have to… We have to make this work. And she's coming over tomorrow. And I want for you all to meet her. But I think I need…time. Tomorrow."

One thing she knew, she would not let her feelings about him mess this up. Maybe her mother was right. Maybe she'd be a bad mother.

But she wouldn't be *her* mother.

"Of course," said Quinn.

"Of course. Whatever you need. I… This is incredible," said Alaina. She looked at her sister for a long moment. "When you realized I was pregnant, you told me that I could make whatever choice I needed to, and that you would understand."

Fia looked down. "I meant it. Because I understood. I understood how difficult it was. To face down the prospect of being a single mother. I understood what it was like to feel overwhelmed by that. I… I just understood."

"I appreciated it, Fia. More than you will ever know. Because that was how I knew that I made the right decision."

She nodded. "Thanks."

"If I had been as young as you were, I know that I never could've done it."

"Landry doesn't agree with you."

"Landry," said Quinn, shaking her head. "You guys were really… Sneaking around and stuff?"

"Yes. We were."

"And you hid it from us. From *everybody*."

"It wasn't hard to hide it from you." Fia let out a breath. "No offense, but you were children."

"So were you," said Alaina.

"Well, not *as much* as you were," said Fia. "I didn't

want you guys to know. First of all, I knew that I would get into huge trouble. Second of all, I...I didn't want to be a bad example. I knew that what we were doing was...not wrong. But it was risky. I was just so... I was so in love with him. I..." Saying it even now made her feel like she couldn't breathe. But admitting it didn't make her feel ashamed. The truth was, it had been difficult to recount all this even inside her own mind because it was just so thorny. But Lila was with them now.

And one thing was certain, there had been no shortage of feelings between her and Landry when Lila had been conceived.

That was weird. To recast it that way.

It was definitely something she never let herself think about before. For obvious reasons.

"We weren't dating really. It was more like..."

She let herself remember. Which was something she never did.

"Hey, Fia."

"Don't tell me you forgot your pencil again, Landry King, because I'm starting to not believe you."

"You're onto me. I just want to talk to you."

She turned to look at him. Landry was the hottest boy she had ever seen. Every time she saw him her stomach tightened. Her hands went clammy. That she was managing to play it cool around him and trying to banter was no mean feat.

"You should help me study for the math test."

"Ask someone else," she said.

"There's, like, two of us taking the math test."

That was an exaggeration, but still.

Their one-room schoolhouse only had a few students in each grade. Even though Landry was nearly a year older than her, she was doing work on his level.

"You want to study?" she asked.

"Yeah. Tonight."

"Where?"

"There's a cabin. Kind of on the edge of King's Crest. We can go there."

She squinted. "How many other girls have you invited there?"

He shook his head. "None. I swear."

So she went. Because she would be a fool not to. And by the end of that first night, Landry had given her her first kiss.

The next time they studied, it had been a lot more kissing than reading. They had their first fight about a boy she talked to after school—who wasn't even really a boy, he was one of the ranch hands, probably eighteen.

"That guy's a creep. What's he doing talking to you?"

"He was just talking."

"He wants something from you. That's how men are."

"Oh, is it? Is that what you want? *Something* from me. Is that it?"

"No. I mean…yeah. But…"

"Fuck off."

She stormed away, and wouldn't answer his texts the whole weekend. And she cried because she missed him.

They made up, and after that, the kissing turned to more. It was like they were the only two people in the world.

She had never wanted to fall in love at fifteen. Her parents' marriage was a mess. They were unhappy, and Fia knew it. And she just didn't want to… She had never wanted to get married young. Hadn't wanted to fall into that trap. Of being married and being unhappy. Because you had kids together, and there was nothing you could do about it.

But she was falling for him. *Did* fall.

She certainly hadn't meant for them to have sex. But she didn't want to say no.

She wanted to say yes. She didn't want to wait. Because being with him felt like a window into something new. Something different. It felt hot and grown-up. It felt like something so far away from Four Corners and everything she'd ever known before. It wasn't fumbling and awkwardness.

When they came together it was magic.

The other girls that she knew on the ranch, a couple years older than her, who had ever talked about sex made it sound awkward. Made it sound like they didn't get a whole lot out of it.

But Fia did. Every time.

It was all she could think about. *He* was all she could think about.

They made love as often as possible. They fought all the time. He was jealous. And intense.

She supposed she wasn't a lot better.

She yelled at him for an hour after she saw him talking to another girl at the grocery store. A girl who must have gone to high school down in Mapleton, because she was their age, but Fia didn't really know her. Because he was just so handsome, and if she wanted him, every other girl must too. It had been flattering when he was jealous in return, because it must mean that he felt the same.

She knew now, as an adult, that was a bad way of looking at things.

She knew now, as an adult, that while it had felt like love then, it hadn't been love. It had been hormones and immaturity. But at the time it had felt like everything. At the time, they let themselves get consumed by it. They forgot condoms more than they remembered them, and at first it felt like they were just going to be lucky.

And then they weren't.

She looked at her sisters. "I broke my own heart. Landry was involved. But it was me."

"I just can't believe it," said Rory. "All this time, we were encouraging you to go have a mad passionate love affair with the man, and *you already had.*"

"I mean, I kind of assumed that you guys had slept together," said Quinn. "But I didn't know you carried on a whole affair."

"We were like toddlers playing with a box of knives. We had no idea how bad we could hurt ourselves with what we were doing. But it all felt real. It all felt like such a big deal."

She'd been depressed before him. Waking up every day had felt hard with the ranch crumbling, her parents' marriage crumbling. Then Landry King had kissed her, and suddenly she couldn't wait for every new day.

"Well, our Landry-Fia saga isn't going to work out the way we wanted," said Quinn.

She frowned. "What?"

"You know we ship you."

"You *what*?" Fia asked.

"It's what you call it when you want two people to get together. A relationship. Ship."

"I know *what it is*. I am not a TV show character. You cannot *ship* me. I am a real person."

"Hey," Quinn said, "you and Landry didn't play by the rules, and neither do we."

"That's not… That's not remotely the same," said Fia.

"Do you need us to stay tonight?" Quinn asked.

"No," she said. "I'm fine."

"I don't want to leave you alone," said Rory.

"Me neither."

She looked at all her sisters. And this was what she had been missing during that most horrible, vulnerable time in her life. She had been missing support.

And she knew she could have had it the whole time. She did.

"Thank you."

Because she wasn't going to turn it down now that she had it.

And as they rallied around her, calling their husbands and letting them know they wouldn't be home, she felt a piece of herself that had been broken for a long, long time knit itself back together.

## *CHAPTER SEVEN*

LANDRY GOT UP EARLY and made himself some coffee. Then he made a second cup of coffee and decided to do something he *never* did.

Venture into enemy territory.

He was going to Sullivan's Point, without making an announcement. He was taking his life into his hands.

But Fia wasn't just an ex-girlfriend anymore. She wasn't even his enemy.

She was his *co-parent*. And he figured it was time for them to come up with a real strategy.

He was going to bring Lila over in the afternoon when she finished her schoolwork, and before that, Fia and himself would probably benefit from a meeting. A *summit*. Landry King liked a plan. He had a plan for how he was going to handle all of this with Lila, and it hadn't gone smoothly.

So now he was on plan B. And this one was going to have to involve Fia, rather than cutting her out. He could acknowledge that his part in that had been a little shady.

And so he would come bearing coffee.

He went to Sullivan's Point as often as anybody, because the lake was there, and they had lots of different events down at the lake. Plus it was where they had their town hall meetings. It had become a pretty normal thing. But even so, he was always aware that he was a stranger in a strange land.

That he was not a single Sullivan's favorite person. And hell, they hadn't even known *why*.

Just that Fia wasn't a fan. So neither were any of them.

What the Sullivan parents lacked in loyalty, their daughters made up for, and then some.

Well, everyone was going to have to get accustomed to his face.

The one place he didn't go habitually was the farmhouse. But then, he never had. It wasn't like they'd had the kind of relationship where you went home and met the parents. No. It was more stopping somewhere in the woods for a blow job in the back of his truck and then continuing on to meet people at the lake and pretend that wasn't what had just happened. Of course, he was an equal opportunity kind of man, and he'd spent just as much time with his face between her thighs as she'd spent on him.

She'd always been pretty. Now that she was a woman, though, if he looked at her too long he felt a kind of deep ache that permeated his whole being. Took over his chest. Took over his whole body.

He didn't care for it.

He had dismissed it as anger for all of these years. But the truth was, he knew.

He had never stopped wanting her. He had wanted her while she stood in front of him and broke his heart all those years ago.

It didn't matter if there were other women or a huge space of time, it didn't change the facts. He had never felt for anyone else what he felt for her.

Justice and Denver were absolute whores. They screwed around with every pretty woman who wanted them. At a certain point Landry had figured he should test that lifestyle out. It hadn't lasted long. It just hadn't…excited him. He felt like he'd peaked at sixteen. And maybe it was the phenomenon of never being able to forget your first. But sex had never felt so sharp or dangerous, brilliant or mind-blowing in the years since.

He was closer to living like a monk now than being like any of his brothers.

The problem was, sometimes he looked at Fia, and he felt more just looking at her than he did when he was actually inside another woman.

Not the best thing to think of as he pulled up to the farmhouse, and grabbed both cups of coffee, then headed up the stairs.

He needed to get himself together.

He rolled up and knocked on the door. The place was so bright now. Impossibly feminine. There were ostentatious lanterns hanging from the weeping willow out front. A table and chairs sat out there, all mismatched and pretty.

It was quintessentially Fia.

He'd always liked that about her. The way that she was just so girly. Tough too, though. But she wore dresses, and she was soft. And it wasn't that he didn't appreciate a horse girl, but Fia just wasn't. And he liked that.

The door opened, and he came face-to-face with those green eyes.

"Is Lila with you?"

"Nope. I just got her set up to do school."

"Oh. I didn't even ask about that."

"Right now she's doing distance learning with the middle school that she was in before. Eventually, I'd love to have her at the schoolhouse here. But she wasn't sure she was going to stay and wasn't sure she was going to like it, plus…"

"You hadn't told me." Her tone was accusing, and that was fair enough.

"No. I hadn't told you, and that needed to happen."

"So what are you doing here?"

"I brought coffee. As a peace offering. I thought… Well, hell. I thought we might as well hash some stuff out."

"Such as?"

"Can I come in?"

She let him pass and closed the door behind him. And he realized they had been alone together just a very few times since the old days. That last time had felt like this too. Like they were too close, like those years were too close to them. Like they were one step away from crying, kissing or screaming. All three of which had been their specialty back in the day.

"Look at us. Having a social call," she said.

"Yes, indeed," he replied. He held the coffee cup out.

"Is it poison?" she asked, squinting.

"No. I wouldn't be that sloppy. I don't have an alibi."

"Good to know." She took the coffee cup from his hand and took the lid off, as if she was checking the cream to coffee ratio. But he still remembered exactly how she liked it.

Damn.

Thinking that sent a bolt of lightning right through him.

He wondered if he remembered how she liked *everything*.

No.

That was not going to happen. They had a kid to

think about. And more baggage between them than the damned *Titanic* could hold.

At least the *Titanic* had sunk.

If their personal ship sank, it could take some of their bags down with it.

They weren't going to have luck that good. He had a feeling.

"I could respect you if you were a murderer," she said. "But I can't respect an idiot."

That was the Fia he remembered from back when. Funny. Sharp.

Beautiful.

He cleared his throat.

"Good to know," he said.

"I think it's good to know where you stand."

"I don't think you or I have ever been confused about where we stood with each other."

Everyone around them might have had questions, but as far as they went, they'd been crystal clear. It had been great, until it wasn't. It had been love until it was hate.

And now it was…civility of convenience?

"Fair. So now we need to what? Lay down ground rules? Is that what you want?"

"It's been a day. How do you feel?"

"It has not been a whole day, actually. But thank you. And I feel… I don't know. In some ways happy. In some ways sad. In some ways shell-shocked. I think I really felt like for the first time in a long while my life had settled. And now I am a mother. I suppose in some ways I am, I have been. But in other ways no. So this is new. Except… I don't know, you've been with her for three weeks. How does it feel?"

His chest went tight. "I pretty much want to cry every day. That's how it feels, Fia."

She looked at him, shocked. "I thought cowboys were allergic to tears."

"It's a kid. *Our* kid. How can you not want to cry? Looking at her, thinking about it. It's... It's intense. Every day is intense. And I know that I feel for her more than she does for me. I'm not even sure if she cares that I'm her father, or if it's all the same to her. And I get what it would be. I do. It was good for me. To hear you tell her that it was okay she wasn't looking for us. Because that hurt me when she said it to me. And you responded better than I did. You change the way I thought about it."

"Look at us," Fia said. "Being civil."

"We blew up over the biggest reason a couple can. A kid. In some capacity I think kids are often the cause of explosions. And now we're trying to be civil for the same reason a whole lot of people try civility. A kid."

Fia put the lid back on her coffee, and bit her lip. "That is true. You're definitely not wrong about that. This is... I don't know. I've been caught between wanting to fall to my knees and give thanks for this, or...cry. I wanted to spare her. From trauma from... She's back with us anyway. And I just want... I want us to make the tragedy she's had to live through into something good. And that means we need to behave ourselves."

Yeah, there was a real sense of *what was the point* that overtook him sometimes too. She was back here anyway. And he could admit it had been part of what fueled his anger when he'd made the decision to keep his choice from Fia.

He was relieved to see her grapple with it too. It

made him feel like he wasn't alone. Which was maybe a strange thing to think. But Fia was the only one he shared this with.

That had been true all these years. And they'd never talked about it. Never dealt with it.

The part of him that carried this felt stuck at seventeen sometimes, maybe for that reason. Because he'd locked it up in his chest back then and didn't take it out ever.

"Agreed. We need to keep it together," he said.

That much he knew.

"So just whatever conflict we have—because you and I both know we're going to have conflict. There's no way we spent the last thirteen years at each other's throats and were just suddenly going to be amazing at conflict resolution."

He laughed. "I guess that's a good point."

"We can't drag her into it. We can't have her feeling like she's somehow responsible for the tension between us."

"I think I've done a pretty good job of making sure she knows we come by the tension honestly."

"We do."

She looked like she wanted to say something, but instead looked down at her coffee.

"What? We're alone. It's free-for-all time. We have to get it out of our systems so it doesn't affect Lila."

Fia looked away. "I was remembering. Some things that I don't always let myself. I know why I was so jealous. I found out that my dad was cheating on my mom, and I basically didn't feel like I could trust men. Anyone. If my dad, who I always thought was a decent guy, was cheating, then why wouldn't my boyfriend cheat? That was why I was continually losing my mind whenever you were with some other girl. Or looked at one. Why were you?"

He huffed a laugh. "Because I was an idiot."

"Sure. Granted. I believe that. But I feel like there was more to it too."

"My dad was a narcissist, and he used everyone's feelings for him to control them. He'd give me something to get my loyalty. Take it away to remind me who was in charge. My mom loved him so much her only choice was to run away. In the end, she couldn't stand the way that he used her feelings. Manipulative. She had to get out. There wasn't really jealousy so much as I was always on the lookout for ways that you could be manipulating me. Because I... Because I would've done anything for you. And I freaked out about how intense all that felt. Teenagers shouldn't..."

"That's the *real* reason teenage sex is a bad idea. Isn't it? It's feelings."

"I think the unintended pregnancy also," he said.

She laughed. "Okay. Fair. The unintended pregnancies are definitely a big one."

"Yeah. But damn those feelings." They looked at each other for a long moment. "I thought I loved you, Fia."

He didn't know why he'd said that.

"I thought I loved you too." The only sound was the ticking clock on the wall. Why the hell did she still have a clock that ticked? She cleared her throat. "Listen, whatever you felt back then, whatever we were, you weren't alone. I...I cared for you. A lot. Looking back on it, I don't really think it was love. It was too immature. I'd like to find a piece of that, though. Now.

And remove it for all the drama, and just find a way forward. Together. For Lila's sake."

It was like a wall fell inside of him.

Lila.

He wanted to talk about her. Brag about her. This was something he couldn't hold back on.

"She's a good kid. She's so cool. When I met her, I... I can't even explain it. She looked so much like you, Fia. It just about damn near knocked me off my feet. I was pissed about it, then. But I was also in awe of it. Now...I'm not pissed about it. I'm not. She's *ours*. We made her. Together. It's a pretty damned amazing thing. Because she's so stubborn, which I think is both our fault. And she's just interesting. I know that we have to thank Jack and Melissa for that."

She nodded. "They were really good people."

"I realize that I denied myself that reassurance by not being able to talk to you about the decision." He looked down. "I cut myself out of the conversation. And I'm still not sure I can say that I'm at peace with everything."

"You're not ready to admit that you think I'm right."

"I don't know if you can call a choice like that right, definitely, just like I can't say keeping her would have been wrong. But I can understand." He sighed. "Do we need to agree? Are you ever going to think that what I wanted was reasonable?"

She shook her head. "No."

"Then why do I have to think that your option was the only option?"

She looked angry then. Mutinous. It reminded him of old fights. And old times they'd spent making up for those fights. "You don't. You don't have to do a damn thing."

"There was a lot I *should have done*, though. A lot of things I've been angry about were my own fault. I could have been part of choosing her family. I could have met them. But I never talked to you about that, I never asked you about them. I never…even asked you about her birth. What she looked like. How it was for you." He was disgusted with himself then. For not asking her about the labor and delivery. How long it was, if she'd had some kind of pain management. If someone had been there to comfort her. "It was easier for me to make you into an enemy," he said, his throat tight. "You're right about that too."

She blinked. "Wow. That's a whole lot of *you're right* from you."

"Don't make it hostile. I'm trying to be fair."

She finally took a sip of the coffee. Maybe finally accepting that he wasn't trying to poison her. "I don't know that there's any point going over all this old ground. We might just have to move forward. Make something new. That won't be so bad. I think there's no… There's no way to logic ourselves into a perfect way of dealing with this. I think we have to be ideological. We need to let go of the past. We need to accept that we are not going to come to a consensus on the things that happened then. And we just need to draw a line under it. And that's not a thing that any normal person wants to do ever. That's certainly not something you or I have been willing to do all this time. But we didn't have a reason. And now we do."

Well, she was right about that too. Dammit.

"Want to come to dinner at my house tonight?"

"You're kidding, right? Wait, *your* house or…"

"Nope. The Kings. The family homestead."

"Why?" she asked.

"I think it would be fun to let them know who Lila's mom is…by surprise."

"You're kidding."

"I'm not. It's different than it was with your sisters. My family already knows I have a kid. And hey, don't you think it would be fun to absolutely shock my brothers? Especially Denver."

Fia and Denver had worked together getting the new iteration of the ranch up and running. He remembered feeling jealous about that. And he and Fia had broken up two years earlier. But old habits died hard with her.

He could see she was tempted by that. "You just want to ambush them with me?"

"A lot of people suspect that something happened with us back in the day. It's not like we were subtle. It's not like we've been subtle a day since."

"Well," said Fia, "I haven't been."

"True. Mostly, it's you."

He looked at her, and he realized maybe for the first time how strange it was. That for a year of his life she had been the only thing he thought about. And that together they had created a situation that had nearly destroyed them as people. And then they'd acted like it hadn't happened. They'd never spoken about it. They hadn't talked to each other. They had just stopped being that piece of each other's life.

It was crazy. It really was crazy.

And now she would be part of it again. A key part. And that almost felt right.

Even if he couldn't explain it.

"What time are you going to bring Lila over?"

"Two o'clock?"

"That works for me."

He nodded. "Then when you come for dinner, you can just bring her with you."

"I would like that."

"All right. Hey." He spread his hands. "Look at us. We had a conversation without having an explosion."

"Pretty mature of us, I think."

"Yeah. I would say."

"All right. I'll see you later," she said.

"Yeah. See you."

He congratulated himself on two things when he left Fia's house. That he hadn't yelled. And that he hadn't kissed her.

He had been more tempted to do one than the other.

FIA FELT NERVOUS. How did you prepare to have your kid at your house for the first time? All of this was just so very strange.

Because of course for Lila, this would never be the same kind of mother-daughter relationship she'd had with Melissa. But it would be all Fia knew. All she understood.

A completely unique experience.

And she really wanted Lila to like the house. She wanted, on some level, for Lila to be impressed by what she had built. So that Lila would understand why Fia had made the choices she did.

And she obsessed about it all day until Landry pulled up in her driveway. She felt like it was kind of a bad precedent that she was back in a space where seeing Landry's truck caused the whole earthquake inside her body. But at least this was about Lila and not about him. She waited outdoors, twisting her hands. Lila got out of the car, with her phone and another handheld device of some kind in her hand, along with a stuffed animal, and what looked like a plastic, segmented slug.

And Fia suddenly realized that while she had once been a teenage girl, she wasn't entirely sure what to do with a teenage girl at this moment in time.

Landry shut the truck door behind Lila, his movements effortless as he came up behind her. And she had some weird kind of schism. A sensation like they were in a life they might've had, but never quite made it to. Not one where they were together. But like they were doing some kind of custody exchange.

God knew that was where they would've ended up.

They could never have gone the distance. Landry tipped his hat. "See you ladies at dinnertime."

She didn't know why that made her smile. But it did.

She tried to suppress it

Which left her with Lila, who was looking at her somewhat suspiciously.

"Hi," Fia said, her stomach going tight.

"Hi."

She was looking up at Fia expectantly, because of course Fia was supposed to be the adult.

"You can call me Fia."

"Okay."

"I thought you might want to see my house. And we could…bake. You like baking?"

"Not really."

"Well. Do you, um, do you know how to knit?"

"No. But…it looks kind of cool."

"Or crocheting. I like to do amigurumi sometimes. And make little animals."

"Oh yeah," said Lila. "I'd like to do that."

"I can teach you. And I can bake. You can watch if you want. I'll get you set up with a round for your crochet."

She wondered if it was normal that she felt a little bit like she was babysitting. There was also a strange, dull ache in her chest that wouldn't go away, that let her know that this wasn't just normal child-watching duties.

Was something wrong with her?

She'd wondered that before.

What was she supposed to feel?

What she felt was impossibly big, but she wasn't sure it was the right kind of maternal. How did you know?

These were the kinds of things normal people could probably ask their mother. But Fia wasn't normal. Her mother wasn't normal. They never had been.

She couldn't call her up and ask her. She'd have to also add, *oh, hey, Mom, by the way, I had a baby just two months after you told me I'd be a terrible mother.*

That would go down great.

She sat down at the table across from Lila and took out some of her crochet supplies, and a very simple pattern for a penguin. She'd taught herself to crochet years ago. It was good for her to keep busy, and at night sometimes she got a little bit overanxious. Especially now with everyone moved out, knitting or crocheting with the TV on was a great distraction.

"Um—" she picked up her hook and started a magic circle quickly "—this is going to be your base."

She spent a few minutes explaining it to her, and she felt like a camp counselor. She wondered when her numbness would ease. There had been a rush of feelings right at first, and then she'd said all these things. The right things, she felt.

And now she felt afraid of what she might do or say. Like she might breathe in too deep and all of this would shatter.

She'd been afraid she wouldn't be able to do this when she was sixteen. So confident she could do it now. But the initial rush had moved over her like a wave and left nothing but little pools of doubt and spiny sea creatures in its wake.

She could do without the spines, to be honest.

She breathed in and they hurt. She looked at Lila and they hurt.

But they passed the day working on their penguins and she felt like maybe it had gone well, because she at least looked pleased by her little yarn creature.

"So what do you think about ambushing the Kings with our presence?"

"I enjoyed ambushing them with mine," Lila said.

Fia scrunched her nose up. "Hmm."

"Are you embarrassed?"

The question cut Fia to the bone. Because of course it would seem like Fia was embarrassed of Lila. And of course she…was.

Not the way Lila was thinking, of course. It was the idea that everyone would know. Because when she thought of how she and Landry were it was all heat and fire and anger. When she thought of them it was so hot and intense.

Exposing.

Everyone would know.

"Not…of you," she said. "It's more… I don't know. No one knows Landry and I were together back then. He's explained the whole ranch to you, right?"

"Yeah, there's four ranches, but they're kind of all one thing. Like a Taco Bell Pizza Hut."

"Yes. We are the Taco Bell Pizza Hut of ranching. But if there was also a Burger King and a Wendy's attached. And we all know each other. We went to school in a one-room schoolhouse."

"Landry said there was a schoolhouse here. I think a school that small sounds insane. I don't even know the names of every kid in my class."

"And that's why I'm embarrassed. We just all know each other too well, and there are no surprises left, really? And now everyone will know…" She suddenly felt deeply immature talking about this to a thirteen-year-old.

*Her* thirteen-year-old daughter.

"It's so silly," Fia said. "It's the history between Landry and me that I don't really want people obsessing over—and they will. I don't know if you've noticed or not, but there isn't that much to do here."

"Yeah, I've noticed," Lila said. "Though it's not like I did much the last year."

"Oh. Yeah. I… What did you do before?"

"Normal stuff. I volunteered at an animal shelter on the weekends. We used to go hiking out of the city. My dad really liked to go to Blazers games, even though they suck."

Fia laughed. "They do suck."

"So bad." Lila smiled. "My mom didn't usually come to the games. But she liked to go to the Japanese garden. She said it was her favorite place to think. She had a membership, and she would take me there sometimes and we would just sit. We used to go to the zoo a lot. It's a really interesting zoo."

The picture Lila painted of a family so close-knit made Fia's chest ache.

It was what she'd wanted for her. But she'd lost it. She'd been affected by hideous trauma.

For the first time since Lila had come to Four Corners, she let herself wonder how it might have been if they'd kept her. Would they have gone on family hikes and trips to the zoo?

She blinked, trying to get rid of the stinging in her eyes. "Well, we don't have a zoo or an animal shelter, but we have a lot of animals here. And there aren't any stadiums, but we have a game day every year where we all compete against each other in things like football and potato sack races and get very competitive. Mostly, we also suck. We don't have gardens like Portland, but we have quiet places in the mountains, and I do have a garden where I grow fruits and vegetables. It's not going to be the same. But I think it could be pretty good."

Then she felt some of the spines inside her retract. She felt some of her uneasiness ebb. Maybe she wasn't the worst at this.

When it was time for dinner, she loaded Lila and the crochet creations in her car and they headed over to King's Crest. The place would be familiar to her again. What a weird realization. It was a new beginning in a lot of ways, but also a strange kind of old echo. A retread. She had to guard those grooves in her heart.

Which had been returned to her, but felt a little bit battered and bloodied besides.

But they weren't in love anymore. If she was honest, in a true adult sense they never had been.

*Obsession* wasn't love. *Lust* wasn't love. She and Landry had a lock on lust, that was for sure.

They did lust very well.

Dammit.

She hummed, mostly to fill the silence, mostly to try to redirect her thoughts.

"It'll be like ripping a Band-Aid off," Lila said sagely.

"I don't like ripping Band-Aids off, though," Fia said.

"Landry would probably say you can't avoid taking Band-Aids off forever or they'll mold. Or a bobcat will come eat your knuckles."

Fia looked at Lila out of the corner of her eye. "Would he?"

"Yes." Lila paused. "You and Landry don't *like* each other, do you?"

That didn't land quite right. She'd…despised him. For years. Hated him, even. He was also the only man she'd ever seen naked.

"It's a little bit more complicated than that."

"Like *him not telling you about me being here* levels of complicated?"

She sighed. She hadn't had any time to think about what kind of mother she wanted to be to a teenager. And she had never let herself fantasize about what it would be like to be a mom to a baby, because that just opened old wounds, and since she hadn't dated since Landry, it had been kind of a moot point anyway.

She had made the farm and the farm store her baby. And she had decided to be happy with that. To be a cool aunt.

Now she was trying to be a cool mom? While she felt like a combination babysitter/failure/maternal figure. Maybe? So she wondered what all she needed to say to the kid.

How much transparency she owed her.

And then she remembered that Lila was thirteen, and Fia had been fifteen when she got pregnant. The truth was, depending on what was happening in their lives, some kids just grew up too fast. She and Landry had been at a dangerous intersection. Adult hormones and desires colliding with teenage brains and coping skills.

Maybe if somebody would've noticed, maybe if one of her parents would have paid attention to her. Maybe if somebody had talked to her. About how feelings could seem savage and fatal when you were that young, but they were only feelings, and deferring pleasure wouldn't kill you. Using condoms was important. Protecting a piece of yourself might be a good idea.

"It isn't very straightforward when you used to… care about somebody very much."

Lila looked sage then. "So you had a bad breakup."

She felt relieved that Lila had managed to make it sound so simple. "Yes. We did. A long time ago."

"Was it over me?"

She bit the inside of her cheek. "Yes and no. We definitely disagreed about what to do, but we would've broken up anyway. I knew that. We couldn't listen to each other. We didn't know how. We weren't raised by parents who listen."

"I can't imagine that. My mom listened to everything I had to say. She was so great. She—" Lila stopped suddenly. "You probably don't want to hear this."

She needed to hear it. To keep imagining Lila in all those happy times. To stop being so tempted to imagine Lila as a baby, as a child, with her. With Landry.

She swallowed hard.

"I do," Fia said, with more gusto than she felt. "It's pretty lucky, actually, for me. That I get to have a kid who knows what kind of mom she wants." She looked away quickly. "I'm sorry. I didn't mean to say it like that. I didn't mean to say it like I was trying to take over. Or erase the mom that you had."

"I know. I mean… I need…somebody."

*Somebody.*

Fia could be that. She didn't know if she'd ever be the best, but she could be *somebody*. She might never be a manicured walled-in garden, but she could be a quiet place on a mountain.

The idea of that made her feel more peaceful than she had all afternoon.

"We all do," said Fia. "And that's what I want to be—that someone for you. So I want to know what you want. Because…I've never been a mother before. And I don't know you, really. I know that my own parents left a lot to be desired. I think they tried. I think maybe. But not…not as much as they should have. Let's just say that. They did not make it easy. And I got involved with Landry partly because we weren't getting any support at home. We needed each other so much because we didn't have anyone else. His dad was awful. His mom left. All of the Kings have a lot of trauma."

"Really? They're all so...great. They don't seem at all like they have competition now."

"Because they worked hard to make something better out of what they had before. It wasn't easy. I know it wasn't. And I respect Landry for that."

"But not for much else?" Lila asked.

"Hey. He and I are going to do the best that we can. The best that we can with what we have. And however that looks..."

"But you were telling me about how complicated it is."

"I think we just need to forgive each other. For what it's worth."

Lila looked at her, far too keenly. "Do you think you can?"

Fia wished she had an answer that wasn't possibly a lie. But parents lied a lot. If she'd learned one thing from her own, it was that.

The least she could do was tell a lie that would make her kid feel better.

"I think we can do anything for you."

And just then she pulled up to the farmhouse, so the conversation stopped.

"This is going to make a scene," said Fia.

"The best thing ever was when he just brought me to the house for the first time without warning them."

Fia gaped at Lila.

"You said he ambushed them with you, but you were serious?" Fia wanted to punch Landry for that.

Lila grinned. "I thought it was funny. It was maybe the best thing I've seen in forever."

Fia knew she shouldn't be bitter about that. That the ham-fisted way Landry was dealing with this was amusing to Lila. While she was trying so hard to be fair and measured and careful.

She sniffed. "I'm glad that you enjoyed the spectacle."

"Are you going to?"

"No. I never wanted the spectacle, actually. But now that we're here... I guess we might as well make a scene."

"I think so," Lila said cheerfully.

And bolstered by the fact that Lila was smiling, Fia got out of the car, ready to make a scene.

## CHAPTER EIGHT

LANDRY HEARD THEM walk up the front steps. And he took it upon himself to open the door.

He had told his family that a special guest was coming to dinner tonight, and he hadn't elaborated. The fact was, he had the sense that they already knew who Lila's mother was. They just hadn't said anything. Because they knew he wouldn't tell them. Not until he was good and ready. And here he was, telling them exactly in the fashion he wanted to.

"Hey there, ladies," he said, letting them in.

Fia's green eyes connected with his, and he felt a strange shift in his midsection.

"How was your day?" he asked, lowering his voice slightly.

"It was good," she said. She looked down at Lila and then back up at him. "It was really good."

"Glad to hear it."

"So where is everybody?"

"I believe about to come storming in here with food."

As if on cue, the back door opened up, and he heard all of his brothers talking. He could also hear Arizona, Daniel and Micah, and he assumed that Rue was there, but you would never hear her over the din of the Kings.

And they all stopped. Speechless, when they walked into the living room.

"I told you that I had a special guest coming tonight," Landry said.

*"Holy shit,"* said Justice, freezing in place. "Fia fucking Sullivan."

He could see Fia pause for just a second, like she was doing a math equation to figure out how to respond. And then it passed, and she smiled.

"Justice fucking King," Fia said in return. "There's a kid present."

"So there is," said Justice. "I believe she's my niece, though, and over the past few weeks she's grown accustomed to the kind of language we use around here."

"Very interesting. It just so happens that I'm her mother, and I am asking you to watch your mouth."

And that was that. Fia had done it. He'd been so pissed at Fia for so long he didn't think he'd ever fully appreciated just how amazing she was.

The lone woman to serve as part of the core, founding board of this version of Four Corners. Denver, Daughtry, Fia, Sawyer Garrett and Gus McCloud had come together when their parents had all cleared off and looked around and seen just how bad it all was. And realized the ranch was going to die if they didn't do something.

They established the system they had now. A way of sharing profits.

Denver had money from professional gambling and he'd invested a ton of it, pumping the ranch full of cash so they could reinvigorate their herds.

The Sullivans had leased land, started gardening,

done whatever they could do to bring capital into the ranch. All led by Fia.

And here she was, holding her own against all the boys yet again.

Lila looked delighted.

He felt…something. Something rise up inside him and grab hold of his throat. An intense kind of possessiveness that he knew full well lived inside of him. This need to gather both Fia and Lila to him and hold them close. To never let them go.

Feeling it now for Fia, that was a hell of a thing. And definitely not his idea.

"What the hell?" Denver asked.

"Don't tell me you didn't suspect it," said Landry. "Can't you see her?"

He gestured between Lila and Fia.

"Yeah, I can *see* it, but… Damn. I just figured…"

"That he had a type?" Fia asked.

Denver looked abashed. "Sort of."

"I expect everybody has a lot of questions. And the real reason that I showed up like this, and indulged Landry and his sense of theater, is that I want to make use of you-all as part of the gossip chain. Tell everybody so we don't have to."

Landry laughed. "Hell, yeah. There's so many of you, spread the word."

"This is quite the small-town scandal," said Daughtry. "And you told us not to say anything about Lila yet."

"I know. Because I hadn't talked to Fia. And listen, our business about the whole thing is our business. Not yours. But feel free to make the rumors real colorful."

"*Nonsensical* even," said Fia. "Everybody will mutter at each other behind their hands and we won't have to put up with it."

"And once it all blows over," Landry said, "maybe you can think about going to school at the one-room schoolhouse. We need the drama to pass."

"Wow," said Lila. "So this is like a *small-town scandal*? Are we a *scandal*?"

"Oh yeah," said Denver. "It's a big one. Because Landry and Fia hate each other. And pretty much always have. At least, that's what we all thought."

"You didn't have a theory on why that was?" Fia asked.

Denver shrugged. "Not really. My brother is off-putting. We all are. We're kind of used to people just disliking us because they do. I figured it was that."

"Really?" Fia asked, looking genuinely confused. "My sisters had been convinced the entire time that Landry and I…" She glanced at Lila. "Well, that we were secretly a *couple*."

"I guess they were closer to the truth than we were," said Justice.

Daughtry snorted. "I knew about you."

"*Did* you?" Landry asked.

"Yeah. I saw you kissing her years ago. Out at the cabin. I was trying to bring a girl there. And you were already there. Son of a bitch."

Lila looked slightly harmed by that information. Fair enough. Landry was harmed by the thought that his brother had seen them.

"Okay," said Landry. "Enough about my personal stuff in front of my kid, please."

"Hey," said Denver. "You brought the personal stuff to the King family. You get what you get."

And that, he figured, was mostly true.

"My mistake," he said dryly. "Really."

But after that, they all went into the dining room, which was already laden with potato salad, rolls and green salad. There were baked beans and pigs in a blanket, and his brothers set meat platters down next to all of it.

This was normal for them. A typical family get-together. They were functional. That was the thing he kept coming back to. They had made a functional family, even without the model of one. He wanted to use that evidence to tell himself that Fia was wrong.

To tell himself that he had been right, and they could've all rallied together and raised Lila.

But the truth was, his father had still been around them. And the thought of his father getting any of his poison near Lila, it made him want to kill the man.

It made him feel kinship to Angus McCloud, who, it had been rumored for a great many years, had in fact killed his father.

And no one would blame him.

So maybe the circumstances had been wrong. But he had offered to run away with her. But then... What would've become of the Sullivan sisters? Because just a couple years later their parents had busted up and then Fia had spent all that time taking care of her sisters while their mother had checked out. He had observed that even though he'd been distant from her at the time.

And maybe he'd even enjoyed her pain a little bit back then.

Because his pain had been the only pain that mattered.

And the real issue now, looking around the table,

looking at all these people who he loved dearly, was that while he admitted that he wouldn't have actually been a good father at seventeen, it made him question whether or not he could be a good one now.

As Fia had said to him, he had really looked at himself as a thirty-year-old, and had said that he could've done this when he was seventeen.

As if he hadn't learned a damn thing. About how hard life was. And if nothing else, he should at least be able to look back on how fragile he'd been as a teenager, and tried to imagine what he might've done with the child.

There was something about being in this house with Fia, which was something he had never done then, that made him face the impossibility of it.

He felt broken. Broken by the realization, broken by the feelings that were pouring through him now.

Daniel and Lila were bantering, and he looked at his sister, Arizona. She had been in love with Micah when she was seventeen. He had only really heard that whole story later. She'd fallen in love with an older man, and when he'd left, her heart had broken. He'd come back years later with a teenage son, and they had found their way back to each other.

She'd been on ice since then. Ferociously, fiercely angry. Arizona had been the kind of person who wore her anger on her sleeve. She had a reputation for being unpleasant in a way that Landry didn't.

But they were the same. He'd been hurt, and rather than looking at any of the rational reasons why something might have happened, he'd let it all fester. Let it turn to hatred. He would let it keep him frozen in the exact same spot he'd been in back then.

He'd let it keep him from being there for Fia. And he'd been angry at her all that time for not loving him enough. But how the hell had he shown that he loved her? He had chosen a fantasy over her.

He hadn't realized that then. He'd been desperate for her to have the baby in part because he wanted to keep her with him. He had felt like her giving the baby away had meant that he was giving them away too.

He was a fucking idiot. He could've been there for her. He could've listened to her. But instead, he listened only to himself.

He was his fucking dad.

And that was a hell of a thing.

Had his dad not realized the kinds of things that he did? Had he not known that everything he did was a narcissistic maelstrom? Because Landry hadn't known. He felt justified. He'd felt like his reasoning was valid.

He'd felt like everything was sensible when it had come from inside of him. And now he was on the outside of his body, watching this family dinner. Looking at Fia next to Lila, and realizing how wrong he'd been to not tell Fia from the beginning.

But his hurt and anguish had been piled in front of anything reasonable. He had been indulging it. He'd been indulging himself.

After dinner, there was pie, but he didn't taste it as he chewed and swallowed.

Daniel and Lila went off to play video games in the next room. And Daughtry kicked back in his chair, looking over at Landry and Fia. "So. You guys are…"

"Co-parenting," said Fia, crisp and precise.

"Right."

"Yep," said Landry. "We're co-parenting. Because that's just how we are. Mature."

*"Copacetic,"* said Fia.

*"A vibe,"* said Landry, smiling. "I learned that from Lila."

"I like it," said Fia.

"Okay then," said Daughtry. "And that's really all you're ever going to tell us."

"Play your cards right, and get me drunk enough and maybe you'll hear the story," said Fia. "But until then, we have a lot of things left to figure out."

"On that note," said Landry, looking at Fia. "Why don't we go outside and have a drink."

"I got some good stuff," said Denver.

He pulled down their famous apple pie moonshine. It was dangerous, because it tasted just like apple pie. It did not taste like what it was. Which was a very, very high proof clear alcohol that they brewed themselves.

It had caused a couple of brawls over the years, in fact.

He poured Fia a measure over ice. And some for him as well.

Then they went outside to the back porch. It was screened then, overlooking one of their larger pastures. They were close to their cows, and Landry had always liked it that way.

Some days he liked cows better than he liked people, if he were honest.

It was hard not to.

And some people would never understand the dichotomy of loving those animals, and raising them for meat. But it was in his blood. The care and keeping of the food they ate. Making sure that they were given good lives. That they were respected for what they gave in return.

Nobody loved cows more than the Kings.

"What is it?" Fia asked, taking a sniff of the liquid in her glass.

"It tastes like pie," he said.

She looked at him skeptically, then took a sip. "Well. It does. It doesn't even taste like booze."

"It *is* booze. Be careful. What I poured you should be all right, but it's a whole thing." He was silent for a long moment. "I was wrong, Fia." He turned to her. "Just about everything. I have gone out of my way to never think about this in a more mature way because if I did, then it was going to mean that all the hurt that I felt over all these years was unreasonable. That I was the one... That I was the one who took a bad situation, a difficult situation, and made it damn near impossible. But I have to face the fact that I was. I am so sorry. I'm so sorry."

She looked down into her glass. "Is this stronger than I think it is, or are you actually apologizing to me?"

"It's what you said," he said. "About the fact that Lila doesn't regret the adoption. I wanted to believe... I *needed* to believe that I could be enough. That I could love a kid in a way that my father couldn't. I needed to believe that the baby would keep you with me." He paused for a long moment. "A lot of it was about keeping you with me, Fia. I told you, I was a mess. And I was being serious when I said..." His throat worked. "I was struggling. Sometimes I had thoughts. About ending it."

He could see the words hit her hard. Life had been

bleak here. It really had. They were a pack of feral kids with parents who ran the gamut from cruel to indifferent. That they'd all made it this far was probably a miracle.

But he'd never confessed that to anyone.

"And I… I'm not using it as an excuse," he continued. "But loving you was the thing that made me enjoy my life. Loving you was what got me through being Elias King's personal experiment. You know he loved it when I felt like things were precarious. Like I had to do something to earn his love, and then he liked to withhold it. Dangle it in front of me. You never did. I was just really afraid to lose it. I was happy when I found out that you were pregnant, because I thought it meant you had to stay with me. And fucking hell, if I could go back and tell that scared, stupid little idiot one thing it would be he didn't love you like he thought. Because I should've been a better boyfriend, and counted on *that* to keep you with me. Not a baby." He dragged his hand over his face. "I realize that the way I've treated you is closer to my father than I ever wanted to be. Bringing Lila back… I did want to hurt you, you're right. And I twisted the truth of it all to tell myself I didn't." He paused. "But I did. Because I hurt, and I wanted you to hurt along with me."

It was honest. Not in a mean or spiteful way, but he could see it hurt her all the same.

"When we were young, we were so angry," she said softly. "We were never honest. If we came close to it, it was always really just us being spiteful. I feel for you. But I can't feel more for you than I do myself. Not about this. Not when my own memories are so clear. So painful. But you…you gave me honesty and I owe you the same. Not to hurt you, but to make you understand."

She took a sharp breath and continued. "Landry, I realize that you aren't lying to me about how much it hurt you that you didn't have Lila. I do realize that. I also… It was the hardest thing I've ever been through. The only way I could survive it was building a wall between us. It was so hard. To need you like that. We were…each other's safe place for a long time. I know, I know we hurt each other too, but we were still able to share more with each other than we did anywhere else. And I had to cut you off. To save myself. I had to build that wall."

She swallowed. "It's been weird to not have it there. It's been weird to be around you again. We spent all these years denying the truth. I get it. I get why you couldn't look at this differently. Because for me it feels a lot the same. I never imagined Lila at thirteen. I still imagined her as the little strawberry-haired baby that I held for just a minute. Because it's like I had to leave it back there. And even though I loved her, even though I carried it with me all this time, I didn't… I couldn't really think about the passage of time. And I really could never bear to look back on all of it. I accepted the lie that we made up, the one we told everyone without even talking about it. That nothing ever happened between us. That we just didn't get along, and I even kind of played into my sister's idea that I just wanted to…jump you."

He laughed, even though it was forced through a throat that felt like it was lined with broken glass.

"Yeah. Well. That was a simpler story, wasn't it?" he asked.

"So here we are. And here this is. You and me and Lila. The secret that we carried all this time."

She looked at him and hesitated. Then she reached out and put her hand flat on his chest. It was the first time in thirteen years that Fia Sullivan had touched him, and it was like making contact with a live wire. He didn't move. He didn't trust himself to move. "I am sorry about all the pain we both felt all this time."

"I'm sorry," he said, putting his hand over hers and holding it there. "I'm sorry for everything. I'm sorry that I was sixteen and stupid. I'm sorry I didn't use a condom. I'm sorry that I loved you like it was a crash test and I was the dummy. I'm sorry for all the stupid shit that ever came out of my mouth."

"Me too. It wasn't just you. You weren't alone in that. Landry, that alone would've left us both scarred. The way that we were… It wasn't…"

She didn't have to finish. He knew. It wasn't normal. It wasn't healthy.

It wasn't common.

They'd had a real, scarring, tragic kind of love. A real Romeo and Juliet kind of thing. And for a while there, it felt like that. Like drinking poison.

He would have.

And that boy could never have been a father. What had he learned since then? What had he done? They were still holding each other's hands, pressed to his chest when he moved even closer. "I don't know if I'm going to be any better at this now."

"I don't know if I am either. I taught her to crochet today." Fia looked down at their hands. "I asked her about the things she used to do with her parents. I wasn't sure what to say half the time."

"I'm not either."

He felt connected to Fia now, like he hadn't for a long time. He searched her face and tried to see if she was less certain than she'd been at first, if like him she felt wrong somehow. He knew he wanted Lila in his life, but he'd been grappling with his feelings of inadequacy and what that meant for the feelings he'd had back then.

He doubted himself.

He wondered if Fia did.

"She said she just needs somebody to be there for her," Fia said softly. "We're somebody."

"Yeah," he said, his heart going tight. "We are."

Fia moved away from him, disconnecting their hold. "I'd like to have her spend the night."

For some reason, internally, he rejected it. But he didn't reject it out loud. "Of course. Anytime."

He hesitated. "Let's… I don't know what all we're going to have to do to get you involved in the adoption process. But I assume that you want to legally adopt her also."

"Yes," she said. "I do."

"I'll find out. I'll call the caseworker tomorrow."

"Okay."

"Let's… Let's hold off on her spending the night."

"Why?" she asked.

"It's just all new and different. I swear I'm not… I'm not…"

"You're just worried," she said.

"Yeah, I know it doesn't really make any sense. But she's had a lot of changes."

He could see that she was resentful. Resentful that he was in the position that he was the one who knew

Lila best at this point. The one who was in charge of making this call.

And he thought about saying something different. He thought about reversing what he'd decreed.

But he had just walked back a whole lot of things. And he wasn't quite ready to deal with this.

"All right," she said. "Can she spend the day with me again tomorrow? I'd like to take her to the farm store. And I would like for her to meet my sisters."

"Yeah. Can I… Can I come for dinner?"

She took another sip of the apple pie. "Yeah. Why don't you come for dinner?"

Right then, as dumb as it was, he felt a little bit like he had a date with Fia Sullivan.

## CHAPTER NINE

SHE DID THINK, as she waited for Landry to come again the next day for them to make the exchange so that she could bring Lila to the farm store, that it was hilarious they were having dinner with each other's families two nights in a row.

If she could find much of anything super hilarious right now. Especially concerning Landry.

He had apologized. It had been tantamount to him saying she was right. He had essentially said that. It was very strange. And not expected at all.

She was excited to bring Lila to the farm store. Because Rory, Quinn and Alaina would all be there.

So as soon as she and Landry pulled into the driveway, Fia was out the door.

She waved and then felt silly. She practically ran up to the car, like a favorite surprise she'd been waiting for had just gotten there. But that was how she felt.

Lila brightened when she saw Fia and jumped out of the car.

She felt like Lila maybe even wanted to hug her, but didn't.

"Are you ready to see the farm store?"

"Yes," she said. She turned quickly. "Bye, Landry."

"Yeah," said Landry, looking vaguely stormy. "Bye."

"What's with him?" Fia asked.

"I dunno. He woke up grumpy today. He had another glass of that apple pie stuff after you left. He was sooooo drunk. Denver had to drive us back."

Fia frowned. "Well, that's not good."

"Don't be upset about it. He was just… He's fine."

She disapproved so, so hard. But she was trying to be careful.

"You like living with him," she said.

"He's great. He tries really hard."

Fia sighed. "Yeah. He's definitely trying really hard." That was undeniable. She couldn't even be petty about that. And she really would be if she could be. Because a little bit of pettiness in that space would be kind of nice.

"He's funny too," Lila continued. "And he let me get a gecko. He can build anything. I've been watching him out in the barn. And he's great with animals. I think that's where I get it from."

She was chattering about Landry, all stream of consciousness like he was the greatest thing ever. Like she hero-worshipped him a little.

If she detached herself from her post-Landry trauma, she could see why a teenage girl would hero-worship him as a dad. He was tall and strong and handsome.

But drunk, apparently, which was concerning. And out of that concern she could not have him drinking.

She and Landry were on texting terms now, which they never had been while they were together, because texting just wasn't as much of a thing all the way back then, especially not with the kind of service they had at Four Corners. But as soon as she got to the store, and got Lila shown around and settled, she pulled out her phone.

Really? You got drunk last night?

Barely, he replied. I wasn't drunk, I had Denver drive us home out of an abundance of absolute caution.

Lila said that you were sooooo drunk. Many ooooos.

I wasn't.

That was her perception. Maybe you need to be a little bit more responsible.

She fired the message off, and stood by it.

We'll talk about it later.

What if I want to talk about it now?

Because this is texting, not talking.

It's the same thing.

It isn't.

She was about to pick up the phone and call him when her sisters walked in. All three of them, red-headed and different, stopped in the doorway, and Lila looked at them. "Oh my God. We all have the same hair."

Alaina made a noise and then rushed forward, pulling Lila into her arms. "I'm sorry," she said. "I know that's very not cool. But wow. It is amazing to meet you."

"Thanks," said Lila, looked bemused. "It's kind of amazing to meet you too."

"We're your aunts," said Quinn. "I'm Quinn. That's Rory. That's Alaina."

"That's going to take me a minute," Lila said.

"It's okay. Just say *hey you*. We all respond okay to that."

"*Hey Ginger* also works," Rory said.

"Not on me," said Quinn.

Quinn always had been the one who wanted to pick a fight.

"How much of the business has Fia shown you?"

"A lot. It's really amazing."

"Agreed," said Quinn. "My husband, Levi, has the ranch that goes just beyond this road."

"She hooked up with him because of the road," said Fia.

"Hey," said Quinn. "Don't make me sound like a road ho."

Lila seemed delighted by the exchange, which was the only thing that stopped Fia from scolding her sister for saying *road ho* in front of the teenager.

Lila seemed to notice Fia's distress. She put her hand on her forearm. "Relax, Fia. I'm on the internet."

"You say that like it explains something," said Fia.

Lila just laughed.

They got her set up on the register and let her ring up a couple of customers, and then they took her to the back where they had extra preserves, baked goods and other delicious things.

At closing time, they went to the root cellar at the house and got out some supplies from there, then brought her inside and started to prepare dinner.

Lila sat at the table watching them all. Her focus was added.

"Why don't you help?" said Quinn, tossing Lila a dish towel.

"I don't know how to cook," she said.

"This is easy. We're making a chicken galette. We already have the dough made. It just needs to be rolled out. We're going to cut up some vegetables, brown some chicken and add some seasonings. Then we're going to bake it in a skillet."

Lila looked skeptical, but eventually joined them, and the pride that Fia felt watching her daughter cook just like they did was...

Maybe this was it. The moment it felt real. Did she feel real now? She felt like crying. Her chest was tight and her eyes hurt, and she felt afraid and hopeful and like it was all too big.

She wasn't bad at this.

Her only experience with a mother-daughter relationship had been bad. As the oldest, Fia had taken the brunt of her mother's frustrations. She'd been the biggest help, and the biggest target. And once her parents had started having real issues in their marriage, Fia had been the one her mother had exploded all over. To the point where she'd sometimes been cruel.

She'd told Fia she couldn't do anything right.

In hindsight, and with age, Fia knew her mom had been putting way too much on her, but at the time Fia had taken it really seriously. She'd let it hit her too deeply.

She'd felt so protective of her sisters, afraid their mother would be mean to them too. She never was. It was just Fia who drew fire. But Quinn, Rory and

Alaina had suffered from their mom being distracted by what was happening with their father and Fia had picked up the slack.

She'd gotten to a better place with her mother in the years after her dad had actually left. It was the in between place that had been so awful for all of them. Like watching someone die slowly. When he'd finally gone, it had been a relief.

She had never managed to have a companionable time in the kitchen with her mom when she'd been a teenager.

She'd *screamed* at her mom in this kitchen, and her mom had screamed back.

Lila was making a galette.

Maybe this was the honeymoon phase. Maybe this was unrealistic. Maybe Lila was still on her best behavior because she was afraid of being sent back.

She wanted to be here, Fia knew that. But would she want to be when she and Landry had to be strict parents? When they had to put their foot down about things? It was difficult to say. Right now everybody was on very careful behavior.

She couldn't see the future. But she could see right now. Right now, everything was good.

A half hour later, Landry showed up.

When he knocked, she held up a finger.

"Just a second," she said to Lila and her sisters.

Then she took off her apron and bustled to the door, slipping outside and closing the door behind her. She felt suddenly like she'd made a miscalculation, because he was standing very close. So close that her breasts tingled, a bit closer to the hard wall of his chest than she had intended for them to be. She didn't think he had grown much since he was sixteen. But he seemed taller. Maybe that was the strength in his shoulders. The depth in his chest. He also smelled delicious. Not like the cheap body spray he'd had when he was sixteen. But like soap and skin and man.

A man she had known once upon a time, and who her body yearned for in that moment.

It was like a pure hit of nostalgia. Of adrenaline and need. A degree to which she hadn't let herself feel in forever.

"Yes?" he asked. His tone jolted her out of her reverie.

"The drinking."

"I had one more little drag of the apple pie. I was a tiny bit tipsy. If I'd been alone, I would have been fine to drive myself back to the house, and even Daughtry would have been fine with it. That's how *not* drunk I was. But because I had Lila with me I decided not to. If she thought I was *soooo drunk* it's because I was messing around with my brothers, and I woke up in a mood, so I think she thought I had a hangover. I didn't."

"Okay," she said. "You're sure?"

"I'm not going to lie to you," he said. "First of all because I've never been performing for you. Not one day in the last thirteen years, have I?"

Grudgingly, she had to concede that point. "I guess not."

"Second of all, because I have been taking care of her for three weeks. And she's doing good. So trust me."

"Okay." She pinched the bridge of her nose. "What did child services say?"

"The easiest thing would just be to have you adopt her after I do. Because I can just let you do it. We don't have to have a whole state involved, inspections, none of that. I just have to sign off on it, as her father."

She wrinkled her nose. "I'm not sure that I like that. You being legally recognized as her parent before I am."

"I get it. If you want to involve the state, feel free. But it's a whole rigmarole. And I already did that part."

"I want to be able to adopt her the day that you do." It was important to her. It felt like an obvious thing from her perspective. They'd created Lila together. She'd come into this world theirs. She didn't want Lila to belong to Landry and not to her, even if it was on paper, a formality. It still mattered.

He sighed. "Okay. We'll start that then."

"Thank you." She felt like maybe they'd made some progress. Because he wasn't telling her that she was silly, even if he thought it was silly. He seemed to actually be listening.

"Smells good, whatever you're cooking."

"Oh. Galette."

"No idea what that is."

"I guess you'll just have to see."

She opened up the door again and let him inside. Her sisters all stopped talking and turned to face the doorway. They were wide-eyed, and looked shocked. As if the specter of Landry King passing into the farmhouse was one shock too many.

Which she could understand. After all the years of Fia and Landry being generally heinous to each other, him being here was akin to Satan appearing at the pearly gates.

"Landry King, everybody," she said dryly. "He's joining us for dinner."

*"Wow,"* said Rory.

Quinn raced to the window and looked out through the lace curtain. "I'm sure if I stand here long enough I'm going to see a pig fly by."

"Adorable," Fia shouted, clapping. "Just adorable. Congrats to you."

"Thank you," said Quinn. "*I* thought that it was adorable. But then, I'm invariably adorable."

Rory grabbed her oven mitts and retrieved the pie. Landry looked at it and then back at Fia.

"Why didn't you just say a galette was a topless pie?" said Landry.

"Because I thought it was more fun to keep you in suspense."

Their eyes caught and held, and maybe it was the inbuilt innuendo that made the eye contact feel heavy. Or maybe it was just the two of them.

Because more of that angry debris had been cleared away, and every time there was another sweep of it, she felt old *feelings* bubbling up beneath.

Old attractions.

She really did not need that. Because they were just now managing civility. She still felt on edge.

They didn't need to introduce that drama. It shouldn't really be surprising that being in proximity to him reminded her of all that chemistry. It shouldn't be surprising the chemistry hadn't gone away. They were hot together. They had been *multiorgasmic* together even as fumbling kids.

Really, they'd never been fumbling.

Landry had always been a master of her body in ways that she still couldn't quite understand.

But they were toxic. Through and through. And the

last thing they needed was to introduce any toxicity into this environment. Not now. Not when they were doing this well.

"Well. Let's eat," she said.

They had a big bottle of sparkling water at the center of the table, which Alaina wrinkled her nose at and went to the fridge and got a can of diet soda.

Then they all served themselves generous helpings of galette. Followed by extra pie and cake for dessert. Because they were always more interested in dessert.

"This is amazing," said Lila.

"Yes, it is," said Landry, his eyes settling a little bit too heavy on Fia.

"Well, I never thought we would have a King at our table," said Alaina.

"That makes it sound like he's royalty," said Lila.

"Oh, we know he's not," said Rory, sounding sharp.

Fia grinned, and so did Quinn. Toothy, and a bit threatening. It made her love them even more than she already did. Part of the reason she'd decided to place Lila with another family had been her need to take care of her sisters.

It warmed her to have them take care of her now.

Even if she knew she had to call them off. Because Landry was Lila's father and they were *being nice*.

"Damn," said Landry. "I didn't realize I was in trouble here."

"Just on the naughty step," said Quinn. "Until you prove that you ought to be off of it."

"I can respect that."

The evening slowed after that, and when it got late, she walked out to the porch with Lila and Landry. Lila went straight down the steps and headed to the truck.

Landry paused, and Fia took that opportunity to try to introduce the idea of Lila staying with her.

"She could spend the night next time," said Fia.

"Let's just wait."

She knew a moment of absolute annoyance.

But she let it go, and instead she tapped her foot on the porch.

"What?"

*"Nothing."*

But she wished it was nothing. Because right then the porch light caught the hollows of his face, and she had a strange moment where she seemed to exist in two realities.

It was like she was back then and firmly now.

Looking at the boy and the man all at once.

Yes, they'd had chemistry. That had never been their problem.

But this strange feeling she had now wasn't a memory. Landry King had never stood on this porch, like a date waiting to kiss her good night. They had skipped all that.

They had never really been boyfriend and girlfriend in that way.

But she could easily imagine it. What could've been. Far too easily.

"Good night," she said quickly, and she turned and raced inside before she could do something extremely dumb. Something she would only regret.

Because if there was one thing about Landry King that she knew, it was that he was a mountain rife with her potential regret. And very little else.

# *CHAPTER TEN*

"Landry. I have my period."

Landry stopped, his shoulders going tight. "What?"

"I got my period," she repeated. "I need some supplies."

He frowned. "Supplies. What… What kind of supplies?"

It was seven in the morning, and Landry was dumbfounded. Not because he didn't know that women had periods, and that it was reasonable and likely that Lila would have hers. She had been with him nearly a month now, and it hadn't really occurred to him, though, until just now. And he also didn't quite know what to get. His sister would. But…he had no idea. He'd never been in a long-term relationship with a woman. He'd never lived with a woman.

But by God, Lila was telling him and she wasn't bashful or embarrassed in the least, and he'd be damned if he made her feel weird about it just because he didn't have experience.

"What do you… What do you use?" he asked.

"I like period underwear."

"I…" He did not know that was a thing.

There was only one thing to do. He texted Fia. *I need some kind of feminine products over here.*

Feminine products?

Lila has her period.

I have pads. I bet she hasn't used tampons.

God in heaven.

She said she wants period underwear.

We'll have to go to the store to get those. And probably Mapleton?

Do you know what those are?

Obviously.

Well, it wasn't obvious to him.

"Hang tight," said Landry to Lila.

Will you please bring over some pads? That should help at least.

On my way.

"Fia is on her way with some pads."

"Great. But I hate those. I usually get the underwear."

"I don't know what those are," he said.

"Are you one of those men who get squeamish about mentions of periods? My mom says that we should be comfortable talking about bodily functions. And that using blue liquid on commercials is a form of shame."

He blinked. "I mean, I'm not opposed to an open discussion…"

"Good," Lila said, making the kind of bold, confrontational eye contact teenagers excelled at. "Because I refuse to be ashamed of normal anatomical functions."

"I don't want you to be."

"*Periods are part of life,*" Lila said, spreading her arms wide.

"Absolutely," he said. "I just don't have a lot of experience dealing with them. Fair?"

She got quiet. And then her eyes filled with tears. "I forgot for a second that my mom doesn't really say anything anymore."

He stopped, kind of unsure of what to do. A tear slid down her cheek and he moved forward, wrapping his arm around her. It was way more important he got this right than what he'd just said about periods. He took a breath, he prayed a little. He tried. "Maybe not. But she said those things to you, right. And they were good things. They became part of who you are, and even if she can't say them to you now, you just said them to me."

He thought of all the bad things his father had left behind inside of him. And he could only be grateful that when she was being formed, his daughter had been given something better. Better than what his father had given her. Better than what he could've given her.

Fia got there in less than five minutes, and she had a big package of pads in her hand.

She handed the package to Lila as soon as she walked in. "Here you go."

"Thanks," Lila said, looking back up the stairs. "I

have to start school soon. Can you get… I need the underwear."

"Yeah. It'll take me a little bit to get back with them."

"That's okay," she said.

"You don't want to go shopping with me?" he asked.

"No. I have school and… I just want the stuff that I'm used to." She looked sad then. And he felt it in his own chest. Like his own heart was crushed. She was confident and bold, and not embarrassed at all.

But she was also vulnerable, and experiencing something she probably didn't really want to experience with *him*.

"Whatever you need."

Lila went upstairs, and they heard a door close.

"I bet you kind of wish she would've spent the night with me now," Fia said, looking at him in a way he could only describe as *gently* antagonistic.

"Kind of," he said.

"I'm going to go over to Mapleton to get what she's asking for."

"I'll go too," he said.

"Really?"

"Yeah. I'll just let Denver know that she's here, and she'll be fine. She's got tons of family all around her. And she's just doing school."

"No. I meant *really* because… You actually want to go on a period underwear buying mission?"

He shrugged. "I need to know what she's talking about. I got a pretty sound lecture on not being ashamed of basic bodily functions."

Fia grinned. "Well, Landry, she is correct. You shouldn't be."

"I mean, I'm *not*, as you know."

He looked at her meaningfully, and her cheeks went fiery red.

He had never been squeamish about sex while Fia was on her period. Hell, he had wanted her all the time. But that didn't mean that he knew the array of feminine products available.

She coughed. "Great. Thanks for the memories. Let's head out to Mapleton, then. We'll buy a couple months' worth so we don't get caught unawares next time."

"Good idea."

They decided to take Fia's car, which got better gas mileage, and they set off down the dirt road after he made sure that Lila knew where they were headed, and that his brothers and sister were on deck to handle anything she might need.

"She got upset earlier," he said. "Because she told me something that her mom said and she forgot to make it past tense. I feel bad for the kid."

"Ah," said Fia, her eyes glued to the road. "You haven't had to deal with this yet, have you?"

She meant the period thing.

"No. It just didn't occur to me. Which I realize betrays my lack of experience with…living with women. But you know, we all had to be super independent. If we weren't, then life was just going to be hard. And my mom wasn't around anymore by the time I was old enough to know what a period was." For the first time he wondered how Arizona had handled all that. It made him feel like a jerk that he'd never wondered about it before.

"I'm sorry. I guess we both have parental abandonment in common." She grimaced. "Even though I was a lot older than you when my parents split."

He shook his head. "It doesn't matter. It's all the same bullshit, no matter how old you are. My parents were—" he pulled his teeth back into an approximation of a smile "—toxic."

It felt like the word had come up a lot lately. It felt like it was a good one for him and Fia, and his mom and dad, and if that wasn't sobering, nothing ever could be.

"Sorry. Wow."

"I really never wanted to repeat the cycle," he said. "That was never what I was asking for. But I would have, wouldn't I? How did you see that back then, when I didn't?"

He looked over at Fia's profile. At her neat frown. The way that her brow pleated as she thought.

"I don't know," said Fia. "Maybe it was because of my dad's affair. Because I found out right around then that he was…cheating."

"How did you find out?"

"I saw him. I saw him *with her*. I couldn't even bring myself to tell you. I just shoved it down and I kept it to myself." She looked at him, just for a moment. "But it made us feel so fragile. So intense."

"It's why you were jealous," he said.

She laughed. "I mean, if you can't trust your dad… why trust your boyfriend?"

It made sense. It gave him a lot more understanding of what had happened back then. Why she'd gone off on him sometimes for perceived slights.

"I get it. I trusted my dad even though I shouldn't have. Even when he proved I shouldn't. I never had one big thing that broke it. It was just…a lot of time. To sit and reflect on why I felt so bad all the time."

"I'm sorry," she whispered. "What a mess."

"Yeah. It was a mess." What he didn't tell her was that he'd wanted her to redeem him. Wanted her to *heal* him. Back then he'd looked at her and seen salvation.

Had his dad seen his mom that way at one time?

It was a sobering thought.

"I confronted him on the affair," Fia said. "I yelled at him. I told him that I was going to tell Mom. He told me if I did I'd ruin everything. So I kept it inside because he told me I had to. Then two weeks later I found out I was pregnant. I was so scared, Landry. I thought… I thought that everything was broken. Ruined forever. I thought about not telling you. I thought about…making it go away. That seemed like the easiest thing. But I knew that I had to tell you. And then you wanted the baby. And… I wish that I would've told you sooner that I had doubts. That's one thing I regret. That I didn't tell you right away that I thought adoption was the best thing. Maybe then you would've had more time to adjust. Maybe then you wouldn't have had a false idea of what I was feeling."

It was sweet almost, the way she was trying to give him credit now. But after all that self-examination he'd done lately, he really couldn't give himself that same credit she was. He'd been too stubborn. Too selfish. He'd seen her pregnancy as a gift because he'd seen it as a way to keep her, a way to heal himself…

He'd seen it as loving the baby, but it had been a very, very selfish love.

He saw that now.

"Nothing could've made me react to that better,"

he said. "Because I wasn't listening. I was feeling my
own feelings. And I was... I was so desperate to prove
myself. To prove all these things. That maybe I wasn't
my dad, that maybe the Kings could be functional.
That you should stay with me." He shook his head. "I
wouldn't have listened. I would not have listened to
you, Fia. Don't tell yourself that you could have done
something different."

"Thanks," she said. "I appreciate it. Back then...
It felt like the house was on fire. Burning all around
me. My life was on fire. And when I handed Lila to
her mother, I felt like I was handing the baby to a fire-
man who was outside that burning building. Like I was
handing her to safety. When you say I gave her up, I
don't know what you picture. But that's what *I* see."

A knot gathered in his chest, and he felt an unexpected swell of emotion behind his eyes.

"Well, damn," he said, trying to breathe around his
feelings. "We were kind of a fucking burning house,
weren't we?"

"Yeah. I just didn't want her to burn in it."

"I know. We can't be that now," he said.

"We aren't," Fia said. "We aren't. I promise. We
are better than that. Because we are older. Because
we have different resources. We won't be a burning
house again."

The image struck him, and it was the second time
in a couple of days that Fia had taken his worldview
and turned it completely upside down. Because he had
pictured giving a baby up as something *cavalier*. Something that you did to unburden yourself. But Fia had
never been unburdened, not a single day. He could see

now what she'd seen then. And he could never fault her for that. Not ever.

Fia turned the radio on, and he wondered if it was to keep them from having to talk more. The unfortunate thing was, they only had heavy truths between them, and that made being together a little bit exhausting. Of course, he was no stranger to having weight between himself and Fia Sullivan. That was just life, as far as he was concerned. It was definitely his life.

But while the song played, it got intimate, a little bit sexy, and he couldn't help but notice the curve of her neck.

Which was not the point of this trip.

Not indulging in the attraction that he still felt for her was definitely part of proving that he was different.

That they had grown.

They were going to co-parent. Like functional human beings. They were not going to get trapped in the bog that was *each other*. Because it wasn't about them. It wasn't about their previous connection any more than it was about his anger. Any more than it was about her resentment.

They had set that aside, and he would have to set the attraction aside too. When she turned her head just briefly to look at him, he saw a glint of something in her green eyes that suggested that it wasn't only him experiencing the feeling. But she would ignore it too. Because she knew that it was the best thing.

They pulled into the parking lot of the big grocery store in Mapleton and got out. It was early morning, so most of the shoppers were older. And it wasn't all that crowded.

They got a cart and went inside, and he was struck

by the domesticity of the moment. He and Fia had never had anything like domestic in their relationship. Not remotely. They had been nothing more than fire and flame. Nothing more than clandestine meetings and big screaming matches. There hadn't been nice dates, or dinners with family.

They had not been this. But then, he didn't even think he'd ever been to a grocery store without an adult at that point.

That was a pretty big indictment of the actual situation.

Fia took them straight to the feminine health products and grabbed two boxes of something clearly labeled Underwear. So there. It existed. He learned something new.

They were also right next to an array of condoms and lube.

Fia determinedly looked at none of it.

"Let's go look at some snacks. I'd like to have more stuff for her. Easy to make things."

"She can always just come to my house during the day."

"I need to have food for her at my place," he said.

"I guess," said Fia.

"There's no 'I guess' about it. She's mostly doing school at my place."

"She doesn't have to. She can do it at mine."

"Yeah."

Fia then went and got her own cart, which felt like an act of defiance, and they started a run of competing supplies.

This was healthy.

They went through the line together and paid. When

they got back in the car, he didn't really know what to say. So he said about the dumbest thing he could have.

"It seems like they have a lot more kinds of lube than they used to."

He *had* noticed that, but it was maybe not the best thing to say to his former lover. His former lover who he was still feeling a whole lot of things for.

"I'm sorry, *what*?"

"Just…a thing I noticed when we were in the aisle with the condoms."

She tapped the steering wheel aggressively with her palm. "I would've assumed that you were a lube aficionado," she said. "Or do none of the girls you bang need it?"

He was shocked, jolted by her mention of other women. And whether or not his seduction attempts required additional lube.

"This doesn't need to be a whole discussion, Fia. It was an attempt at small talk."

"An attempt at small talk about *lube*. Interesting. *Interesting choice*."

"I'm filled with nothing but interesting choices."

"For sure."

She let that ride, thank God. The only sound in the car was the tires on the pavement.

"So. How many women have benefited from your expertise since me?"

He thought he'd said the worst thing possible. But no, *she'd* gone and done it.

He was floored by that question. And also, he hated it. He did not want to talk about sex with Fia. Not now, not ever.

"None of this is about us."

"You're right. I'm sorry. I shouldn't have asked that." She paused for a beat. "I don't actually care."

"Good."

"It's… But you can't go bringing a lot of women home when you have a teenage girl living in the house."

So she did care.

"I'm not tempted to, thank you," he said.

"It's just, I imagine that it's curbed your lifestyle a little bit."

"I think you make assumptions about my lifestyle that are not actually true."

"So. Then you can answer the question."

"Very few, Fia," he said through gritted teeth. "Does that make you happy?"

She looked at him sidelong. "What do you mean 'very few'?"

For God's sake. Whatever. He didn't care. He didn't have any pride about it one way or the other.

"Three?"

"In thirteen years?"

"Yeah. I don't—" he let out a hard breath "—get a lot out of it."

"You're serious?"

"Yes. I'm serious. I tried. After the wound healed a little bit, I tried. I was… I was only disappointed. By the whole experience. It's actually distinctly depressing to feel like you will never have…"

He didn't know if there was any point in finishing the sentence.

She didn't say anything more.

"You're right," she said softly. "This isn't about us."

He felt wounded. By the whole conversation. By all that it forced him to reveal.

"How about you?" Because he felt like it was fair. Because she'd asked him.

"No one," she said.

He looked at her, and he couldn't figure out what the hell to say to that. His stomach was tied up in a knot, a knot that seemed to extend up his chest, wrap around his lungs, make it impossible to breathe.

"You're kidding," he said. "More than that, you have to be lying."

"I'm not lying. I didn't… It seemed dangerous. After you."

Because of course she was the one who had gotten pregnant. Of course she was the one who had to carry the physical consequences of that. He had been so sure that he was affected by that in a unique way. He had been so certain that he was the one that was scarred by it. Fia hadn't even had sex since she was sixteen. And sure, it had never been the same for him. But he'd done it. He'd gone out and taken some lovers and tried to forget her, using sex. Using other women. And she had been just so…devastated by what she had experienced with him it had actually ruined her.

There were circumstances where a man might take some pride in ruining a woman for all other lovers, but that was not what this was.

This was about *scarring* somebody. Taking one of life's joys and stealing it from them. This was about the harm that he'd caused that he'd never been able to acknowledge.

It didn't mean that he hadn't been hurt.

But Fia had never tried to deny his hurt.

He'd tried to deny hers, because like she'd said, he had needed a villain. It had been convenient. It had been expedient for him to make her the villain, because then he could oversimplify everything. Then he could make it all easy.

But it wasn't easy, and it never could be.

"Damn. I really fucked things up for you, didn't I?"

As apologies went, it kind of sucked. But it was the refrain echoing in his soul.

"There were two of us involved in that relationship," she said.

"But it didn't help. The way that I reacted to everything."

"No. It didn't help. But we can't keep rehashing it. We can't keep going over and over…"

"We can, though. Until I get it all sorted out inside myself. Until I…reckon with the fact that I hurt you. All the ways I hurt you. Because all I have thought about for years is the way that *you* hurt me, Fia. But I never looked deeply enough at the way that I hurt you. I looked at you and saw the person who was in control of the decision. The person who was in control of whether or not we became a family or broke apart. That wasn't fair. It was never fair. And it becomes clearer and clearer to me when you say things like that. You haven't even had sex with anyone else. Because you were so…so scarred by what happened. By the consequences. I'm sure that the way I treated you had something to do with that."

"I don't know… Don't. Don't make it sound like you were evil. Or abusive. You weren't. You were fundamentally a pretty good boyfriend. Until everything went to hell. Or at least, you were as good as *I* was. I was the one who screamed at you all the time, every time you talked to another girl. I was the one who was so obsessed with you that I started sneaking out every night to see you. You *never* pressured me for sex. I jumped on you. I was the one who told you it was okay the times you didn't have a condom. I bear as much of the responsibility for what we were as you do. Yes, the whole thing surrounding Lila's birth…and the way that you held it against me, *that* we can interrogate. But don't act like you victimized me. I own responsibility for us."

"I don't really get how you do that." He looked out the window, every feeling on the spectrum shifting through him. "How you act so fair. How you let me be so many different things, but I only let you be one."

"Because I've had to," she said. "Because that's what it's like to be a woman in the world, Landry. Because it's what it's like when you find yourself pregnant as a teenage girl and you have to go through all of your options. You have to be able to see things from a lot of different angles. And…it's what I had to do in my family, too. I had to be able to see things from everybody's point of view. Because my parents…"

"There was no scope for complex thinking in the King household. You agreed with my dad or you were out on your ass."

"How…how did you all end up with the ranch? I mean, I know your dad was in prison for a while after…"

"That's not what we were talking about," he said.

"No, I know. It's just not interesting, though. How I survived. Why I'm able to think about things this way. It's because I went through something really hard. And I knew that I wasn't a villain. So I had to learn to think of myself in a more complicated fashion. I don't think that's actually unique. I think it's survival. I think we both had to do our fair share of that. It sounds like you had to look at things black-and-white to survive."

He ground his teeth together. "Yeah. In a fashion. My father wasn't abusive in the way that Seamus Mc-Cloud was. The McClouds survived worse than we did, don't get me wrong. But he made everybody around him feel like they were walking on eggshells all the time. He set himself up to be the smartest, most important man in the room. He was gregarious and interesting when he wanted to be, and he was a tyrant at other times. But again, not in the way that he made you feel afraid. He made you doubt yourself. Made you doubt your own strength. Made you question everything. So yeah, I chose black-and-white a lot of the time, because my dad splintered things. Because he made me question reality. Denver wouldn't let him come back after he got out of jail. He paid him to leave. That's the only real thing our dad ever loved. Money and power. We made it clear he didn't have power anymore."

"He… Denver has money?"

"Yeah," said Landry. "You started the whole collective with him, do you not know that?"

"I always thought that big injection of cash he gave was from the Kings."

"No. It was from his pocket. There was nothing here. Everything our dad made was from his drug running, his illegal gambling and loan sharking. It was all dirty money, and the ranch itself…that was a front. It was dying. Denver did what he had to do to get it back on track, and he made it clear to our dad that there was no place for him here. He was a narcissist who overplayed his hand."

"I… I really had no idea. Not the narcissism thing,

I did know that. I mean, maybe I didn't think of it as a diagnosable condition, though I know for him it was on that level."

"It's tough," he said. "Because I've spent a lot of time hoping I'm not my father. And I realized I'm more him than I'd like to be. I acted in a way that would've made him proud. I'm sorry about that."

"You're not your father."

"Hell, I might be, Fia. What do I really want to have a kid for? Is it to shape her into something that's mine? Is it to prove myself right? I'm not sure that I can trust my own motivations. It's messing with me because I'm not sure what my dad thought about anything. I imagine him as some kind of Machiavellian figure who knew that he was manipulating everybody around him, but now I just wonder if he thought he was justified. That scares the hell out of me. That I could be him and not fully realize it. That what I was doing was making a cast of villains to avoid looking at the fact that I was one."

"I told you. Don't oversimplify it. You aren't a villain. You never were. I care about you, Landry. I always have. Even though I'm angry at you. I didn't fall in love with a narcissist when I was fifteen. I saw that you were hurting. That you were a kid with a lot of feelings, and nowhere for them to go. No wonder you were so angry."

"It was hard not to be angry. He would tell us we could do something, have something, and then tell us he never said it. He would forget all birthdays. And then get angry if we forgot his. If we didn't make a big song and dance about the patriarch. He talked about the cost of raising us. What we owed him. How much more money he'd have if they didn't have all those kids. When my mom left, he said it was us. I knew it was him. I knew it wasn't us. But then you have to wonder why she didn't come back. Ever. Because we are grown now, and he's not here. And she's no contact for what reason?"

"It wasn't you," she said. "And you're not your father. Look at the lengths you went to to get your child."

"I don't understand how you can say that."

"Because I can believe that both are admirable things. My giving her up, and you wanting to make space for her in your life. And I can believe that what you did was a little bit petty while also acknowledging that you did it out of love."

"Shit," he said. "I feel like an emotional preschooler next to you."

"Because the world only demands men ascend to the emotional level of the preschooler, Landry. That's the problem. So if it seems outrageous to you, it's only because I don't think you realize how much is asked of women. But let me tell you, being the one ranch with only women, being the only woman on the board for Four Corners, I do get how different it is."

He found himself considering that position she found herself in yet again. The matriarch in many ways. This woman who was strong enough to hold her own with men. He had never appreciated how much more work she did. There was so much he didn't know. Hadn't considered. She made him feel like he'd been walking through the world with blinders.

And maybe it wasn't narcissism.

But damn, righteous anger was a hell of a drug. And it didn't make your vision clear.

"Well, I don't like the idea of being an emotional preschooler. Particularly not given that I'm raising a thirteen-year-old who has to be a woman in the world. I need you. You know that right. Because I don't know what *period underwear* is, and I don't know how to navigate all this. I didn't have a woman in my life for long enough. And poor Arizona had to acclimate to what we were. Feral."

"Well, I want to be part of this. Of Lila. Of her life and your life."

"Maybe tonight would be a good night for her to spend the night," he said slowly.

"Really?"

And he felt something inside of his chest loosen. A fist.

"I'm not in control of this, or her. I have to stop thinking of myself as the primary parent. I'm ashamed, Fia. Of myself. Because the truth is, that part of me was firmly rooted in my seventeen-year-old thinking. But I am a grown man. And I can certainly look around and see that this is different than I thought it was. And that what I wanted was…" He sat there for a long moment, trying to figure out how to say what he wanted to say next. Because it had been a feeling inside of him and nothing more for a very long time.

"Back then I wanted a sure thing. I wanted firm ground. Because I didn't have anyone who felt safe in my life. My mom left, my dad was volatile. And you and I felt so fragile. I saw a kid as something that would glue us together. I saw it as a simple, uncomplicated love. I could just love a child and they would love me. Hell, I loved my dad even though he hurt me. And I was convinced that I would never hurt a child of mine. Not ever. I was certain of that. And now here I am with her, she's thirteen and she's complicated. The love that I feel for her is so all-consuming, so intense. It's painful and brilliant all at once. I know that I couldn't handle it then. But I was so desperate. I was so desperate for something that felt cut-and-dried. But this isn't, of course. It never was. I was a fool to think that I could…"

"You wanted to control something."

"Yes. And most of all, I wanted you to look at me and see a hero. Because I wanted so badly to be a different kind of man than my dad was, even then. And you saying we weren't in the right place to raise a baby felt like you rejecting me, as the father to your child, as your boyfriend. It made me feel like I couldn't possibly be better than my old man. That made me feel like I must be a liability. And so yeah, I made you the bad guy, because I didn't want to be."

He took a deep breath, and he felt like there was ground-up glass in his chest. He could barely breathe.

"I'm sorry," he said. "I'm sorry for hurting you."

"I'm sorry for hurting you."

The words were simple, a balm for those wounds.

He felt differently now than he had a few days before. It was amazing what a conversation could do.

Well. And a very strong motivation to actually listen to each other.

They just hadn't had it before. They had no reason to forgive each other, and now, they did.

Though he did feel in the end of all things, he was the one who possibly needed forgiveness more.

He might've had his reasons, but that didn't mean he'd behaved right.

"Well, I can ask her if she wants to stay at your house for a couple of days, do her school there. You're right. There's no reason she can't."

"Thank you," she said.

They finished the drive in companionable silence. And for the first time in a very long time, he felt like he'd said the right thing to Fia Sullivan. Even more important, he felt like he'd done the right thing.

## CHAPTER ELEVEN

"I THINK WE should have a birthday party for Lila."

"Her birthday isn't until May. Also, Thanksgiving is in two weeks."

Fia sighed and crunched her phone between her shoulder and ear as she straightened up a display in the farm store, keeping one eye out the window on Lila, who was standing in a group of chickens with a look of delight on her face. "I know. But she turned thirteen in foster care, and I just think that we need to make sure that something special happens to mark that. She needs a real birthday party. With her family."

Landry made a musing sound on the other end of the phone. It was weird how much she talked to him now. They had talked more in the last few weeks than they ever had. In all honesty, their teenage relationship had not been based on conversation. It had been hormones and feelings. A *lot* of feelings. But feelings all the same.

"Yeah. That sounds like a good idea. Who all would we want to invite?"

"Well, your family and mine, obviously. I wonder if we should try to invite some of the kids that go to the school? Since eventually we want to integrate her there. When she's ready."

"Yeah. That is true. Is there anything more awkward

than being a teenager and being forced to interact with teenagers you don't know?"

Fia laughed. "Okay. Granted. Maybe you can find out from Daniel if there are one or two people he might think are good to invite for her. He knows her pretty well now."

"Yeah. They get along great. He loves taking on that older cousin role."

"Perfect," said Fia. "Then he can play older cousin and we can figure out a couple of people to invite."

The rumor mill had definitely done its job on Four Corners. Word had spread about her and Landry's child. And Fia had intentionally *not* taken a couple of calls from her mother. She was certain that by now one of her sisters had talked to her mom. But she just didn't have it in her.

They'd come to an okay place. Not a place of talking all that often or anything, but Fia had visited her mother in Hawaii a couple of times since she'd moved there. There was no good reason to turn down a trip to Hawaii. Not even childhood trauma.

But they didn't talk about those dark years when her mom's marriage had been crumbling and Fia had been doing her best to hold things together while falling apart.

She'd never been able to figure out quite why she'd made her mother so angry. She probably never would. That was okay. She didn't need to.

She didn't need to rehash the past any more than she already had to right now.

"Are your parents ever going to come back?"

He asked that as if he could read her mind. That was the strange thing about Landry. They really hadn't done a good job of communicating when they were younger. She wasn't sure they did a great job of it now. But he seemed to know what she was feeling and thinking almost as often as she did. Maybe that was why it had felt like such a betrayal when he hadn't agreed with her then. On the most important thing. The most essential thing.

She swallowed. "I doubt it. I think we're just going to have to accept that Lila doesn't have functional grandparents. Though, it sounds like she didn't before either. Jack and Melissa were isolated from their family. I don't know why. They didn't say. I just know that she didn't have other relatives."

"Yeah," he said. "At least we have... Well, all of us."

"Yeah," she said. "Obviously I'll make the cake. And we can handle a few other aspects of the food."

"We've got dinner," said Landry. "It'll be great. A big teenage birthday party. Hell, it's kind of a first birthday party for us."

Fia was suddenly gripped by regret. Anguish. His words forced her to imagine a chubby one-year-old sitting in front of the cake with a single candle. Her grip slipped on the phone.

"Fia?"

"I'm here," she said.

"Are you okay?"

"I wish... I wish we had pictures of her. I'm sure they're...somewhere. But what happened to all of her things? What happened to everything she had to give up when she went into care?"

"I can try to find out. But I have a feeling if it was easily accessed her caseworker would have said." He sighed and Fia felt it across the distance. "I have a feeling finding it would be somewhat miraculous."

"Well," she said. "I guess we're in the middle of something some people might call a miracle. You know, centered around tragedy and regret."

His voice lowered. "Do you have regret, Fia?"

"Don't you?" She was doing it. Turning it back around to him. She did that. She made it about what kind of father he would've been. She avoided thinking about what kind of mother she might have been.

"Of course," he said. "I regret the way that I handled things with you. How can I not? I let myself get steeped in regret this whole time. But I ignored too many things. I ignored what my part in all of this could have been, should have been. Most of all, I didn't take care of you."

It was such a simple, stark statement. And she felt nearly undone by it.

It was what she'd wanted. To have Landry take care of her. Because of all the people in her life, she had loved him the most. She knew not to count on her parents. They had always been more interested in themselves than in their own children. But Landry had been *hers*. And she had needed him. She had clung to him like she did because she'd needed him. And then when she'd needed him most he'd become her enemy.

"Fia?"

"I'm just thinking. Sorry. I did need you. That was the worst part, Landry. Well, it wasn't the worst part. But of some of it. When I was sleeping at Jack and Melissa's in the room that was going to become Lila's, I just wished that I could call you. I just wished that you would be there to hold me. I didn't wish that

I had my father. I didn't wish I had my mother. I just wanted you."

She was grateful for the distance they had. For the fact that he was on the phone, and Lila was outside safely. The fact that her store was empty. Because her heart felt like it was crumbling.

Because she loved that child outside, but still felt some distance. Some hesitation. Because she was a whole tangle of memories she wished she had, and memory she didn't want.

Because the man on the other end of the phone had been her sworn enemy for the past thirteen years, but was also the only person who had shared this with her in any capacity. Because in many ways he still felt like the closest person to her, even when he had felt like the most distant.

Because she felt justified in the decision that she had made to give Lila up. But she felt sad.

And with Lila here she couldn't defer the sadness.

"I'm here now," he said. "It's not going to erase the last thirteen years, but it's something. I hope."

She thought of all the life she'd lived since she'd taken that pregnancy test. She'd had to grow up, stand firm. To love sacrificially. She'd gone to stay with Jack and Melissa, where she'd experienced a kind of stability she'd never imagined before. A stability and care she'd brought back to her sisters, and had carried forward in the way she cared for them.

She'd found strength she hadn't known she'd ever possessed, which had helped her when it came to forming the Four Corners collective, doing battle with the men when necessary to make sure that Sullivan's Point got what it needed to survive and thrive.

She'd started the baking business. Planted seeds, grown gardens. Opened a store.

She'd given her daughter up, and while she'd known it had been best for Lila, she'd also done what she could to make it matter in her own life too.

"The hardest truth is…is we don't need to erase the last thirteen years," she said. "We've done a lot. A lot of work on our ranches. A lot of work on ourselves. Lila was out there having a whole life. It wasn't *nothing*."

There was silence between them for a long moment.

"No," he said, his voice heavy. "It wasn't nothing."

*It just didn't have you.*

She thought that while looking at Lila. She thought it with Landry's breath in her ear on the phone. She wasn't sure which one of them it applied to more. But then half the time she still couldn't figure out the nature of her feelings for Landry.

"Saturday night. Let's do the party. I'll make sure that all my family is available, but who are we kidding? None of us do anything off the ranch."

"Untrue. Your brothers like to go out to Smokey's."

"That is true. I just don't care."

She was pondering yet again the conversation they'd had in the car. About the way that he didn't enjoy hooking up. She wondered if he was just built that way. Or if it did have something to do with her.

She didn't ask.

"Okay. Well, I will make some plans. What presents should we get her?"

"I have an idea. But don't get mad at me."

"Why would I get mad at you?"

"Because you're going to accuse me of stealing your thunder."

"I will not," Fia said.

"I thought I would give her a horse. Back at CPS I mentioned that we had horses and she lit up, and she really likes coming out with me on the ranch and riding," Landry said.

"Okay. That isn't fair. My name has to go on the tag for that."

He laughed. "I think that can be arranged. And then I think maybe we need to do a family trail ride."

The word settled strangely in her chest. A family trail ride. He meant her. He meant him. He meant Lila.

Lila made them family. Maybe that wouldn't be true for everybody, but it was for them. For the situation. She wasn't quite sure what to do with that information. With that feeling.

"Why don't you come by later? You know, when it's time for you to drop Lila off. And then we can choose a horse together."

"From your horses?"

"Actually, I was thinking I might call Gus. I know he's got some great, gentle animals. I know he needs a lot of them for the equine facility, but I heard him saying something about taking on some new rescues."

"I can call my sister about it. You know, since he's my brother-in-law."

Landry laughed. "Yeah. I guess he is. I can't get over that one."

"Why not?"

"Okay, I think at this point everybody knows we would be the most unlikely couple on Four Corners. But I think Gus and your sister would've been a close second."

Fia frowned. "Because of their age difference?"

"That, and… The everything about Gus."

"Yeah. I would've agreed with that. But it's amazing how good they are for each other. He just loves her. Actually, that's true of all my sisters' men. Nothing could be more of a relief to me."

"You really had to take care of them, didn't you?"

"Yes. When everything imploded it was… We were adults when our mom left, but she had checked out way before that. And once Dad left somebody had to see to the running of the ranch. He'd left so much baggage. And so many enemies. He's not as widely loathed as your father, but he did some shady, underhanded dealings. Levi Granger hated my family for a reason. And thankfully, my sister sorted that out by falling in love with him, but yeah. There was just a lot. It was a lot to take on when I did. I was never more grateful that I'd made the choice to give Lila up than during all of that. I couldn't imagine trying to be a mother to her while I was trying to mother my sisters and get everything in order. Start up the collective with Sawyer, Denver, Daughtry and Gus."

"I'm not the oldest, Fia. So the responsibility, all of that, it was never going to fall to me. I'm the youngest. I think there are some difficult things in that. The ways in which the people around you don't include you in decision-making. We were the same age, hell, I'm a little older than you, but I wasn't included in the making of Four Corners as it is now because everybody above me had more decision-making power in our family. I didn't have the responsibilities that you did. That's not an excuse. But maybe it's part of why to me things always seemed a little bit simpler." He blew out a breath. "My life was simpler. People don't like admitting that. Hell, I don't like admitting it. Because of course you feel like you work hard. Like you're doing everything you can. To look over and see that somebody else is dealing with more, and with more grace than you manage on a given day is difficult."

She closed her eyes. "Thanks. You are right, though. These years haven't been nothing."

"No. And you know what's even better? The next years won't be either."

She looked out the window at Lila again, who was now dancing around the chickens looking happier than Fia had ever seen her.

"No. They won't be."

## CHAPTER TWELVE

FIA MADE ARRANGEMENTS for them to go over to Mc-
Cloud's Landing and choose a horse for Lila. Landry
felt strangely nervous, and he couldn't quite pinpoint
why. Whether it was about trying to choose the best
animal for his daughter, or about seeing Fia again. In
which case it wasn't nerves. It was something else entirely.

It was amazing how quickly he got back to his
thoughts being consumed by that woman.

But he saw her face in his daughter every day. She
was inextricably linked to the biggest thing in his life.

And she herself was quickly becoming something
major in his day-to-day.

He didn't talk on the phone. He had spent an hour
on the phone with Fia earlier.

And then again later when they had discussed their
plans for tonight.

Lila was with his family, and Denver was going to
see her home when she was tired. But he didn't think
he would be that long at McCloud's.

He pulled up to Fia's house in his truck. The place
really had never looked better. He stopped to admire
the gorgeously manicured fenced-in gardens. A cor-
nerstone of the farm store that the Sullivans ran.

There were flowers and fruits and vegetables. Cherry trees, apple.

He was musing on that when he walked up the front porch and knocked on the door.

"Have you ever thought about getting a greenhouse?"

She blinked. "Well. Yes. I have definitely looked at some beautiful old-fashioned-looking greenhouses online. Because who doesn't want an orangery like a fancy Regency miss?"

"You could grow more things year-round. Citrus even. Avocados."

"I *could*," said Fia. "But I've always felt like we needed to stick to local and seasonal."

"It would still be local and seasonal if it was in your greenhouse."

"Fair," she said. "But I don't go to your ranch and tell you that you should have bison. You have cows."

"I do," he said. "But maybe I would get a bison."

"Then maybe I'll get an avocado."

They looked at each other for a moment, and he tried to ignore the swift kick in his chest he felt when her green eyes sparkled with humor.

"Come on. Let's go. Gus is expecting us," he said.

"Yep," she said, closing the door behind her and heading down the steps with him. They got into his truck. And there was something about that that felt quintessentially old-school Fia and Landry.

Being in his truck with her. He felt compelled to make her laugh. He'd done that. Back then there had been a lot of laughing.

They hadn't exactly talked very deeply about the things that were going on in their lives. They had been an escape for each other. In that sense, he had known that things weren't great at her house, because he knew that he didn't share what was going on at his own.

So he had accepted that what they were was a break. From the lives they didn't want to be living. They chose each other. They chose those nights out in the cabin. Furtive escapes during the day in his truck.

It had felt like the real world. The real thing.

His house was just a place he had to go sleep.

Fia had been his home.

He turned his thoughts away from that particularly raw realization.

"Memories," she said, sighing.

He was taken off guard by her absolutely unerring ability to speak his own thoughts out loud.

"How did you do that?"

"What?"

"Know exactly what I was thinking."

She leaned forward in the seat. "I was thinking the same thing about you earlier today. You always say what I'm thinking."

The truck went over a pothole in the road, and they pitched forward and back. "Maybe our thoughts are just both headed down the same road most of the time. Because what we're living in is definitely a resurrection of a shared past."

"Definitely," she said softly.

"We just pretended it didn't happen," he said. "How did we do that? Now we talk about it every day. I think about it every day. From morning to night. Every day. I go over it. Us. Lila. The way that we hurt each other."

"Me too," she said. "I don't know. Survival, I guess?

The same way that my parents just left here and barely acted like they had kids at all?"

"Maybe that's how you protect yourself when you know something is too messed up to untangle. Even if your parents came back, would you guys forgive them?"

"It depends. First of all, my mom and my dad aren't the same thing. Second of all, I think me and my sisters all had different experiences with our parents. The younger girls really worshipped my dad. Especially Alaina and Quinn. Rory less so. But she was never so much the rancher. She was kind of the nerd. The bookish one. She spent a lot of time with Gideon and his family, because she didn't even go to school here like the rest of us. She sort of had a life outside of this place, and I think part of me was envious of that. Sometimes I didn't. And I also never could see my dad as an infallible figure. I was way too aware of the issues he and my mom had. Because she told me. I was the oldest. I was the sounding board. I never wanted to do that to Lila." She looked over at him. "We were so dramatic sometimes. I never saw them in us back then. I couldn't imagine that the connection my parents had shared at one time was probably *sexual*. Gross. Who wants to think that? I thought that you and I were unique. But… When I imagine what our relationship would have looked like once a child was in the middle of it…"

"You think that's what we'd be like."

"Exactly. So, if my parents came back, would I forgive them? No. Because I think that you should be able to trust her parents, and I've never been able to trust mine the way that a child should be able to trust their parents. I had to take care of them. I had to bear their burdens. I can give them space to be part of Lila's life if they decide they want to make an effort, and if they're good to her." She sighed. "I don't need to *punish* them. But at the same time I will never be able to have the relationship with them that a child should be able to have with their parents."

"I get that."

"Maybe my sisters feel differently. It's okay if they do. Like you said. Being the youngest is different than being the oldest."

"Yeah. I did not have the best understanding of who my father was. It took a long time. Denver and Daughtry were my idols, and they worked with him. They believed in his…mission, I guess. My dad seemed like a good guy to me. It seemed wrong that our mom left him. He painted himself as the victim and I believed it. Then I wondered why I felt bad after I spent time with him. And I wondered why I made so many mistakes and made him angry at me. Everything that he did I felt like was my fault. When I found out that you were pregnant, that was when I realized I wanted to be a different kind of dad. That was when I thought…"

"What?"

It was painful. To think. To feel. "I wanted it to save me. I wanted to prove to myself that I wasn't him. Because when I tried to imagine the stuff he did to me being done to a child of mine, it made me so angry. It was when I realized that what happened was a kind of abuse. That the reason I didn't want to be alive half the time was because of the way my dad treated me. And that no parent should ever make the child feel like that."

The car was silent.

"I am… I'm really sorry I didn't understand that," said Fia.

"I barely understood it, Fia. Why should you?" He breathed out heavily. "You and I didn't know how to talk. We knew how to fiercely defend our own feelings. Our own space. We didn't know how to let each other in, not really."

"I don't think I know how to do that still," she said. "I've been an island for a long ass time."

She said it with a kind of bland humor that resonated with him. He laughed. "Yeah. I get that. My whole family is made of violence. So I get it. I mean, we're close. We get together. We eat together. But we don't talk about the past. In some ways it's a lot like us. You and me. What we did back then. We just constructed a new reality to live in, and we don't really go over the one we left behind. What's the point?"

"And now we're both having to do a whole lot of dealing with the past. No wonder we feel uncomfortable."

He chuckled. And just then they pulled into McCloud's Landing. He was kind of grateful for the reprieve. Because the conversation was nothing if not heavy.

Gus was out there waiting for them, along with Alaina and the baby. Fia smiled and took her niece into her arms, and Landry knew a moment of tense emotion.

Because it was a reminder of what they'd never had. It didn't matter. Like they'd just talked about. The last thirteen years hadn't been nothing. They hadn't been a blank space. They'd grown, they'd changed. They had made Four Corners better, and they had made themselves better. And what was the point of any of it if they didn't make the most of it now. If they didn't let go of the regret to the best of their ability.

"Thanks a lot, Gus," said Landry. "You're really helping us put on an extravagant birthday. We've got a lot to make up for."

Fia ducked her head and pressed her cheek against the baby's head. He wondered if what he'd said had felt pointed. He honestly hadn't meant it to be. But he supposed he had to earn her trust. Why should she believe that he wasn't taking shots at her?

"I've got three horses for you to consider. They just came in from a rescue. All older. Very docile."

They walked over to the stalls with Gus and spent the next few minutes meeting the new horses. There was a paint, a black quarter horse with white socks and a star on her forehead, and an Appaloosa with a bright blue eye. Normally that breed wouldn't be his pick based on temperament, but she seemed like a total sweetheart.

Fia seemed drawn to her too.

She was pretty. Gray and speckled, unique looking.

"I think we're both fans of Genevieve," said Landry, stroking the horse down her nose.

"I think so," said Fia.

It was the easiest agreement that the two of them had come to…maybe ever.

And that was a relief.

Because of all the things, they didn't need to be having a fight over something they were trying to do that was good.

With the choice made, they said goodbye to Gus, who agreed to bring the horse over on the day of the birthday party. And it felt like something. Felt like doing something to heal some of the wounds. Some of the scars of the past.

He wanted to. Lord knew he did.

And not just with Lila. Not just with himself. Fia had needed him, and he hadn't been there for her.

He made a promise to himself then and there that that would never be true again.

In some fashion, she was his, and always would be.

He would never treat Fia that lightly again.

## CHAPTER THIRTEEN

THE DAY OF the party they were working at being sneaky and also getting everything together as efficiently as possible. Fia was ferrying a cake over as soon as Landry came to get Lila, and she had a free moment to be sneaky. She had managed to shape the cake into a gecko, and that had been a whole feat of sculpture. Piping the little scaly bumps onto him had been fun.

And he looked amazing if she said so herself.

They were doing a little bit of a complicated dance. Lila had spent part of the day with Fia, and then she would be going back to Landry's, but then also thought she was going to the King farmhouse for dinner, which was where the party would actually be. And that was where Fia would meet them all.

Landry pulled into the driveway, and Lila rushed over and gave Fia a quick hug.

Fia just stood there and then watched as her daughter ran out the door to the car.

"Bye," she said, processing that feeling. The hug. Which hadn't been the first time that they had ever hugged, but had been the first time Lila casually initiated the contact.

Fia still felt...like everything around her had to be temporary. Like this couldn't be real.

Like the cake she had made might vanish, no matter how much work she had put into it. No matter how much work she had put into making the process feel real.

Because how could it be real?

Lila being here. Her and Landry working together. It felt like it might all evaporate. The truth was, the last time she'd been this happy, it had all evaporated.

It was so easy for her to cling to the toxic parts of her relationship with Landry. Because it was the toxic parts that had killed them in the end.

But he had also made her into someone confident. Someone who had felt beautiful. He had given her stretches of happiness in a time when she had been happy at home.

She knew that she had done the same for him. That what they had done for each other wasn't small.

It was just that it had gotten lost. In hurt feelings and anger. She had likened their experience to toddlers playing with knives. And in the end, they had been two teenagers trying to defuse a bomb. There had only been one way that it could end. In an explosion.

One that had devastated them both. One that had left fallout that had long-lasting implications.

So she held on to the hug, because there was still all the other stuff. Because even though things were progressing, she still felt...

Was there ever a point where you felt adequate?

And in this circumstance, was there ever going to be a time when she felt secure, or like she wasn't...

She closed her eyes.

Lila patently hero-worshipped Landry.

She seemed to enjoy Fia.

But it was difficult to get a real read on her.

Landry carried the wound of what felt like abandoning a child deep inside of him. And even though
he said he understood everything now, she wondered
if that was still there. And it also made her wonder if
Lila might carry around some resentment of her too.

No matter what she said.

She had gone through so much.

*What-if* had been Fia's enemy for a very long time.
It was very, very hard to stay away from asking what-
if right now.

The truth was, she had wanted to spare Lila from
going through any pain. But she hadn't done that, had
she?

It made her feel like she'd failed. Even though in
many ways she felt like she had succeeded, this end
point made her feel like she'd failed. Having Lila back
here made her feel like she had failed. And at the same
time she wanted her here.

It was an impossible circle of things. Realizations
and feelings.

And at the center of it all was Landry and the fact
that her feelings for him could never be anything like
straightforward.

She sighed heavily and went to her bedroom—
where she had hidden the cake—to gather her things.

She had to accept that this was the beginning, and
not dwell so much on the past.

But she couldn't escape the feeling that there was
something in her past she needed to get a grip on in
order to move forward.

She just wished she knew what it was.


IT WAS A pretty full house, the entire King family including Arizona's husband and stepson. Rue was also

there, an extension of Justice. Rory and Gideon, Levi and Quinn, and Gus and Alaina were there, and she knew that the horse was in a trailer, ready to be brought out at the right time.

Daniel was in a corner talking to a couple of girls that Fia didn't know, but they must have been his recommended picks for the party. She did sort of wonder if he had chosen based on who he wanted at the party, because that was the amount of trust that Fia put in teenage boys.

Not for nothing.

Denver made his way over to her, and she braced herself. They hadn't actually had a conversation by themselves since the revelation about her being Lila's mother. The problem was, she knew Denver in the context of setting up the Four Corners collective. Because of that, she really was not surprised that he had something personal to say to her on the subject.

"All right," she said, rolling her eyes. "Get it out."

"What?"

"I had the feeling that you wanted to say something kind of snarky about the fact that I hooked up with your brother?"

"That is the least interesting part of the story, Fia. You two had a baby, and she ended up back here thirteen years later. That is vastly more interesting than whatever teenage shenanigans you two had going on."

He was right, and she felt silly that she had assumed otherwise. It was just that to her, the whole thing with her and Landry kind of loomed large as far as revelations went. Obviously, it wasn't as big of a deal to somebody like Denver for whom hookups were not that significant.

"Okay. Then what?"

"I was just curious how you were doing? I know it's been a lot of years since we actually established the collective. And you and I never had the easiest time communicating." He looked in the direction Landry had gone. "I kind of get why now."

"I was never mean to you."

"Not *mean*, per se. But we were not close."

She squinted. "I'm deeply suspicious of cowboys."

"Especially cowboys with my last name."

"Right. Well. Fair assessment."

"You were holding a lot on your shoulders. I don't know that anybody ever gave you all the credit that you deserve. For being eighteen and stepping into that room with men who were older than you, and hard-headed, and making the case for what Sullivan's Point needed. And now I realize you were doing that just two years after having Lila, after having all that happen with Landry. It really was amazing. And what you're doing now, that's amazing too. I am pretty damned impressed."

"Well, thank you," she said. "I hear that you're secretly rich?"

His eyes widened and he took a step back. Then he seemed to recover himself quickly and shifted and smiled. "Depends on who you compare me to."

"You contain multitudes," she said.

"Not really. Ask around. I'm pretty basic."

"You've been a good uncle to Lila. I can see that you're taking care of her."

"Listen," he said, his tone heavy. "My dad didn't take care of much. He broke things, he didn't build things. He has blood on his hands in my opinion."

He sighed. "Let's just say my dad has a lot to answer for. I'd like for some of it to happen in this life, but if it's just in the next I'll take that too. But I try to build things. For my part. Leaving it better than it was before. Not worse."

"As far as I can tell, that's what you're doing."

"You too." He looked at her for a while. "Our dad was really hard on Landry. He didn't give him any quarter to make mistakes. To grow. I'm always amazed at how good he is. How smart. Because living the way that we did, it can kind of beat you down. It can make you doubt everything that you believe, about yourself and about the world. But you know, Landry just thought up this thing to rehab some of the buildings on the property, and to expand our business. That whole finding your niche thing. He thinks outside the box, and I actually think when you've been through what we have, it's difficult to do that. Because growing up with a dad who criticizes everything you are puts your brain in a cage. It's the best way I can explain it."

"I get it." She said that easily, but she knew that she needed to turn over exactly what he just said. "I mean, I do know him."

He was right, about Landry. Landry was forward thinking and focused. He was smart when it came to improving the ranch.

When it came to their personal interaction, his brain had been stuck in a cage.

And she could understand why. He'd actually explained it pretty well.

But it made her wonder how much that was true of herself.

Because even though her parents had been different

than their father, they had definitely created an environment where their emotions were more important, demanded all the attention.

It limited you.

It limited what you could imagine for yourself.

Just like when she had found out she was pregnant and all she could imagine was being her parents.

"Oh, I see headlights," said Denver.

She knew that they were here.

She turned her focus to the door. And then, it opened.

"Surprise," everybody yelled.

Lila's eyes went round. "What's this?"

Fia went over to the side table, where the cake was. "It's a new birthday. Because we know that you didn't have a great one this last year."

Lila blinked seriously. "Oh. Thank you."

"Of course."

She stood there, and she wondered if Lila would hug her again. But she didn't.

She wished that she would. But maybe she was too overwhelmed.

Instead, she shrank back, she clung to Landry, which made Fia feel heavy in her chest.

She knew she should just be grateful that Lila had somebody she could lean on. It didn't feel that way. Not all the time. Not right now.

She had the terrible feeling that because Lila just came in the afternoon, Fia wasn't the only one who occasionally felt like it might just be babysitting. Something temporary. Something less than actually being a parent.

It was Landry who started singing, and everyone joined in, and Lila looked brighter then.

They led her into the dining room, where all the food was spread out.

Daniel managed to take it from there, pulling Lila into the group.

Fia felt some of the tension in her chest ease.

But she still felt like she was having some kind of strange out-of-body experience.

Landry came over to her, and leaned in and whispered in her ear. "Are you okay?"

"I'm fine," she said, turning to look at him. Their faces were closer than she'd realized.

And she found it hard to breathe.

"Are you?"

"Yeah," she said.

"Why do you look so sad?"

"Why do you care?" she asked, knowing she was being bratty.

"I've always cared."

That made her feel like she'd been stabbed in the chest. She tried to be like when she'd said that. Somewhat flippant. But it had come out heavy, and that his answer had been heavier than she'd been expecting.

And it made her feel things.

"This makes me feel like we should have red Solo cups full of beer," she said. "A big house party like this. Without our parents."

He chuckled. "We're the parents."

It was so sobering. She looked over at the kids, who were talking and laughing.

"Do you get the sense that she's happy she's here?" she asked.

"She looks happy now."

"Yeah. She does. She looks really happy. I never know... We get along well. We have a nice time together." She realized that she was pulling strips off herself and exposing her insecurities to Landry, and the Fia of just a few weeks ago would hate herself for this. But she didn't have anyone else to talk to about it.

"What don't you know?"

"Does she still feel like this is foster care? Does she really want us to adopt her?"

"She doesn't really have a lot of other options."

"No, I know. But what does she *want*?"

"We didn't get to choose our parents. She doesn't either." He tried to smile, but she could tell that he didn't think it was worth the effort. "I mean, I get it. This is complicated. Depending on how you feel about fate or whatever, it really becomes a whole thing."

That made her feel sour. She tried not to show it. Because he was right. When you brought fate into the mix, everything got extremely muddy. She didn't need it to be muddy. She didn't want it to be. She wanted things to feel clear.

She wanted to feel completely confident in the decision that she made in the past and completely certain of her footing now.

And looking at Landry always made her feel that quandary of emotions that she'd been mired in from the time they were kids.

"I feel like it could still all go away tomorrow."

And part of her thought it might be easier. Because she learned how to live a certain kind of sad. She had learned how to live missing a piece of herself, but having that piece returned to her, and having it bring up all the other things that she still missed, all the things that still weren't healed. That was difficult.

"Me too," he said. "Every morning, I wake up and I go up the stairs and knock on the door and…I'm afraid. I'm afraid she's going to be gone. I'm afraid that it was a dream. And yeah, I recognize that maybe this isn't a dream for her. That's hard too. I don't want her hurt."

"Me neither."

His voice was heavy now. "But she didn't get to choose. And I like to think that maybe we're not the worst option."

"Me too." When she looked over, she saw that Lila wasn't there.

She went over quickly to Daniel. "Where did Lila go?"

"Oh. I don't know. I think just to get some food?"

Except she wasn't around the food.

They still had her present to give her.

And… Fia's heart started to pound. She knew that she shouldn't get panicked. But she felt…panicked. Because she couldn't see her child. She didn't know where she was.

*She's not a toddler.*

No, but something was wrong. She could feel it. Lila had been edgy since she had come to the door.

*I'll be right back*, she mouthed to Landry, then swept out of the room and looked around the living room.

Then she slipped outside.

She looked across the yard, and she could see a small, slim figure sitting on a swing, her head bowed low.

Fia let out a sigh of relief, and then she ran across the yard. "Lila," she called, jogging to where she was.

Lila lifted her head. "What?" She wiped her tears on her arm.

"Are you okay?"

"No," she said miserably.

Panic hit her, full in the chest. She'd messed this up. By trying to be too much too soon she'd messed this up. "I'm sorry. Maybe the birthday party was too much. I wanted to do something nice for you."

"It was your idea?" Lila asked.

"Well. Yeah. I'm sorry, though. Maybe we should've told you."

Lila shook her head. "No. It was a really nice thing to do. I appreciate it."

"What's wrong?"

"I just… It's hard to believe sometimes. That this is my life."

It was so funny. Of course, not funny funny. Nothing about this was funny. But just the connections between herself and Landry, and now Lila. The way that they were all grappling with this in such similar ways. The way that their thoughts were often linked.

"Me neither," said Fia. "Sometimes I can't believe you're real. I can't believe you're here."

Lila's eyes went round. "Really?"

"I know it's hard to imagine when you're thirteen, but… You don't really feel on top of everything when you're an adult. I think that's the saddest thing I've learned. I gave you up because I didn't think I could possibly do right by you when I was sixteen. And I'm twenty-nine and I don't feel a lot different. That's kind of upsetting."

"I was hoping that eventually you just felt like you knew everything."

Oh, how Fia wished that were true.

"Sadly no. And it must be hard for you. Because you've been through so much. Losing your parents is hard enough, but having nowhere stable to be, having to move through so many different houses..." She took a deep breath, and decided to ask the question that had been burning inside of her, the one that hooked into her own insecurities, her own worries. "Do you feel like I'm babysitting you?"

Lila didn't look up at her. "I feel like you're another foster family or something. It's weird. I've been bouncing around so much the last year that everything kind of feels like that. None of this feels real. I didn't really know what to do when my social worker said that they found Landry. That he was my biological father. I..."

Suddenly, Lila started to sob. Great racking sounds that moved through her small body. And Fia didn't know what to do. She didn't know what to say. So she got down on her knees, and she pulled her off the swing, into her lap, hugging her. Holding her. "I wanted you both to find me. Because I didn't have anybody. Not in the whole world." And suddenly two fat tears rolled down her cheeks. Landry hadn't mentioned this at all. Her crying. Her being emotional.

Fia felt frozen.

"I just thought it was a nightmare. That my parents were dead." She sniffed loudly. "I kept thinking I'd wake up, or hoping I'd die too. And my parents' families were bad people. Dysfunctional and into drugs and alcohol and they'd never wanted me to go with them. But they didn't...have anyone picked to take care of me. And that started to make me angry."

Fia felt like she was stranded in a wilderness,

searching for wisdom. "They probably couldn't even think about the possibility of not being there for you. They...they waited for you. They wanted you so much."

"I know. But then I didn't have them and... I didn't have anyone. I'm the one who asked my social worker if they could look for my biological parents."

"You...you did?"

"What's the point of even being adopted if your biological parents can't come rescue you?" She sniffed again. "And then he did. And I'm so afraid... I'm so afraid that he won't want me if I'm not good enough."

Fia's heart broke right then. Into tiny little shards that cut her inside.

"Landry has wanted you since before you were born," she said, her voice catching. "You...you have to believe that. He would never not want you."

"And then you're here. You're *here*. When he came to get me, I didn't even want to ask him about you. I was afraid that maybe you were dead, and I couldn't stand hearing that my biological mother was dead. Because I already lost my real mother and... I'm sorry. I just..."

"I'm not dead."

"But you didn't want me." Her voice was small. "I was never upset about that, not ever, because I knew you gave me to good parents and I didn't think I'd need you, but I need you now and it scares me."

Fia felt tears well up in her own eyes, but she didn't want to shed them, because the poor girl was already feeling out of sorts, and watching an adult cry was likely to send her over the edge. If there was one thing that Fia did remember from being a thirteen-year-old girl it was that her own emotions were uncomfortable enough. She really didn't need a trusted adult's emotions thrown into the mix. And a strange adult? For all that Lila was expressing her desire to know them. To love them, it was most definitely a strange adult kind of situation.

But she felt gutted, because that was her fear. That Lila was afraid Fia hadn't wanted her.

"I wanted you," she whispered. "But I wanted to be a different person for you. And I didn't see a way I could do that. So I had to give you to someone else. I didn't want you to have to grow up while I tried to do the same. And I don't know if I'm grown up enough now, or good enough or…anything. But I do know that I love you. I have loved you since I knew you existed. Standing up to the boy I loved, fighting for the future I thought you should have, was the hardest thing I ever did."

"I know. I…I was raised to respect what you did for me. My parents wanted to make sure I knew I hadn't been abandoned or unloved. They always said I had more love in my life, not less. But then…you have a life. And I wasn't part of it, so it makes me scared that you'll decide you won't like…me."

"Every decision I've made from the moment I knew about you was for you. And even when it cost, it was worth it. Landry and I have decided to adopt you. To make you ours. I promise you, I will stand as firmly in this as I did in giving you to your parents all those years ago. It was hard, Lila. I wanted to snatch you back, but I didn't. I knew what I had to do for you, and I did it. And this? This is for you and for me. This gives me back something I lost. I love you. I have loved you. I will love you."

She promised it, like a vow. A refrain. One that came from the depths of her.

"Have you told Landry any of this?" she asked.

"No. I didn't want him to feel like he had to keep me. Why would I want that? I don't want that. You guys gave me up. But when he came to get me, he said he never wanted to give me up, and then I kind of hoped that maybe… It was something that he really wanted."

"Let me tell you something, it was never a matter of *wanting*. Landry really wanted you. I really wanted you, but for me it was a matter of knowing what I wasn't capable of. But I'm twenty-nine now. I have a financially solvent business. I'm not a sixteen-year-old freaking out and crying every time some girl talks to Landry."

Lila shifted away from her, back to the swing. "You were seriously in love with him, weren't you?"

That cut like a knife.

"Yeah. I was. I was very seriously in love with him. But it was not healthy. It was very toxic. If we were a YA book people on the internet would cancel us."

Lila laughed, watery and shaky. "Oh no. Please don't talk about cancel culture. Stop. It's what everyone does to try to be relevant."

"I was just making a joke."

"Well, whatever. It's played out."

"Sorry," she said. *"Scathing."*

"I'm thirteen. Scathing is kind of my vibe."

"Right. Great." She let out a long breath. "We both want you. And there's no question of returning you. We are absolutely 100 percent committed to this. Because I know there's legal paperwork required for us to actually make you ours. But the thing is, you are. You're ours."

"I don't know… It's hard."

"I get it. You probably feel like you're not being loyal to Jack and Melissa. To your mom and dad. But you didn't choose to lose them. You're in a really difficult place. One that nobody ever wants to be. But you're in a lucky one too. Because you fell, but you have a safety net. Two other parents who really want you. Who want to have you. Who…who love you already, Lila."

"How? You don't even know me."

"I didn't know you when you were growing inside of me either. I didn't know you when I held you in the hospital. For just a few seconds, before I handed you to your mom. I didn't know you then, but I loved you. And every decision that I made was all about how much I loved you."

"I never really worried about it. I mean, in the sense that I didn't feel like my parents dumped me off or gave me away or anything. Because I had such great parents. That it didn't matter what my biological parents did, or how they felt. I was just glad I ended up with the parents I had. And I didn't look at it as being very different from being born. It's kind of random, right? You don't get to choose. So, I never worried about it. Because my mom and dad made such a big deal out of how much they loved me. How much they wanted me. It wasn't, like, creepy, you know, where they acted like they were saints because they chose me or whatever. They just made it so clear that I was theirs." She lowered her head. "But then when I didn't have anyone… I realized how much I needed you."

"You have us. Believe me, kid. You do. We are very glad that we found you. I know Landry never let go of you. And I didn't either. Just in a different way than him. I kept you with me."

"It's really brave. I think. I always have. I didn't mean to hurt your feelings when I said that you didn't want me. I know it wasn't that. I always thought... If it ever happened to me, I'd want to be brave like you were. Be able to do the right thing."

"Feel whatever you feel. Like Landry said before, when you're thirteen, it's completely all right to not know what you think or feel about anything. You don't have to. We don't know everything. Why should you?"

"I don't know. I guess because it just feels like the last year I've had to take care of myself and figure out what I want. But you're right. I didn't choose it."

"No. And it's not what I would've chosen for you. But I am really grateful that you're here. And I can feel both of those things. You can too."

"Okay."

They sat there for a while longer. "Do you like the birthday party?"

Lila nodded. "It hurt because it was too nice. Because it made me realize how much I want to be here."

Fia wiped a tear off her own cheek. "I hope it shows you how much we want you here."

Lila nodded.

"It's time to open presents," Fia said. "Are you ready?"

"Sure."

"I think everyone got something for you."

"His family is so great. So is yours."

"Yeah?"

"Yeah. I love them."

She realized it was easier for Lila to say that than it was for her to say that she loved Landry and Fia. But Fia completely understood that. Aunts and uncles were something that people were used to having lots of. As far as parents went… That was a little different.

She could see that this whole thing was going to be a difficult process. Because of course it was. They were people. And all of this was not easy.

Then of course there was the added factor of her and Landry.

It hadn't really hurt her feelings to hear all the things that he thought. She already knew them. She also knew that he had listened to what she'd said. And that was a start, maybe.

"Why don't we bring everyone out here?" She was conscious of the fact that Lila would probably feel like a spectacle walking back into the house after having vanished.

"But aren't the presents inside?"

"Not all of them," Fia said. "You stand right here."

She went into the house and grabbed Landry's arm. "You and I will have to have a talk later. But don't worry about anything for now."

"You can't just say don't worry. That instantly makes me worry."

"That's not logical."

"I'm beginning to understand this whole parenting thing is not that logical."

"Well. No. But we can do the horse now."

"Okay," said Landry, addressing everyone in the room. "We got a very special gift for Lila for her birthday, but she's going to open it outside."

Gus took that as his cue and went outside with his truck keys.

Everybody else poured out of the house, and Landry and Fia went to where Lila was.

"We have something really special for you," said Landry. "We can't give you back all the things that you used to do. But we can do new things. We want to do new things."

That was when Gus pulled his truck around from behind the house.

"Here we go," said Landry.

He went over to the horse trailer and opened up the back.

And in the light shining from the porch, Fia could see the beautiful Appaloosa exit the trailer. The horse was so beautiful, honestly. She was a dream for anyone.

"What?" Lila asked.

"You love animals more than anyone I've ever met," said Landry. "So I thought the best thing for you to have… We thought the best thing for you to have, would be a horse of your own."

"Really? Are you kidding?"

"I'm not kidding. This is Genevieve. She's kind of an old girl, but she's even-tempered."

"Let's do some riding now," said Daughtry, clearly ecstatic over the surprise for his niece.

"She can't ride now, it's dark."

"I'll just lead her around in a circle," said Daughtry.

"Yeehaw," said Justice, and his brothers set to work in all their enthusiasm.

Lila looked at him. "Can I?"

"Get on, scrap," he said.

And Lila did.

Denver helped her up onto the horse, and Justice ended up leading her in a circle with a rope, like it was a kid's party pony.

He stood back with Fia and watched.

"Well, here's a first we're getting to experience," he said.

She touched his arm. "She was overwhelmed. Because she wants to stay with us. Because she's afraid that…" Fia's voice broke. "She *did* want us to find her, Landry. She felt so alone. She…"

Fia started to shatter. Started to cry. In the shadows, Landry wrapped his arms around her and pulled her close. Like it was the easiest, most natural thing in the world. She melted into him, like she'd done it a million times. She had. It had just been so long ago, but it felt as right now as it had then.

"It's okay," he whispered against her temple, his breath hot on her skin.

"It's not." Fia gulped. "She was scared. And lonely. She *needed us*. She didn't have anyone for a year. I'm just so sorry that she went through all of this. But so… so glad that she wants us. And it feels wrong to be glad about that."

"Not wrong," he said. "You love her."

She nodded against his chest. And that was when she became aware of how strong he was. How good it felt to have them hold her. Landry had always felt like homecoming. He had always felt like the thing she wanted more than anything else.

She'd been apart from him for all this time. She'd been trying to weather all this pain without his arms around her. It had been the most unjust thing in the world. That she'd had to go through the worst pain of her life without him. That he'd caused her pain, and couldn't be there to help her fix it. It was just *so hard*. It felt so good to be back with him. To be held by him.

She looked up, and again, their mouths were so close.

It was like they were the only two people then.

Like being fifteen then.

"Landry," she whispered.

She heard a cheering sound, and they looked over in time to see that Daughtry had planted his hat on Lila's head.

"There's a whole audience over there," whispered Landry.

"Yeah," she said, stepping away from him.

"Let's plan a horse ride with Lila. Maybe give it a couple days?"

"Yeah. Let's do that."

"I'll see you then."

"Yes."

Like they were just civil acquaintances. Like they hadn't both been looking at each other's mouths.

And then he left her. Melted into the crowd watching Lila ride.

Fia stood back. Feeling torn, feeling separate. Wondering what all she was going to have to keep holding back to stay standing.

Because she couldn't melt into Landry, no matter how much she wanted to.

She couldn't give in to despair over what she felt for Lila. She had to be strong.

She'd been strong all this time.

She just had to keep doing it.

# CHAPTER FOURTEEN

THE COUPLE OF days that Fia spent with Lila were great. Lila was in a little bit of an emotional state. After her breakdown on the swing, she'd been cheerful at the party, but teary, and that mood had continued over the next few days. But Fia didn't mind babying her. It wasn't exactly how she had imagined her intro into motherhood, but it was nice. To be able to care for her. To be needed.

She was an interesting kid. She overthought a lot of things. She cried over movies, but was far too interested in true crime for someone her age. She cared very deeply about animals, but also loved bacon. She talked quite a bit about her gecko and of course about Genevieve.

They had plans to go on a short trail ride today to get Lila used to her.

"Did you have a dog or cat before?" Fia asked, while they waited for Landry to show up with the horses.

She looked away. "Yeah. I had a dog named Sunday. But I couldn't take her with me when I got moved into care. She went to a shelter."

Fia kept thinking her heart had already broken enough times. But then something like this would prove to her that a heart was an endlessly breakable resource.

Lila, sweet, caring Lila who loved animals so much, had lost her dog along with her parents.

"Oh."

"She was a lab. She was such a great dog."

"Do you remember which shelter she went to?"

"Yeah. But it was a long time ago."

Fia made a mental note that she was going to try to track that dog down. Of course, a well-behaved lab like that was likely snapped up quickly in a shelter, but she also knew that dogs went back to shelters often.

Landry texted her to check on Lila, and she ignored the way that her heart lifted.

Have a couple civil conversations with the guy, and it felt like she was back in high school.

Well. Not quite. She hadn't ripped his clothes off. And in high school she would have definitely done that by now.

She ignored a pulse between her thighs.

Why had she told him that she hadn't had sex since they'd been together? She had no idea why. Except she'd been so shocked by his admission that there had been so few women for him.

His brothers were registered hound dogs. She had kind of assumed that he was the same. She had let herself be wounded by it. Victimized herself often by imagining Landry seducing women and discarding them. Fortified herself with it. She had decided that it was best to think of him that way, so that she couldn't actually feel jealousy.

But she wanted to know more. Why was hooking up not something he enjoyed?

If memory served—and she knew it did—he'd always had a very strong sex drive. Granted, he was a teenage boy, but he'd been a teenage boy when they'd broken up too. So it stood to reason he would go out and carve a swath through the willing populace with his penis.

It was just strange to her that he hadn't. And continued to not.

She wanted to think that it was about her. That she had ruined him for other women.

She never let herself think she didn't hook up because he'd ruined her for other men. She felt like the experience had ruined her for love. And casual sex was definitely not on the menu, considering she knew what the consequences could be. Considering she knew that she specifically lost her head when she was high on desire.

That had been what she told herself anyway.

But Landry…

And now she was fixating. Great.

That wasn't healthy. Particularly when they needed to be fixating on *their child*.

Fia and Lila were sitting on the front steps of the farmhouse when Landry pulled up with the horses.

"There's an easy trail we can take just off the dirt driveway," she said. "We can ride around Sullivan's Lake and back."

She and Landry had spent a lot of time at Sullivan's Lake. On the far side away from everyone, under the trees. She really needed to stop.

"Sounds good." He got all three horses out of the trailer, and Fia smiled. It had been a long time since she'd been on a trail ride. Horses weren't part of the daily life at Sullivan's Point.

And in general, she was glad of that. It was a lot of maintenance.

But it would be nice to take a ride.

As for Landry...

She watched him help Lila up onto the back of Genevieve. And then he began to give her instructions

"This is an easy ride. She's going to follow the trail. And you will be following my horse. Fia will be behind you."

"Okay," said Lila. "I'm good, Landry, you don't need to worry."

"It's my job to worry about everything," Landry said, grinning.

Fia was getting flushed, and she knew why.

It was sexy, watching Landry be so good with Lila. It was that dad energy. It was undeniably hot. A man being a caregiver.

But the other problem was that Landry himself was just undeniably hot.

His whole cowboy thing had always done stuff to her.

That white hat, his tight shirt. His tight jeans.

Standing next to the horse now, he looked at ease. In his natural element. And he was showing her, in a thousand different ways, that he was actually an amazing father.

*Maybe he would've been a good one the whole time. Maybe the problem was you.*

That hurt. Jabbed her unexpectedly.

She had told him that she was good with complicated emotions. But there were some that she didn't like.

"It's a great day," she said, overly cheerful.

"Yeah," said Landry, looking at her with a funny expression on his face. "Great."

Probably because he could tell that she was being overly bright for some reason. But didn't quite know why.

She mounted her own horse, and they began to ride in single file.

Lila, for her part, was looking excited, all around. "I'm actually doing it," she said. "I'm actually riding a horse."

"Yeah, you are," said Fia, feeling exceptionally proud.

Of all the things this girl had been through. Of all the things she had overcome. She was resilient.

*She's like you.*

The unexpected nice thought about herself nearly sent her tumbling off her horse.

Maybe that was true. Maybe she had given her daughter something of herself other than that stubborn chin, her hair color and her eyes.

Maybe she got some resilience from her.

And what she really hoped was that Lila would never need that resilience because of her and Landry. Because God knew they'd both had to be resilient, in part because of their parents.

The scenery around them was beautiful. Familiar, but it made her ache every time.

There was something complicated about being a Sullivan. There always would be. Because her family legacy was this land. But it was also the people. Who had been imperfect. Difficult.

"Our families founded this ranch in the 1800s," said Fia. "All together. And there have been a lot of different stories on this land. A lot of failures. A lot of triumphs. But it keeps going. It always keeps going."

"Landry told me his ancestors were gamblers," Lila said.

Fia looked over at Landry. "They were indeed."

"How come your parents aren't here?" Lila asked.

Fia looked at the scenery a bit more determinedly. "My dad moved to California. He wanted to live at the beach. He wanted to live with a woman who wasn't my mom. There have been several other women since then. My mom ended up moving to Hawaii. She kind of lives in a commune? I don't know. She's happy. Actually, she's happier now than I've ever known her to be."

That had always made her feel a little bit torn. That her mom was happiest away from her kids. But the fact was, she just didn't love the ranch. She never had.

"The ranch was my dad's," Fia continued. "The name was my dad's. She couldn't bear to still be here, living a life she hadn't chosen. But Rory, Quinn and I, it's in our blood. We love it. Alaina loves it too, but Gus is in her blood a lot more than this place. She's a McCloud now."

Landry looked behind her. "I guess that's another problem we had. I never could've made you a King."

He was teasing, but it made her chest feel sore. "Sullivan through and through," she said.

He must've seen something in her eyes, something that made him want to look away, because then he did.

She tried to breathe past the tightness in her chest.

"When the Kings came out West," said Landry, "the family had ten children. By the time they got here, two were left. It was a hard trek. The land cost them everything. And that was why they were so committed to it.

It was on that drive out West, through all that adversity, that the families met. And I think we stuck together more out of sheer stubbornness than anything else."

"Wow," said Lila. "They lost eight children. That's so sad. Is that why they started…all the gambling and stuff?"

"I think so," Landry said. "I think they'd done good their whole lives and suffered hardship anyway. I think they lost touch with what they believed in. Life was hard then. It's a different kind of hard now. When you really believe in something, you fight for it." He paused. "I don't know that I would've fought for it at the expense of my children, though."

"They didn't know," said Fia. "They didn't know before they started out, and after they'd made it out here, losing so much… They had to make it worth it."

He'd never thought of it that way. It gave him a little more compassion for how his family had started out. They'd lost what mattered. They'd lost family. Maybe that was why money had become more important later on.

"That's true," he said.

"You know so much family history," said Lila. "I never knew any. I mean of the Gates family."

"I'm sure they have some."

"It was tough. They both made breaks from their family. There was no contact. Because their families were so toxic."

Landry exchanged a glance with her. Probably due to their own toxicity with each other. Well, and with their parents too undoubtedly. Landry was definitely no contact.

"So they just didn't really act like our family history mattered much. Because they were making a new legacy with me."

"You are definitely that, Lila," Landry said, his voice getting rough. "You're their legacy. The legacy of lives very well lived, even if they were too short. Because you are very cool."

"Yes, you are," Fia agreed.

They rode on until they reached the lake. Lila took her shoes off and stepped cautiously toward the water's edge like she was considering testing the temperature.

Landry and Fia hung back with the horses, settled under the trees.

"How are you after the other night?" he asked.

"Emotionally damaged." She smiled. "But what else is new?"

He chuckled. "Absolutely nothing." She felt a pull toward him. She looked into his eyes, then down at his mouth.

Again.

Like a magnet.

Like it was inevitable.

"Fia," he whispered.

"Don't," she said. "Landry, everything is going really well."

"I know." But they wanted each other. There was no point pretending or trying to hide it. They wanted each other, and there wasn't a hell of a lot of anything they could do about it. It just was. It sat between them. Obvious and strong.

"Think of all we gave up for her to get to this point," Fia said. "Think of all we gave up when we didn't have her. What are you willing to give up now that she's here?"

"I'd give up anything," he said.

"Me too."

Lila came scrambling out of the lake after about five minutes of being ankle deep. "It's so cold."

"Yes, and it stays that way until it gets miserably hot around here," Fia said.

She was grateful when Landry moved away from her. Grateful when she could breathe again. The ride back was nice. Quieter. And Landry loaded the horses up and drove them back, while she and Lila spent the rest of the afternoon at the farmhouse, until it was time for Lila to go back home. She wanted something more. She wanted to not feel like the secondary parent. Especially after the conversation she and Lila had had, she wanted her to feel like she had a more permanent place at Fia's house. Maybe that could be a topic of conversation for her and Landry sometime over the next couple of days.

She'd already weaseled him into letting her stay the night so maybe…well, maybe they could talk about the balance of things now.

When it was time for her to head back to Landry's— and Gort the gecko—Fia packed everything into the car, and they drove over together.

When she walked in, Landry was standing at the stove with a dish towel thrown over his shoulder. He was literally wearing an apron. And he could not have looked hotter.

Was she really no better than this? She had made all that commentary about women needing to be complex. About maturity and all of that.

And here she was. Drooling over him like she had back then.

Like she was the same. When she needed to be different.

Because if she was the same, then maybe she wasn't up to any of this.

She needed to be better and different. It was important. Very important. She had to keep Lila's needs elevated above her own. She had lived on the same ranching land as Landry all this time, and she had managed not to fixate. She had managed to not check him out, she had managed to not be a slave to her baser desires.

So, like, what the hell, man?

"Hey," he said. "Glad you're back. Will you stay for dinner, Fia?"

"Yeah, Fia," said Lila, fixing her with her intense teenage stare.

"Sure," she said. "I'd love to."

Even though she needed distance. She couldn't deny Lila. Lila wanted to spend time with her. And that was sweet. It was lovely. She knew more about what Lila wanted and thought about them than Landry, though, as far as she knew.

She was caught sometimes between keeping Lila's confidence on that, and talking to Landry.

If they were a couple, she would've had to tell him. They weren't, though, so she had kept it a secret like Lila had asked her to.

"What are you making?"

"Well, it's no topless chicken pie," he said. "I'm just pan-frying a couple of steaks."

"You ever have your cholesterol checked, Landry?"

"Yeah," he said. "Cream and beef does a body good."

Well, it certainly did his body good, though she didn't want to say that. She shouldn't have even thought it.

"I worry for him," said Lila.

"Fia probably doesn't. She probably wishes I'd drop dead."

Lila went white-faced.

"Sorry," said Landry. "I'm sorry."

Lila shook her head. "It's okay."

He moved away from the stove and went over to hug her. The tender gesture made Fia shiver.

"Sorry that he's so insensitive," said Fia.

Lila laughed. "He is, though. Though he did tell me that a bobcat probably wouldn't eat me. Only a bear would. He thought that was pretty tender parenting."

"I'm just being honest," he said. "And I think that living in the wilderness hinges on honesty when it comes to animal-related injuries and devourings. You don't need to worry about being eaten by a bobcat. At least not in your entirety. Bears, cougars, I would worry a little bit more."

"Wolves?" Fia asked.

"There aren't enough wolves to concern yourself with," he said.

"I don't know," said Fia. "I feel quite concerned with wolves. All fairy tales suggest we ought to be."

"I think those wolves might be a metaphor," he said.

"For what?" she asked.

He looked at Fia, his blue eyes blazing into hers, and he lifted a brow. And it was like he had spoken the words. He didn't need to. But they expanded inside her all the same.

*All the better to eat you with.*

Yeah. She knew exactly what it was a metaphor for. She knew exactly what young girls were being warned about when walking in the woods. And it certainly wasn't bobcats.

After all, walking to a cabin in the woods had been Fia's downfall. She had definitely let the big bad wolf eat her.

And the way he was looking at her now?

Lord.

"I should be having my background check completed in a couple of days."

"Great," said Landry.

"So it should be full speed ahead for us to be both adopting Lila."

"That's so weird," said Lila. "I'm getting adopted twice. And this time it's by my biological parents."

"Life is weird," said Landry. "That's for sure."

"I think it would be more believable if I were a secret princess."

"It's definitely believable," said Landry. "A secret princess with a throne made of stuffed animals and the gecko adviser."

"Gort is a lousy adviser. Because he cares about nothing and no one but himself. And crickets," Lila said.

"Well. Of course crickets. Though he hardly cares about them in a way that's good for their health."

"That is true."

They had the pan-fried steak and green beans, and Lila went upstairs to go spend time with her lizard. Fia tarried. Even though she didn't have a reason to.

"Want to sit outside for a spell?" he asked.

Somewhere in there, she should feel like there was

a warning. Because she knew better than to go sitting outside on porch swings with Landry King. Because it was those hot blue eyes that had caused her all manner of trouble in the first place. But here they were, grappling with something entirely new, entirely different. So why did some of the feelings in her now feel so... familiar. Old.

The image had flashed through her mind before. Of their anger getting scraped aside. Demolished. And when that happened, it was unveiling some of the desire.

That old need that used to consume her, control her. They couldn't afford that. But she still said yes.

"Drink?"

"Sure." At the same time her subconscious told her no.

But she accepted a bottle of beer from him, and they went out and sat. "How were the last couple of days?"

"Good. They were very good. You know... This has been amazing. I'm starting to feel like it's real. It's taking time. I don't know if this is a honeymoon or what. But I like it. She told me today that when her parents died she had a dog named Sunday. And that Sunday had to go to the shelter. I want to try to track her down. I mean, I know that there are very low odds that she's in the shelter network anywhere. But I do want to know where she ended up. Because I think it would be good for Lila to know she's okay."

"We should get her a dog."

"Yeah. We should. We can do that."

They rocked back and forth. In theory, now, they had nothing in common except for Lila. Except they lived on this ranch. Worked on this ranch. She knew he'd been with three women besides her. He knew she'd been with only him.

"So the barn, you're renovating it... I do want to invest in it."

"You do?"

"Yes. I was just bitter at you because you gave me grief over the farm store."

"Is that all you were bitter at me about?"

"No," she said. "But you know that. I... Why did you do that? With the farm store. Why were you trying to get in the way?"

"I was being serious. I wasn't doing anything to you."

"I have a hard time believing that."

"Well, it's true. I swear, anything to do with the ranch, I would never let our business get in the way of it. I told you, Fia. For the most part, I let myself be cold where you were concerned. And that included anything to do with the ranch. If I had thought that we could make room in the budget to finance the farm store, I would've said."

"But your brother is rich."

"Yes. And it's up to him what he wants to dump that money into."

All right. Fair. She felt slightly cowardly that she had been behaving out of pettiness, while he had not.

While he had been sincere in his objections to the farm store.

"I'm doing it for Lila," he said. "Like I said, Denver has money, but he can spend it on what he wants. It's not up to him to finance Lila's education. But I want to. I want to leave her something significant."

"It's not just going to be you. It's going to be me too."

"Well, in that way, it's the collective, isn't it?"

She nodded. "Except in this case is just you and me."

"True."

"I didn't know that you had dreams for expanding King's Crest. Have you always?"

He shook his head. "No. For a long time, I wanted to survive. And then I wanted to keep toiling here out of spite. So yeah, I guess I did do some things out of spite. I wanted to show our dad that we could make it better than him. The legendary man himself couldn't do a better job taking care of this place, and we could. And we did that. Then, I started to realize I might need to want more. Because I had a kid. A kid to leave a legacy to."

"So this whole time you'd been out here just trying to prove to your dad that he wasn't that great?"

"Yes. And I get that that's stupid. Because he's never going to believe that. He's always going to see it as his foundation. So everything that came after it is his too. Just like we are. That's just how he is. He's never going to be anything more than that. He's never going to see it as anything more than that."

"My dad just never even thinks about us. I don't think he has ever once looked back. And my mom was just so devastated she couldn't handle it. I tried to have some sympathy for her for a long time. I tried to frame it as her sort of doing the opposite of what I did with Lila. She removed herself because she was on fire inside our house. Does that make sense? She was so devastated by the divorce that she couldn't be the best version of herself here. So she had to go off and find something new and different. To be better. Because her being there didn't benefit us anymore. But now I look at Lila, and I just don't see it that way. I would never..." She looked up and their eyes met. "Whatever we do, it has to be for Lila."

He nodded slowly. "Agreed."

"We have to try. To do better. To be better."

"Definitely."

But the whole time she looked at him, she couldn't help but have her gaze drawn to his mouth. She couldn't help but feel a stir low in her stomach. And it was so wrong. It could not happen.

Because she would never be her mother. Not ever. She would never leave her child because she couldn't deal with something.

"This is why I avoid you," he said.

Damn him. For speaking the truth of the attraction into the space. Her making it impossible to deny. For making it clear.

"I mean, not the *only* reason," he said. "But definitely one. We both know it's not the best idea. In fact, I believe that we just discussed this earlier today."

"In general, yes. But right now? It's actually the worst idea. Impossible."

*"Damn straight,"* he said.

"But why don't you like to hook up?"

He laughed, and lifted his beer bottle to his lips. "Well, that is a loaded question."

"Is it? Because you threw it out there."

"Days ago," he said, as if that would mean she wasn't thinking about it on loop all day every day since.

"But I've been thinking about it," she said. "And

don't tell me you haven't been thinking about what I said too."

"Maybe we need to make a deal that we only talk about Lila."

"Too late," she said.

He looked at her, his gaze hot. Searing, even, and part of her wanted to run. While another part of her wanted to lean in. All the way in.

"Fine. I don't like to hook up because it has never felt the same. And I compare every woman that I look at to you. And that's the problem. I told myself that I hated you. I think it was close enough to being true. But the problem is that I never stopped wanting you. Even with all the anger that I felt. I wanted you. Even with all the hard feelings, I wanted you. I've never been able to be neutral. I tried. I told myself I was just different than my brothers. Not everyone likes casual sex. But the truth is I see a woman, and no matter how beautiful she is, she's not you. I kiss a woman, and it's not *us*. Sex just feels…like a shadow of what we had, and it makes me ache for something we can't get back to. I hated the way that felt. It wasn't worth getting off."

She tried to breath. It was almost impossible.

"Maybe now will be different. Maybe now that we kind of peeled back some of the layers. Demystified it. Maybe we were stuck. Like you said, you hadn't ever thought of Lila's adoption in a new way because you were stuck at seventeen. Maybe *we* were stuck, and now we won't be."

"Will it be different for you? Because there hasn't been *anybody*."

That bastard Landry King.

She cleared her throat. "Yeah. I know. Because like I

said, it's different for women. It's not just about whether or not I'll enjoy it—but I might not, satisfaction not guaranteed. I have to actually worry about so much more. About the potential for being a victim of violence, about pregnancy. And it has never felt like something I wanted to jump back into. I get that this isn't… It's not the way people want it to be. But there are too many deep consequences and worries women have to bear alone for it to be as casual as it can be for you, and we might not even come." She tried to laugh. "And I am far too familiar with some of the consequences."

He nodded slowly. "Yeah, I get that. I really do. But all this time, and you haven't found anyone else? You're not sixteen anymore."

"I know. But maybe…maybe what you said is also a little bit true for me. I can't imagine feeling the way that I used to, and you know what, I'm not sure that I want to. There's a…cost benefit analysis here that I can't make math out. I feel very much like I'm the kind of person that loses her head with men. So maybe I'm just not allowed to."

"With men. So you think it would be the same with any man as it is with me?"

"I don't know. I haven't disproven that theory. So it really could be." She leaned back against the porch swing. "Maybe men are just my Achilles' heel in general."

"Bullshit," he said. "You've resisted every man who has crossed your path. Except one."

"A testament to my strong will."

"Right. And do you look at other men and feel what you do for me?"

"Sawyer Garrett's pretty hot."

"That's not what I'm asking you, Fia. When you look at Sawyer, does he make your breath go shallow?" He looked at her, his eyes getting intense. "Does he make your stomach tight, your heart flutter?" As he spoke, those very things began to happen to her. "Does he make you wet?"

*Damn.*

She nearly inhaled her beer. "Landry," she said, looking over her shoulder, as if Lila could come walking out at any moment.

"It's an honest question, Fia. Because I seem to recall you whispering that to me after school one day. That you were wet from looking at me. From imagining what we were going to do later."

"I was an idiot. I was young. And I don't even remember that."

"I do. In detail. Because I remember all of it. I remember how much you wanted me. I remember how much I wanted you."

And she felt herself getting wet now. She felt that tug of arousal between her thighs, felt like she'd been shot clean through with an arrow.

It was disturbing. He was damned disturbing.

Also, it was the hottest thing she'd experienced in over thirteen years. So she wasn't rushing to get away.

"We agreed this was a bad idea."

"We are not known for making great decisions with each other."

"No, we aren't," she said. "Which is why it should be a no."

And she shouldn't be excited by it. This little detour from the straight and narrow. But dammit all if Landry didn't tempt her, and if he didn't make temptation seem like an event in and of itself.

"Maybe. But I'm staying over here. I'm keeping my hands to myself."

"Bastard."

*That bastard Landry King.*

"You're so pretty. I haven't let myself really look at you for quite a while."

She felt a hitch of offense in her chest. She wanted to push at him. Push against that.

"Really?" she asked. "I look at you all the time. It's fascinating. Because I know your body. I know it better than I know my own. But I also know that you've changed. You're not a kid anymore. I wonder all the ways in which you might be different."

"There you go," he said, his voice husky. "That's the Fia I know. Never back down from a challenge."

She met his gaze. "Are you hard?"

He growled, turning to face her, his full focus on her now. Arousal in his blue eyes. "Yes."

"Good."

He didn't look down. Didn't look away. Didn't look ashamed.

"Are you wet for me, Fia?"

She tried not to look shocked. She tried to keep her eyes on his.

"Yes," she said, squeezing her thighs together and shifting her hips.

"Good. When you get back home tonight, I want you to go upstairs, take off all your clothes, and get in bed. Open your thighs wide and touch yourself. Use your fingers. Think about me."

She bit the inside of her cheek. "What if I use a vibrator?"

He let his head fall back. "Yeah. Do that. You got a big one?"

She smiled, even though she felt like she was being tortured. "I didn't see any point downgrading myself from my real-life lover."

"So it's big, then."

Yes, it was. And she had always felt like she deserved the indulgence. Because she might not have wanted to go out and find another lover, but that didn't mean she didn't have a sex drive. She had a decent one, thank you.

"Does that mean I can demand that you take a shower and move your hands all over your own body?" she asked. "Wrap your hand around yourself and imagine that you're inside me?"

"Yes," he said, the word nearly feral.

"We shouldn't touch each other."

"No one's touching anyone," he said.

"No. Because that would be a bad idea," she said.

"It would be a very bad idea."

She was so turned on and she couldn't see straight. She wanted to stay with him, and she wanted to leave, and she could tell by the glint in his eye that he was caught between the same competing needs. To go satisfy himself, and to marinate in this moment.

It was not ideal.

"I guarantee you," he said. "That when I come tonight it's going to be better than any of the sex I've had in thirteen years."

"Except no one will get hurt."

"Yeah."

Were they lying to themselves?

She *knew* they were.

Why was she drawn to him like this? Why did she want him like this? Why couldn't it be someone else? Anyone else. Sawyer Garrett was hot. And yes, he was married now, but it could've been him. It could've been any number of hot men on the ranch. It could've been some of the ranch hands. Men from town. But no one had ever gotten her going the way that Landry did.

It was easy for her to marinate on the emotional scars that he'd left behind. The truth was, she'd done a lot of that. She thought a lot about the feelings. Because thinking about the sex was dangerous. Thinking about the feelings made her want to run from him and never speak to him. It made her want to never reconcile with him.

Thinking about the sex? That made things feel a lot more questionable.

It made her feel a lot weaker.

It made her feel a lot more susceptible to making very poor decisions.

Because she was only a woman after all. A flesh and blood woman looking at the finest damned man she'd ever seen in her life.

And she knew full well it was about more than just the physical shape of his face—though it was perfect—or his body, though that was perfect too. She knew full well it was chemistry. Strong, undeniable chemistry that they could not reason on out or rationalize.

Which was really damned annoying.

"I'm going to go," she said.

"Text me," he said.

"Okay."

She drove home, and then she followed his explicit instructions, shuddering out his name when she came.

And then she did in fact text him.

Fuck you.

Good girl.

She shoved her phone under her pillow, and pretended that she was awash only in shame. And not excitement. Not the greatest sexual peak she'd experienced in years.

There was no room in her life for this right now. This was a one-off. Everything between them had to be about Lila. It was the only thing that would work.

They had just been talking about their families tonight. Lila could never feel insecure the way that they had. She could never feel like the kid that Fia had been. That peacekeeper trying to move back and forth between two parents who just hated each other.

And Fia could never be her mother.

This woman who had self-immolated when she had children to take care of. This woman who had surrendered all of her happiness, all of her everything to a man instead of being there for her children.

Hell. She was still doing that.

There was a reason that Fia had never confided in her.

Bitterly, sitting there in bed, naked and slightly ashamed of herself, she let that truth wash over her.

She hadn't been able to confide in her mother.

She hoped that Lila would confide in her. No matter

what. No matter what the issue was. She needed her to. Wanted it more than anything.

She wanted to be better. Do better. For her child.

It was the single most important thing to her.

It was so damned important.

And this... This had been an aberration.

At least she and Landry hadn't touched each other. They hadn't crossed that line. And they wouldn't. She would make sure that they didn't.

Because it would be a very, very bad idea.

And definitely not one they could afford.

So she decided to ignore this. Pretended it hadn't happened.

It was what Landry had done to her all these years.

She had to protect herself. That was the thing. And she couldn't regret it.

## CHAPTER FIFTEEN

THEY'D PASSED THANKSGIVING BY, which had been rowdy since it had been a combined affair between the Kings and the Sullivans. Lila'd had a great time, though when they'd gotten home she'd cried because Thanksgiving made her happy and sad. Because last year she'd been in foster care and that had been saddest of all, but neither year had Jack and Melissa. And it just hurt.

They'd turned the corner into December, Christmas lights going up on the barn at Sullivan's Point and all around town.

Then they finally got their court date.

Landry was pumped and ready.

It had been a good distraction, knowing their paperwork was in and processing and all they were waiting for was their day in family court. They were going up to Portland, which was where her case was centered.

And it had given him a reprieve from thinking about Fia. And the way that she'd about blown his head off that night they'd talked each other into a frenzy on his porch swing.

She hadn't mentioned it after that. In fact, the next text she'd sent him had been something wholly innocuous, and it had been like they'd never engaged in that sexually charged conversation to begin with.

And like they hadn't gotten off while thinking of each other, just like old times.

Though it hadn't been isolated pleasure back then. They'd have just sneaked out to find each other. They'd have *had* each other. Back when they were teenagers, they'd taken what they wanted.

Reckless.

Heedless.

Unfortunately, now they understood things like consequences and emotional fallout.

Which was a real libido killer.

Or *should* be.

But he'd been on edge ever since.

He knew that it was not what he should be thinking about now.

But he found he did. At least once a day.

Maybe because his life didn't look anything like it had just a few months ago, and he was still blown away by that. Still completely flabbergasted by the truth of it.

He and Fia had both gotten calls about the date.

They were doing it together.

The social worker understood their situation, and she had been very supportive of them and the whole process. It had been fairly expedited as far as these things went. But considering that Lila had no other guardians or prospective guardians, it had been pretty easy.

Lila, for her part, seemed subdued about heading up to Portland.

"Aren't you excited?" he asked. "Adoption! IMAX theaters."

"It's just weird," Lila said.

Of course it was. Because for her, it had been home once upon a time and now it wasn't.

"Sorry," he said.

She shook her head. "It's okay." She paused for a moment. "Landry, I have to tell you something."

For some reason that made him hold on to his breath. "What's that?"

"I actually *do* want to be here. I did want you to find me. And I was afraid that once you did you wouldn't actually want me. So I pretended like I didn't care. I felt guilty too. Guilty finding a way to be happy when…"

He understood that. His whole life was tangled up in that kind of emotion.

"Don't feel guilty."

"Fia already talked to me about it. I told her… I told her about this. At the birthday party, I told her how much I wanted to find both of you."

Fia had told him some of this, of course. He was grateful she'd been there for Lila. That she'd been the right person for Lila to reach out to then. He appreciated Fia in that moment on a level he hadn't yet.

For her intuition as a mother.

*She had it all along, you just didn't appreciate it when it conflicted with what you wanted.*

*She always knew what Lila needed.*

"Well, I'm glad you're here," he said, his throat tight. "I'm glad that you want me."

"I'm afraid of going back there. I'm afraid I'm going to have too many memories. I'm afraid I might forget how to be happy here. Because I've been happy. I don't want to lose that."

"Lila," he said. "You can be happy here. You deserve it. That's what Jack and Melissa would've wanted for you. Your mom and dad loved you. More than anything. Look at the way that Fia was. How she said she was glad that you didn't miss us. That's the way that parents love their kids. Fia understood that earlier than I did. She understood that really loving someone is selfless. It's not about what you get back from it. It's just about that love. That's why Fia gave you to your mom back then, and hoped that you would be happy without her. You have to know that your mom would want that for you now. Your dad would too. It's what I would want for you, Lila. If you hated it here, I would want you to go be where you could be happiest."

He realized then that wherever that was, he'd follow her. Because he would sell out. He would move to Portland. He would live in a suburb. He would uproot his entire life and everything he'd ever imagined he was for her.

Being her dad was a bigger part of him than anything else he'd ever been.

"I'll sell the ranch," he said. "My stake in it. I'd move wherever you wanted me to. I'd live with you here or Portland, wherever."

"Really?"

"I can't be happy without you, kid. You're my family. You're mine. I love you like hell. But yeah, if you hated me, I would want you to find another family."

She seemed to consider that.

"I know you're right. Because my mom and dad were the best. And I know that they wanted me. And that they wanted me to have a happy life and to have all of my dreams. I do know that." She sounded too old then, and entirely too weary.

He hated fate for making her that way.

He hated that he didn't see a way this could have turned out better. Because at seventeen he really couldn't have done this.

So that brought them back here.

"I was too immature to want that for you back then," he said. "I clung to this dream that I had, and it wasn't about you. It was about me. I can see now that sometimes loving somebody with everything means being willing to let them go."

He looked up and saw Fia standing in the doorway. She had tears on her cheeks.

"Wow, that's…wow, Landry," she said.

He stood, his stomach pitching when he saw her. When he looked at her beauty. He didn't think there would be a time when Fia Sullivan didn't affect the landscape of his soul. "It's true. I was too idiotic to realize it before. But I get it now."

"You really do."

"Come on," said Landry. "We've got an adoption to get to. We're about to be a family."

His eyes met Fia's. It was weird. They were about to be a family. Kind of. They were each adopting Lila. But they weren't a couple.

It was for the best.

They would always be bonded together by Lila, though. That had been something painful and sad in the past, and now it meant something joyful.

It couldn't quite mean what he'd wanted it to when he was a teenage boy.

Maybe he had to let that go to. Maybe they both would.

Maybe they finally would be able to.

Finally.

They booked a hotel with an indoor swimming pool, and got connecting rooms. Lila would be in Fia's room, and Landry would have one to himself. They went to an IMAX movie and to the Old Spaghetti Factory, and then Lila spent the evening swimming in the pool.

Fia, much to his chagrin, didn't even seem to be driven to put on her swimsuit to get in the hot tub. He decided that he would, though.

He noticed that she was staring at him, almost a scowl, from the plastic chair by the pool.

"Don't be a hater," he said. "You could join me."

He pretended it was about her wishing she was in the hot tub and not her being mad that he was shirtless. Though he had a feeling she was mad about the shirtless thing. Because he had a feeling that she was mad at him too.

"I'm good," she said, testy, pulling up the mystery book that she was reading so that it covered her face.

He chuckled, and lay back in his chair.

Then they all walked together to the elevator and up to their rooms.

He put the key card in the door and met her gaze as she did the same. There was something vaguely erotic about it. "Good night," he said.

She pulled her card out ferociously, and the door light turned green. "Good night."

And tomorrow was adoption day.

And that would be better than IMAX, the Spaghetti Factory and knowing that he got under Fia Sullivan's skin.

FIA WAS HAPPY to finally meets Lila's caseworker, Angela. They shook hands in the front of the courthouse, and the woman gave her a warm smile. "In all my years in child services, this is the most extraordinary case I've ever seen."

"Yeah. We're pretty sure nobody would believe it if we tried to sell it."

"Definitely not," she said. "I'm proud of you both for agreeing to co-parent like you are."

"They're great at it. They get along and everything," said Lila, sparkling.

Fia felt like that was not strictly true. But she wasn't going to say that, because they were being praised, and she thought that was probably a good thing, and she should go ahead and just let them get praised.

"Are you ready?" Angela asked.

"Yes," they all said.

The process itself was quick. It was like she imagined a justice of the peace wedding might be. She had written a small letter to read. And she turned to Lila, her heart pounding so hard she thought everyone could hear it.

When she'd given her beautiful red-haired baby up to her mother, Fia's heart had overflowed with love and words she didn't think she would ever get to say.

Now she had a chance to say it.

All of it.

"'Lila, I have loved you since the moment I knew you existed. I gave you up knowing that I had to want better for you than what I could give at the time. I love that your mother made you into the girl that you are. She will always be the one who raised you this far. She will always be so important. And so loved. Not just by you, but by me. I'm so grateful to her. So thankful for her. And I'm so pleased that I see her shining out from your eyes whenever I look at you. Because it's the things she taught you that went into making you who you are. It was everything I ever wanted for you. And now I want to do her justice. I want to do the best job that I can for you. I know that you'll make her proud. But I want to make sure that I do too.'"

And then Landry surprised her by pulling out his phone and reading to them both. "'I'm going to protect you both. And protect this family. Because it's the most important thing in the world. You both are. From here on out. This is it. The buck stops here. I'm going to be the best dad that I can be, Lila. And I know that I'm going to make some mistakes. Hell, I already have.'" He looked at the judge, checking to see if he was getting a scolding face for having said the word *hell*. "'But I promise to love you enough to make up for them all. Because you're worth it. And I promise to keep growing into the father that you deserve. The father that you need. Every day. I'm not going to stay stuck in the things that I believed in the past. I'm going to learn, and grow. For you.'"

Her heart felt bruised. And just so filled with joy. Because it was the best thing he could have ever promised.

Far from feeling like she was still parenting with seventeen-year-old Landry, she felt like she'd found a partner who was truly going to do the best job imaginable.

"It's very rare to have such a touching story in court," said the judge. "It has moved me, more than I can say. And I am happy to say that you are now officially adopted, Lila Gates."

They had opted, for now, to keep Lila as Lila Gates.

Someday, she might want to change her name. Maybe. But they had wanted to honor Jack and Melissa.

They had wanted to honor how much Lila loved them. And how much she didn't want that love to fade. Love couldn't be greedy, and even if Fia wanted her and her daughter to have the same last name someday… She didn't need it to happen now.

*Well. You wouldn't. Because you and Landry aren't together.*

That was true. But that was okay. It really was. They didn't need to be together. They didn't need anything more than what they were.

They exited the courtroom, and Landry held their papers up high.

Other couples in the waiting area clapped.

Then Landry hugged Lila, picking her up and spinning her around, and Fia felt like she left her body. Because she had never seen anything so damned attractive as that man overflowing with joy over having his child.

Their child.

*Theirs.*

And she knew a moment of pure unadulterated joy that she didn't allow to be invaded by guilt or regret or *what-ifs*, that Lila was theirs. That they were a family. That she had the second chance. This opportunity to be a mother to her daughter in this way.

Because she knew sacrifice. Sacrificial love.

What a wonderful thing to be able to love like this.

Landry had booked them into a fancy restaurant for lunch, and she enjoyed watching Lila give him pointers on what to order, since he wasn't familiar with the type of cuisine, and she said that it was her favorite.

And only then did she remember the way he looked last night.

Shirtless in the hot tub.

It was a very shallow thing to notice. There were so many other things about Landry that were attractive, if she was going to lean into noticing what was attractive about him, and not try to be above such things. His abs should be the *least* interesting thing about him.

He was a good dad. He was protective. He had written a beautiful statement for Lila in the courthouse.

But *his abs, though*.

And his *chest*.

He was everything that a woman could ever want.

He had been the boy that her fifteen-year-old heart had raced for, and now he was exactly the man that her twenty-nine-year-old self wanted to climb like a tree.

And it could not happen. They had just said vows, not to each other, but to Lila. To a judge and a case-worker. They had just pledged themselves to making this family. It had to be bigger than attraction.

Bigger than abs.

Landry professed each new Thai dish they tried his favorite. The sun streamed through the window putting a halo of gold around Lila and Landry. Fia couldn't actually remember the last time she'd had so much fun.

Except that she could. Riding in Landry's truck when they were teenagers, blasting the radio. Kissing each other while they drove, even though it wasn't safe.

Memories tinged with gold and magic.

It was with him.

It was always with him.

They went to the zoo and walked around until Fia's legs were about to fall off. Lila screeched and cooed over every animal. But somehow and most especially, the prairie dogs and the naked mole rats.

Fia was left questioning why anyone could possibly be that impressed with a rodent.

Especially a naked one. You couldn't even scratch it behind the ears.

She did not relate.

But she didn't say that.

They left with so much memorabilia from the gift shop, Fia wasn't sure how they were going to fit in the car.

And a balloon. A very giant balloon. She blamed that one on Landry, who was clearly trying to recapture something with such a frivolous purchase. She couldn't blame him.

They'd missed a lot.

But today they were working to make up for it.

They got into the car and drove back to the hotel. They were all exhausted and starving again in spite of their giant lunch because of all the walking they'd done.

"What if I order a pizza and some bottles of soda, and we rent a movie from this antiquated pay-per-view system?" Landry asked.

"Sounds good," said Lila happily.

Watching a movie in Landry's hotel room might've been illicit when they were teenagers, but tonight they were going to have a teenager with them.

So it shouldn't make her feel all intense.

"Yes, sure. Lila, why don't we go to the pool while we wait for the pizza?"

"Sure," she said.

Fia tried to read her book, but she was just going

over the words. Over and over again. They meant nothing. They felt like nothing.

Then Landry texted to say that the pizza had arrived.

"Come on," she said. "It's time to eat."

She bundled Lila out of the pool and took her into their room to get changed. Then, when they were in their pajamas, she knocked on Landry's door.

He swung it open. "Come on in."

"What movies are there?" Lila asked.

"There's a couple that are still in theaters. Superheroes."

"Lame. But okay," said Lila.

"How about this one? It's a mystery. Big cast. Should be fun."

"Oh yes, that."

They got the pizza and the bottles of Coke. For some reason Fia felt so restless she couldn't stand herself.

"I'm going to go get some ice," said Fia.

She got a bucket full of ice, filled her cup all the way to the top and poured her soda in. Which was exactly how she needed the ratio to be for her to enjoy the drink.

Then they settled into watching the movie.

About midway through, her ice began to wane.

"I need to go get more ice," she whispered. "You don't need to pause it."

She got up from the bed she had been lounging on, and Landry sat up from the bed he was on. She waved a hand. "It's fine."

She slipped out of the room and walked down the hall, and only then did she notice how much tension she was holding in her chest.

Definitely Landry's fault.

She went to the ice machine and then turned and nearly ran into him.

She clutched the ice bucket to her chest, her heart thundering. "What are you doing here?"

"I decided I wanted popcorn," he said, gesturing to the vending machine behind her.

"Oh. Of course. Right."

"We haven't had a chance to talk about today."

"No. We've been too busy *doing* today."

His blue eyes were too sharp. Too keen. She was afraid he could see that she was thinking less about the adoption than she should be, and more about *him*.

"You good?" he asked.

"I'm great."

She was. There was just the tension. But that didn't need to mean anything. It didn't need to be anything.

"Yeah. True." He brushed past her and went to the vending machine. He smelled so good. What was the matter with her? Why was he dominating her thoughts and feelings like this? Why was she perpetually sixteen with him?

That this was a permanent state with Landry did not thrill her at all.

"Landry," she said.

At the same time he said, "Fia."

"You first," he said.

"Today was really special. Thank you."

"Yeah. It was."

And then suddenly, he was moving toward her, intent in his dark blue eyes. He wrenched the ice bucket out of her arms and set it in the catch tray of the ice machine. And then he wrapped his arms around her, lowered his head and kissed her.

# CHAPTER SIXTEEN

HOLY HELL. She felt like she had been dipped in flames.

Burning.

She remembered what she'd thought about her mother. Self-immolation.

Well, this was immolation by Landry King. And she didn't think she had the fortitude to stop it.

She hadn't been kissed in thirteen years. She hadn't even wanted to kiss anybody. Because his lips were the only lips she wanted.

Because his mouth was *home*.

Because she could admit that now, even though it cost her. Even though it made her feel like she was insane. Even though she knew it was completely against everything that made any kind of sense. Against what they decided.

He kissed her like he was trying to make up for lost time. Like he was trying to add passion back to all those years that had been a desert. A wasteland.

He cradled her face, his tongue parting her lips, sliding against hers.

She needed this. She clung to his shirt. She felt how hard he was. How strong and muscular and *everything*.

Landry King. The boy who had lit her on fire. The man who continued to.

The father of her daughter.

*The father of her daughter.*

They couldn't do this. They had to be a family. And they could not be trusted. Not with this. It was a box of matches, and they might have learned enough, and changed enough to try to be parents now, but she wasn't sure if they were enough to try this, and they had to be sure. They were both so stunted in this way. They'd never tried it with anyone else.

Maybe because they'd broken something in each other all those years ago.

But he was still kissing her. And she was still letting him. Hell. She was still kissing him back. Even though she had already decided they had to stop.

She had decided that. She knew they had to.

But she couldn't.

She *couldn't.*

She couldn't make her hands release their hold on his shirt. She couldn't stop her lips from clinging to his.

This was everything, and so was he. A huge part of herself that she had covered up years ago. That she had imagined she might have cut out with a knife, but it had always been there.

Part of the grooves that Landry had worn into her soul that she could never quite be rid of.

This need. So bright and intense and shocking.

Need she hadn't felt in so long she had thought that maybe it didn't exist inside of her anymore.

She was wrong. She was so wrong.

But finally. Finally she did exactly what she had to do. Finally she managed to extricate herself from him. Not because he was holding her so tight. Because she couldn't bring herself to let him go.

Her lips felt swollen, her heart pounding fast. She

was slick between her thighs, and she could feel how hard he was. Pressed against her like an iron bar.

"Please don't," she whispered.

"I had to."

"No. Because we have to be better than this. Because we have to be *parents*. And not… Not this. We can't be human torches for each other. Because… It's the same. That's the worst part. It's the same. It doesn't feel any different. I just thought… I thought I wasn't all desperate for sex because I was older. I thought I was over it. But apparently I'm not. You kiss me and it's all the same. You say something dirty to me, and I can't help it. The whole… The thing that happened on the porch swing. It's just the same stuff. We can still get in each other's heads. We can still hurt each other this way, and we have to be better than that."

"What's better than this?" he asked. "Seriously, Fia. What's better? I haven't felt like this… Not since you."

"What's better? Today was better. The zoo and the courthouse and Thai food. It was better. The movie that we're watching. It's better."

"The movie really is only okay."

"You know what I mean, dammit. You know what I mean. It's better than us trying as hard as we can to burn each other out again. It's better than us being fools over hormones. We make a really good team when we're being reasonable and rational. When we're talking. When we're this… It's all we are."

"Are you, twenty-nine-year-old Fia Sullivan, going to look at thirty-year-old me and tell me that we are not different than when we were kids?"

"Yes," she said. "With this. With just this. Because tell me… Does it feel different to you?"

"Yes," he said. "It feels better."

The words lit her up. And she really wanted to be done being lit up. She wanted to be over this. All of it. She wanted to somehow be past this moment. Back on stable ground. But maybe that was a lie. Maybe there was no stable ground with them. Maybe there never had been. Maybe it had always only ever been this. This shifting lava bed of hot endless need.

But no. They had been more these past few weeks. They had been co-parents. They had been sensible. Responsible.

"The caseworker and the judge both said that they had never heard a story as amazing as ours. Angela said she was so proud of us for doing this. And we can only do it because we aren't broken by each other anymore. We cannot let that happen. Not again, Landry."

"Okay," he said, taking a step back. "I'm going to listen to you this time. Because I didn't before. I want you, Fia. Time and anger and distance and all of that hasn't changed it. Common sense hasn't changed it. So maybe you're right. Maybe that means it's something I shouldn't want. Something I shouldn't indulge in. I'm not going to argue. And I'm not going to punish you for not giving me what I want. I'm different. And so was this."

"To what end, Landry?"

If he said marriage and more babies to love, she might be too weak to turn him away. But somehow, she knew he wouldn't.

"Just being together for a while," he said. "Just feeling alive like that again."

She shook her head. "Not good enough for me. It's not enough."

"And I'll give you what you think you want. But I still want popcorn."

"Okay."

She moved aside and let him get his bag out of the vending machine. Then she stood there, feeling hollow. And when he left, she finally picked up the ice bucket and filled it. She should stick her face in it. Try to get a handle on herself.

She had acted like an idiot. Worse, she had acted like her sixteen-year-old self. She didn't know why she was like that with him. Well. It was that thing. That thing that had always been. But they had to be more to each other now. They had to be better. They had to be...

She had spent so many years without sex. She didn't need it. Why did it always feel like such a big deal when Landry was involved? Why did it always feel essential?

She let out a breath. And she tried to visualize the room she had just left. The two beds. Landry sprawled on one, Lila sitting on the floor against the bed. And her bed. They were a family. A different sort of family. But functional.

So much more functional than her parents. And his.

What their parents had proved was that when there was conflict between the father and the mother he couldn't continue to work together as a team. That when the romance between them ended they couldn't continue to have a family.

That was why it was so important that she and Landry not...

It was important.

She picked an ice cube off the top of the bucket and crunched it, not caring that her dentist would yell at her because it was bad for her teeth.

A lot of things were bad for your teeth. And people did them anyway. She didn't see why she couldn't nervously crunch ice if necessary.

Then she walked down the hallway and went back into her room, and then to his by the connecting door.

He didn't look at her when she came in, and she squinted.

He was doing that thing. That aloof thing that he did.

But at least it wasn't filled with hatred and anger. It was just... The way that he put on a show, she supposed.

So she lay down on the bed, put ice in her glass and poured herself some more soda. And did her best to try and pay attention to the movie. Did her best to pretend that she wasn't completely consumed by whatever had just happened.

*It was a kiss. Deal with it. You're a twenty-nine-year-old woman. And it is hardly the first time you've ever kissed him.*

But she had trouble. And she had even more trouble sleeping. Landry was awakening needs in her that she just didn't want him to awaken. It wasn't fair. She hadn't asked for this.

But maybe there was a lesson buried in there somewhere. They had Lila. She could hear Lila breathing in the bed next to hers. Deep and steady.

Maybe there were always difficult things mixed in with the good things.

Counterbalances.

She wasn't entirely sure.

One thing she did know was that her life had all the external trappings of being together. That it hadn't felt this deep, this resonant in a long time.

She loved her sisters. Loved her family. Her friends. But this was something more. Something deeper.

And she realized that whatever was happening between her and Landry, she nearly welcomed the struggle. Because at least it felt honest.

Maybe that was actually what this was. Emotional honesty. All the difficult things being dragged to the surface and dealt with.

For them, attraction was part of it. Maybe it always would be. But maybe they could find a place for that too. A way to handle it that wouldn't break them.

He had listened to her. Even though her body had very much not wanted him to.

It would be so easy to let him sweep her away. To almost demand that he didn't listen to her when she said things like *stop*. Because part of her would love to be able to absolve herself of the responsibility of the kind of tangle they might get in. To claim that he had bypassed her objections and made her lose her head.

They were different now. She thought back to the way he had listened.

They were different now. The heat might be the same. But they weren't.

She fell asleep with that repeating in her head over and over again.

LANDRY COULDN'T LET go of the kiss. Which was sort of ridiculous when you were hanging out in the world's most basic continental breakfast room watching your daughter get free hotel waffles out of one of those weird dispensers where you poured the batter into a Dixie cup and hoped for the best. Fia was across the way at the coffee dispenser, and he was already half-way through his second cup, sitting in front of a plate of bacon and eggs. Which had earned him more commentary on his potential cholesterol from Lila and Fia.

Fia was acting so normal. And he felt anything but. He felt scalded. Scorched. But he wanted to give her exactly what she needed. What she wanted.

He wanted to prove that he wasn't a dumb kid anymore. Though hell, last night he'd felt like one.

Kissing wasn't like that with anybody but her.

It couldn't be. Not ever.

She was something else altogether, and their attraction was something new. Even though it was something old.

That didn't make a whole hell of a lot of sense, but he found that sense wasn't really in his wheelhouse when it came to Fia Sullivan.

Their eyes met when she turned around after filling up her cup of coffee, and he felt a streak of heat go through him.

She smiled, but it was a tense smile. One that became more natural when her path intersected with Lila, and they sat down with him at the table.

"You excited to head back home, kid?" he asked.

"Yeah," she said.

"Are you still feeling good about being stuck with us?" Fia asked.

"Yes," said Lila. "And it wasn't as bad coming back here as I thought it would be."

"We can come back and visit," said Fia. "Personally, I think Landry is a big fan of the zoo."

"Oh, hell yeah," said Landry. "Naked mole rats all the way."

"Naked Mole Rats All the Way is my new punk rock band," said Fia.

He laughed, but it wasn't even just that. It was something deeper. Because there was something nice about connecting with her this way. Reminding himself that it wasn't all sex and screaming back then. They had actually liked each other. Gotten along as friends in some ways. Ways like that.

"Excellent," he said. "It can open for my band, Economical Basilisk."

That was a deep cut from back in their teenage days. Someone had mentioned not being able to afford a dragon, because it wasn't in the budget. And Fia had responded by saying they could maybe swing an economical basilisk. Which Landry had replied it was his new band.

It was strange that he could remember that now, when all those years, he hadn't.

"Wow. Sounds like a lame show," said Lila.

"I guess you're not punk rock," said Fia.

"Absolutely not," said Lila. "I'm a Swiftie."

"Who isn't?" Landry asked.

"That's a good question, Landry," said Fia.

It was good to be on this kind of footing with her. They'd kissed, and they were fine.

They got in the car to drive back to Four Corners, and Fia put Taylor Swift on, as they had all established that they were fans, and some of the lyrics scraped a little bit too close to his bone. Because there were some deep, wrenching truths about breakups. And he knew that while he had been in a lot of pain as a result of theirs, he had caused a lot of it too.

But then thankfully they moved away from some

of the breakup-era songs and gotten into something a little bit lighter.

His brother texted him to ask them an ETA, and he gave it when they were about an hour away.

About forty-five minutes later, his brother texted with instructions to meet them at the town hall meeting barn.

"They're planning something," said Landry, reading the text to Fia.

"That sounds ominous."

"It's probably not *ominous*. But it's definitely going to be raucous."

Lila looked bemused as they continued on toward Four Corners. And when they pulled up to the barn, there was a giant banner hanging on the outside, wreathed in greenery and Christmas lights.

*Welcome home, Lila.*

Lila's eyes went wide and glassy. "What is this?"

"I don't know," said Fia.

And then, everyone was pouring out of the barn. The Sullivans, the Kings, the McClouds, the Garretts, and all of the ranch hand families.

There were tables filled with food, and the band was already playing on the stage outside. There were outdoor heaters blazing to combat the chill, and wreaths, ribbons and Christmas lights on the outside of the barn. The tables were laden with festive food and candles.

It was everything for the Christmas party, donated to this instead.

"'Welcome home, Lila,'" Fia read out loud.

"Welcome home," Lila repeated.

"I had no idea they were doing this," said Landry.

"Me neither," Fia said.

It was the damnedest thing, seeing the Kings and the Sullivans next to each other. They were the family that was always furthest apart. Because of Landry. And now, they were the family that was closely united. With a child between them. Because of Landry. A child they had just adopted. A child that the whole ranch was welcoming into the fold.

"I'm afraid you're one of us," said Landry.

Lila had tears streaming down her face. "Yeah," she said.

"You okay?" Fia asked.

"Yeah," said Lila. "It's just hard to believe. I haven't had a home for a year. I never expected that. To not have a home. So I know what it means for real. Knowing that I get to stay. That this is it. That this is where I get to be."

"With us," said Fia.

"And everybody," said Landry.

They got out of the car, and they were rushed by the crew. The Sullivan sisters took turns hugging Lila, and Alaina even hugged Landry. Quinn and Rory declined. It didn't really surprise him. Denver handed him a cup with an unknown alcoholic substance in it. "Congratulations," he said. "It's a girl."

Landry looked at his daughter, feeling dumbstruck. "I guess it is."

And that was when he realized. This was the baby shower they never got to have. As much as it was Lila's welcome home.

This was that celebration they never could have had

when they were nothing but dumb teenagers. When everybody would've judge them. And Fia most of all.

Landry wasn't one for church, but he could recall a sermon some years before where the pastor had quoted a verse that said God would restore the years the locusts had eaten. He hadn't understood what that meant.

But he did now. Because yeah. There'd been famine. There'd been things that were chewed up and spit out. Good things demolished and destroyed, like Lila's family.

But there was restoration too. A kind of giving back. And he could accept that, while also realizing that this wouldn't have been what he'd have if he had held on to Lila all those years before.

And it was an incredible gift to be able to see that restoration.

That renewal of all that was good and bright and beautiful.

"You know," said Denver, separating him slightly from Lila and Fia. "I still can't quite believe you went through all that when you were seventeen, and never said anything."

"Probably because I knew that I was being a dumb-ass," he said. "And if I shared it with you, you would probably just side with Fia. And I didn't want you to. I didn't want anyone to. I wanted to be angry. And I wanted it to be uncomplicated."

"Hell. I get that. I do. But I just... I feel bad that I didn't realize."

"Back then what could anybody realize except what our dad wanted? We weren't trained to pay attention to each other. Look at poor Arizona. She had a whole heartbreak we all missed. None of us knew how bad that accident affected her. In a lot of ways it was very similar to what was happening with me. I just kept it to myself. It was easiest. And I knew it would be easy to keep it to myself when we were all trained to just… view our lives as survival of the fittest."

Denver nodded. "I mean I guess Fia had a whole pregnancy."

He snorted. "Yeah. So whatever was going on in the Sullivan house was hardly better than ours. Different. But painful in its own way. Very painful."

"I really didn't think you'd ever had a thing with her."

"You didn't? Why did you think we had issues with each other?"

Denver shrugged. "Didn't really think about it, to be honest."

"You're hilarious, Denver."

Denver shrugged. "Listen, as a man who has his own life and his own resources, I get it. Sometimes living in a place like this, it feels better to keep a little bit to yourself."

"We wouldn't know how to do anything but keep things to ourselves," said Landry.

"Well. True enough."

"It's weird," said Landry. "Inside, I made a lot of my identity about what I lost. About what I couldn't have. And now that isn't the case. I have a family. I have my daughter. And there's Fia…"

"You going to marry her?" Denver asked.

"No," said Landry. "It hasn't even…"

"Why?"

His brother asked that question like Landry was a

dumbass. Like marrying her would be the clear and obvious choice.

"What the hell does marriage mean, Denver? It didn't keep her parents together, it didn't keep them here. Sure as hell didn't help our mom and dad."

"True. But there's something to be said for... I don't know. Bringing her into King's Crest. Making her part of everything."

"Who would that leave at Sullivan's Point? The place is Fia's. Alaina is with the McClouds. Quinn and Rory moved off campus. They have their own homes. Fia has always had a tough situation. She is the matriarch of Sullivan's Point. If she's not there, it's nothing."

"All the better," said Denver. "We could absorb it."

He wanted to punch his brother for that.

"You know that can't happen. Anyway. Even if she did consent to marrying me..." He shook his head. "No. Look, there's no reason to do that. No reason to put marriage on the table. She and I aren't even in a relationship. We sure as hell don't even know how to have a functional one."

"But isn't it tempting? To simplify things?"

"Let me ask you something, Denver."

"Shoot."

"Have you ever been in love?"

He didn't even pause. "No."

"There you have it. You've never been in love. You ever thought about getting married?"

"Also no. I made a little something of myself, but I fail to see how that could be complemented by marriage. Which frankly just sounds kind of torturous to me. But then, I also don't have a kid."

"That you know of," said Landry.

Denver scowled. "Fuck you."

He clapped his brother on the shoulder and separated from him.

Marriage. That was rich coming from Denver.

They had never seen a traditional family work.

As far as he was concerned, the traditional family was a bullshit lie. Something designed to keep men and women at odds. And hell, he'd done a much better job just in the last few weeks than he'd managed to do as a teenager, than his parents had managed to do for the entirety of their marriage, balancing being a father, and… All right, so he and Fia didn't have joined lives, really. But she felt like a partner. Felt like someone who was part of his family now. Linked to him.

He thought about that kiss. Damn, that had been hot.

But she'd said no. Unequivocally. And he couldn't argue with that. Nor would he.

Because he'd screwed things up enough between them without pressing the attraction that was still there now.

Yeah. He felt some kind of way about her. But that was messy.

They had the friendship part now. That was what was important. He would never have guessed that they could get to this point.

He wanted to do everything in his power to preserve it now.

He wanted it more than he wanted to kiss her.

He was almost entirely certain of that.

The bonfire was going strong, and people had gathered to dance. He looked over at Fia. He had always wanted to dance with her at a bonfire. Not in recent years. When he had spent most of that time glaring across the expanse at her, letting his anger burn hotter than the flames.

But when he was younger, and they'd been engaging in a torrid, secret affair, he definitely had. And now?

Now they were family.

He held his hand out and looked at her. "Come on, Fia. I think it's about time we had this dance."

FIA DIDN'T KNOW how to respond to that. Except she was drawn to him before she could formulate an answer.

Part of her had always dreamed of that. Of dancing with him at the bonfire, like they were one of the couples.

Well, a long-ago version of herself had.

And it had always felt tricky and sharp and sparky in the years since.

Because no matter how much she hated him, she wanted him too. That had been, and always would be, the most difficult part of Landry King.

But right now… This was a celebration. So maybe it was the perfect time. The perfect time to cross the space and take his hand. Except even as she did, she knew it wasn't just about making a show of being united. It wasn't just about Lila or the adoption or the joy of the party.

It was about the fact that she was drawn to him like a moth to the flame. That she was inexorably tied to him. No matter how much you might want to pretend otherwise. His hand against hers set off a chain reaction inside of her. The whole landscape shifted that left her rearranged. That left her undone.

She tried not to show it, of course. Tried to breathe through it. Even as he drew her up against his body for a moment, before sending her away, and pulling her back. It was a light-footed dance. And the air around them shouldn't feel sick. It should just be fun. But as they were spinning, she felt herself getting busier and busier. She felt the world shrinking down to just them.

And when he spun her, all she could see was the stars, the fire and Landry.

Everything was so clear.

She wanted him.

It was as simple and complicated as that.

They would never have been here. They would never have been dancing, if not for Lila. And yet their connection wasn't only about Lila.

It never had been. They'd needed something no less than their daughter to bring them back to this point.

Or maybe there was no *back* about it. Maybe it was something wholly new. Wholly different and wonderful.

Maybe this was the first time they had ever been quite like this.

She looked up at him, at his sculpted face half illuminated by the firelight. They couldn't move toward each other, not now.

But she could feel the pull to him.

And could feel him being drawn to her in return.

Lord, that man was everything. He just was.

*He can't be everything. He's Landry. You already know how it goes.*

Maybe that wasn't fair. Maybe this was their chance to heal as many things as they wanted. Maybe this was their chance to renew and reclaim. They had both admitted that other relationships hadn't been able to happen for them. And she wondered how much of it was because they had both been trapped in the most difficult, traumatic time of their lives.

But now they had moved past it. They had made something new.

They had their daughter at the right time.

Maybe there would be a chance for them to…

She wasn't silly enough to believe that they could do love and marriage. The simple truth was, she had never actually seen that work out. She knew he hadn't either.

And she would never risk what they were building with Lila over dreams spun from fantasy and well-placed lies. You couldn't count on having a double miracle. They were being given a second chance. In a deep and profound way few people could have ever expected. You couldn't test the limits of something like that. You couldn't test the limits of hope and faith and love when you had been gifted with more than any one person could expect.

But there was heat between them. And she did want to test the limits of that.

She had fantasized only last night about him pushing past her barriers.

About him pushing them both past the brink. Past sanity. And she knew that was childish. The behavior of somebody who couldn't stand by their own decisions. She could.

In many ways she had always been able to trust herself. And only herself.

She knew what she had to do when it came to Lila. Even though she had wanted more. Even though she had wished that she could run away with Landry. She had known the right thing to do. And she had doubled down, turned inward, handled it all without ever including another person in those moves she'd made. Not after it had been clear Landry was going to oppose her.

She had known she could count on herself. So perhaps she needed to trust herself now. That was a tangled thing. A sharp thing. Because she had also always blamed herself for getting into the situation in the first place. And maybe that was where she needed to have more kindness for her past self. Because even her present self couldn't reject this. Couldn't say no to this. Even her present self felt swept off her feet.

Was it so wrong to miss that feeling?

She looked at the bonfire, just for a moment. And then back at him. A wildfire was deadly. Sweeping through the trees. But the bonfire was simply a good time. When they were teenagers, their desire had been a wildfire. Because it had no parameters. No boundaries. It had been only and ever a raging inferno. But they were older now.

The bonfire could stay put. Exactly where it was supposed to.

She swallowed hard and put her hand on his chest.

She watched his jaw firm. To anyone else, it only looked like they were dancing still. But she could tell that he felt the shift.

"Fia…"

"Landry," she said. "Look at me."

He did. His blue gaze hot and hooded. Filled with their own flame.

"My twenty-nine-year-old self thinks maybe we should try to approach this differently," she whispered.

"My thirty-year-old self is wondering what you mean by that?" he asked huskily.

"This exists between us. Whether we do something about it or not, right?"

"Seems to be."

"And there's no point denying it. We've already slipped up. We are not hiding it. But then, we never were. Half the ranch thought we'd already slept together. The other half thought we were going to."

"Apparently not my brother. He says he didn't wonder about us at all."

Fia huffed. "Well, how nice for him."

"Truly."

"This thing between us," she continued. "It's real, whether we explore it or not. And we know it's there. There's no way of denying it."

"Say what you want," he said, his voice hard.

"You," she answered.

"When."

"Tonight. After the bonfire."

"Where do you want to meet?"

"You already know."

"I want you," he said. "I have. Every damned day since we broke up." No one around them could hear them talking. Landry's voice was a low growl, intimate, only for her to hear. The talking, laughing and music rose above them. Swirled around them. Created an intimate cocoon. "I tried to get you off of my mind by sleeping with someone else. It didn't work. Made me feel sick. Later, when time had passed, I decided to do it just because it seemed like the thing to do. But it was never you. It was never this. Nothing ever could be, Fia."

"Maybe we just need this. Maybe we need to do it.

At least one time. Maybe we need to finish it. In a way that's not all broken and shattered."

It felt silly to think that sex could shatter them now. They were parents. To a thirteen-year-old girl who needed them. They were bonded. In a way that was so deep, so profound, she knew she could never go back to living on the same ranch as him and ignoring him no matter what passed between them.

They were different now.

Whatever happened, even if it went badly, they would take the time to untangle it. Whatever happened, they would find a way. It was about the safest form of throwing caution to the wind that she could even think of. Even as Landry looked at her, all sultry and dangerous, she felt that.

And she was at a loss for words. She wanted to kiss him, but not here. Not in front of everyone. She wanted to kiss him, but that needed to stay between them. She wanted to kiss him, but she couldn't risk doing that in front of Lila. Because this wasn't some easy version of *The Parent Trap*.

This was life, real life, with dangerous, delicate emotions, and they needed to guard them.

But there was also real need. Real history between herself and Landry, and she wanted to unravel it all. While he unraveled her.

She wanted him. She wanted to bring all that they'd ever been. In all that they were now, and let them both get burned alive by it.

A time and a place to fling themselves into the fire. Knowing and experienced. They finished out the dance, and her heart was beating hard. She was breathless, and it wasn't just from spinning.

He went over to his brothers, and she stood on the outskirts for a moment. Lila was actually sitting and talking to one of the other kids, and it made Fia's heart feel two sizes bigger.

Alaina edged over to where Fia was and sat. "Is something going on between you and Landry?"

"Did you just get tired of not being able to say your very favorite refrain?" Fia asked.

"No. It's only that it looks like there's something going on between the two of you."

Fia sighed. "I never stopped being attracted to him."

"That's some high-stakes poker, Fia," said Alaina.

"Oh, I'm aware," she said. "But we've been through... everything."

"Yeah. You have." Her sister looked at her carefully. "Should you have to go through any more?"

"I thought you were a big proponent of my hooking up with Landry."

"Well, that was kind of before I knew how difficult what you went through was."

"Yeah, what I went through was difficult. So trust that I can handle just about anything now."

"Listen," said Alaina. "You do not have to tell me about the allure of the cowboy. Or the trouble they can get you into."

She frowned. "Do you mean Travis?"

Travis was the biological father of Alaina's baby. But Gus had married Alaina. Gus had truly become Cameron's father. And the love of Alaina's life.

"I do not," said Alaina. "That wasn't sex appeal. That was stubbornness on my part. No. Gus was undeniable. When I needed to have a cool head. When I needed to be measured. Reasonable. And instead I fell madly in love with him, and took all my clothes off for him."

"Well, I am *not* madly in love with Landry. I'm realistic about Landry."

"Actually, Fia, I think maybe don't be realistic for once. How long has it been since you've had a good time?"

She looked around, at the barn, at the party. Lila.

"Actually, I've been having the time of my life for the last few weeks."

"Well. Might as well keep it going with a bang."

"Very nice."

"Just be careful," said Alaina.

"Neither of us is in any position to give the other safe sex lectures."

Alaina laughed, doubling over. "True."

She got up and crossed to Gus and their baby, kissing him on the cheek and taking her daughter into her arms. She loved watching them together. Really, she loved watching all of her sisters with their partners. And she ignored the tug in her chest that tempted her to think that she could have the same thing.

It was different. She and Landry were different. But tonight, they were going to have something even better than love. She had yet to see evidence that love could be permanent. But this? This was about the most long-lasting thing she'd ever experienced. This need for him.

Why not indulge it?

Who was she kidding, pretending to rationalize. There was no rationalizing this. There was nothing but need.

For the first time in a long time, there was nothing but need.

It made her feel like she'd slipped into an old pair of jeans that somehow still fit. That she loved even more for that reason.

Tonight, she would have Landry King. Tonight, everything really would go full circle. And then, she would be able to move on. And they would be able to make their family.

And everything would be fine.

# CHAPTER SEVENTEEN

FIA DROVE LANDRY and Lila back to his place. Now he just needed to get Lila to scurry up the stairs so he and Fia could sneak down to the old cabin. They could probably do this in the bedroom. The house was probably reasonably soundproof.

He appreciated the nostalgia of the cabin, though. And the practicality of it. Because while he was pretty sure the sound wouldn't travel from that room over to Lila's… He also had no idea how intense this was going to be. For the first time in weeks, the biggest thing on his mind wasn't the stress of fatherhood. The joy of it. The intensity of it. For the first time, everything was Fia. His need for her obscuring everything else.

Fia was invited upstairs first, though, to help feed Gort crickets, which he had to admit was an amusing pursuit. The little leopard gecko always wiggled its tail before it shot across the cage to grab a cricket, and seeing such a tiny predator in action was always entertaining.

"If Gort was alligator sized he would definitely eat you," he said to Lila.

"No. He wouldn't. But he would eat my enemies."

"Woe unto your enemies, Lila Gates." He patted her head.

And then he and Fia made their way downstairs.

"Lila," he called out, "I'm just going to head over to the farmhouse for a bit."

"Okay," she said.

Fia looked at him, raising an eyebrow. He shrugged.

These were the kinds of innocuous lies you had to tell kids for their own good sometimes, he figured. Because he couldn't say "I'm about to go bang your mother until neither of us can breathe." No. You couldn't say that. That was emotional trauma. That was psychological damage that no one was going to recover from anytime soon. It just didn't need to happen. So a little white lie was the best thing here, as far as he was concerned. They walked out of the house and down the front steps. And then, on impulse, he grabbed Fia's hand. And ran. She ran with him, clutching his hand, the desperate need to make it to the cabin as quickly as possible powering them both.

And when they arrived in front of the cabin, they stopped, and he looked down at her. Tears were streaming down her cheeks. He cupped her face and wiped them away. "What did I do to make you cry?"

It had been such a common thing when they were teenagers. Her tears had been his fault far too many times.

"Nothing. It's… Nothing is this, is it?"

He shook his head. "No."

And then, beneath the clear sky, he gathered her into his arms and kissed her.

But this time he knew that they weren't going to stop. This time he knew that Fia Sullivan was going to be his.

He enveloped her body, kissing her deep and long, sliding his tongue against hers. She tasted so familiar, and new all at once. She was everything. All of his memories, sweet and bitter rolled into one. She tasted like heartbreak and first love. She tasted like cotton candy. So sweet against his tongue. Like possibility and failure. Like hope and triumph.

Like regret. So much regret.

And he took it all in. He didn't try to blunt any of it. Didn't try to spare himself, didn't try to block himself.

Not from this. Not from the intensity of it. Not from the truth of it. He had spent all this time telling himself that he hated her.

When it was just this poisoned love that he'd never quite been able to shake. But he knew that it wasn't the kind that people built houses out of. Knew it wasn't the kind they made families with. And on some level he always had. But he wanted her to rescue him. From himself. His own feelings. His own needs.

What a child he was.

He thought that wanting was enough. But of course it wasn't. Tonight, it would be, though. Tonight, wanting, needing, craving was all there was going to be.

He shifted his hold on her, felt the luscious press of her breasts against his chest.

He ached for her.

An ache that spanned thirteen years. An ache unfulfilled. Because sex had never been anything unless it was with her.

Because desire had never been more than a flicker unless she was the cause of it. The source.

Then he propelled them both into the cabin, closing the door behind them. That old bed that was still in the corner, and even if the place was a bit dusty, it was good enough for him.

He held her tightly and then smoothed his hands down her waist, her hips. Suddenly, it hit him. She had carried a child in the years since he'd been with her. It had changed her body. Changed the shape of her profoundly.

Reverence, awe, need welled up within him.

He pushed her shirt up over her head.

He lit the camping lantern so that he could see, because God knew he wasn't going to have Fia Sullivan naked under his hands without being able to see clearly. There were faint silvery lines on her stomach, and he fell to his knees, kissing them, moving his thumb over them. There was nothing to say. He looked up—her eyes were closed, her expression pained.

"You're beautiful," he said. "More beautiful than I remember."

"I'm definitely not a teenager anymore," she whispered. "There's been some wear and tear."

"I'm not a teenager anymore either. And I don't need you to be unmarked by these years. That part of you. Part of your story. Part of our story. You're the most beautiful thing I've ever seen."

He went back up onto his feet and unhooked her bra, casting it to the side. He let out a curse, short and swift. She was everything he could've wanted.

She had been shaped by the years into just the kind of woman he craved. Because it was her. Always her.

With her pale skin, freckles on her breasts, silvery stretch marks.

She was absolutely perfect. Absolutely awe-inspiring.

He undid the snap on her jeans, then the zipper,

pushing them down her legs as she kicked her shoes off, and he managed to take off every stitch of clothing.

She was naked in front of him, that red triangle of curls between her legs a glory he had never thought he'd see again.

He moved to her, cupped her breast, smoothed his thumb over her nipple, and she gasped. His heart was pounding so hard he thought it might burst through his chest. He had nothing. Absolutely nothing inside of him. No thought, no speech. It was like being before a transcendent work of art. It made him question his own humanity in the face of it. His own significance.

Because she was Fia Sullivan, and she was everything. Because she was the most beautiful woman on God's earth.

And that was the truest damn thing.

Because she was everything. Absolutely everything. He kissed her mouth again, her neck, as he continued to move his hands over her curves.

Luxuriating in the feel of her.

"You are perfect," he whispered.

"Landry," she whispered against his mouth. "Take your clothes off."

He moved away from her and gripped the back of his shirt, pulling it up over his head.

Fia's eyes went wide.

"Damn," she said. His lips curved into a smile, and he kicked his boots off as he undid his belt. As he took off his jeans and underwear.

And he could see that reflected appreciation in her own eyes.

It was a wonder. A damned miracle. Perfect for each other at every age, he supposed.

And this, whatever it was, would fuel his fantasies from now on.

She had already ruined him for everything and everyone else.

So this would just make it complete. This would just make it more profound. He was all right with it. He really was.

But it wasn't just desire, there was an emotion swelling up between them that he knew they both felt. Because it was like another person standing in the room. As obvious and present as either of them.

He reached out and cupped her face. "Fia…" He moved his thumb over her bottom lip. Words failed him. There was nothing he could say. She was the woman who he had hurt the deepest of anyone in his life. She was also the woman he had cared more about than anyone in this world.

He had failed her.

In that way, he was like his father. He had a chance to be good. To love her the way that she needed, and when given that chance he hadn't listened. When given that chance he had failed. When given that chance, he had been nothing but selfish, extraordinarily so. And there were no words for that. There was nothing but this deep groaning in his spirit. Another strange thing he was sure that he heard in a sermon, and he didn't know why in hell church was on his mind now. Except that this was spiritual. Not just physical. Except that his soul was sure as hell involved if there was such a thing, and the divine felt present now more than it ever had.

He wanted to tell her that he was sorry. He wanted to drop to his knees and beg for her forgiveness. He'd asked for it several times over the last few weeks. What he felt now… It was more than sorry. It was sorrow. For the way that he had failed to be there. For the way that he had absolutely lived up to the King family name.

He wanted that name to mean more. He wanted it to mean better. But they couldn't just want that. They all had to be it. Including him.

Now though, he couldn't find words. Now though, he had nothing but the deep, intense need to be closer to her. So that was what he did. Kissed her. Until there was nothing but them.

He kissed them both firmly into the present. And even though the past was still there with them, it wasn't the biggest thing. The memories weren't the most important thing. Weren't the most vivid. The brightest thing was her mouth on his. Her soft, naked body pressed against his.

"I stole a condom from Denver," he whispered against her mouth.

"What?"

"I don't just have them lying around," he said.

She laughed. "Oh. I'm… I'm on the pill."

It was just very basic of him that he was thrilled to hear that. Because he wanted to slide inside of her with nothing between them. With no barrier. He already knew that Fia hadn't been with anyone, and he had been with very few people, and not for a couple of years. He let out a long breath. "Well, that's good enough for me if it is for you," he said.

"It is," she said. "But thank you. For thinking of me. Thank you for protecting me."

"Of course."

There was no *of course* about it. Because he hadn't

done it back then. In so many ways. He just hadn't fucking done it.

He kissed her again, then and there, then picked her up and set her down in the little bed in the corner.

He parted her thighs and kissed his way up her leg, pausing at the tender skin of her instep, her knee, right up by the center of her desire.

"Landry," she gasped.

Then he nuzzled those curl and licked into her damp heat. She gasped, holding his head as he started to taste her.

He remembered this. The best thing. Intoxicating and wonderful and all he'd ever craved back then.

That glorious honey between Fia Sullivan's thighs. She'd been his first.

And she was the only one who had ever mattered.

He tasted her now, knowing that. Reveling in that truth.

She gasped as he moved his thumb over that sensitive bundle of nerves and then down her slick crease, pushing it deep inside of her. And then trading it for two fingers.

"Landry," she gasped again, gripping his head, then his shoulders, her fingernails digging ruthlessly into his skin.

He still remembered. Just where to lick her. Just how to suck her. With them, it had always been something that transcended experience. He had a sense for her body, just like she'd had a sense for his.

It had never felt like two kids getting into trouble, not to them. It had always felt like more. It had always felt like everything. Just damned everything. And it did now too.

She was sweet and slick and perfect beneath his tongue, and he pumped his fingers in and out of her willing body, until she shivered and shook, until she cried out his name and her fingernails drew blood on his shoulders. His name was a prayer on her lips, and it was balm for his soul. Balm he hadn't realized he needed. A triumph he hadn't realized he been missing.

It was like a piece of himself had finally come back home.

Because Fia Sullivan was saying his name in the throes of ecstasy, and there would never be anything as great as that.

He moved up her body, kissed her hip bone, her stomach, both of her breasts, before sucking a nipple into his mouth again, until she arched up off the mattress. Then he moved back to her lips, rubbing his nose against hers before kissing her deeply.

She wrapped her legs around his waist, urging him forward. The head of his arousal pressed against her tight opening, and he began to sink into her.

A lump caught in his throat, along with driving, inexorable need.

Home.

All he could think was that he hadn't been home for thirteen years. And here he was. Inside of her.

Her arms, her legs, her soul wrapped around his.

"Fia," he whispered against her lips.

And then he began to move, driving them both toward the brink. Filling them both with pleasure.

And something beyond that. Something bigger. Bigger than everything.

He flexed his hips forward, and she gasped, and

he did it again, and again, his movements becoming hard, intense.

"I need you," he spoke against her lips.

"Yes," she whispered.

There was nothing but the sound of their need. Skin on skin, their raging heartbeats. Mingled breaths.

Her fingernails drawing blood on his forearms.

He wanted it to hurt. As much as he wanted to feel good. He wanted to be torn in two by this endless, yawning need inside of him. Oh, how he wanted it.

"Fuck me," she whispered.

He growled, driving his hips forward.

"Oh, Landry," she said.

And when she clung to him, crying out her climax, her internal muscles gripping him tight, he lost himself. He buried his head in the crook of her neck and poured himself inside of her. His orgasm a roar, echoing in his head. Thirteen years of need coalescing just then. Into this endless glory.

"Fia," he whispered against her neck.

"That was amazing," she said.

He pulled her against him, overwhelmed. Overcome.

He wasn't a man who gave a lot of thought to his emotions. At least, he hadn't over the past few years. By design, really. Because all of his emotions had been pretty toxic. And had he looked too closely at himself he would've seen his father a long time ago.

"I'm sorry," he said.

"You said that."

"But I really feel it," he said. "The way that I... The way that I broke what we had."

"I think what we had broke because it was crushed

beneath the weight of something that was too big for either of us. The thing is, I can't hate you for handling something wrong when you were seventeen, because if I think we were too immature to be parents then I guess I have to admit we were too young to handle our relationship with each other too."

"But that isn't an excuse for what I did..."

"We can keep going over and over all of it," she said, tracing lines by his eyes, down the side of his mouth.

"What are you doing?"

"Just checking where your face has aged."

He laughed. "I think most of it is from the last few weeks."

"I wouldn't be surprised. We've lived in the past for a long time. Let's stop."

"That easy?"

"No. But the past just isn't as important as where we are now."

He let out a loud sigh, and he kissed her forehead. "This is perfect."

"It is," she said softly.

And there was something, something expanding in his chest. Feelings, words. But he knew he couldn't say them in an empty fashion. He was cautious about it. Because his father had used words of deep emotion to manipulate the people around him. He had never hesitated to say that he loved his wife. That he loved his kids. All while demonstrating something completely different, and that was the kind of boyfriend Landry had been back then.

He would never use empty words. Not again.

He would make sure that he showed them good and well first. He would make sure that he really knew what he wanted. Because he didn't trust himself. That was the thing. How could he? How could he after the bullshit he pulled?

Fia snuggled against him, and he held her. Let himself doze for about twenty minutes. "I've got to get back," he said.

"Yeah."

It felt wrong. To part from each other. To have Fia sleeping in a different house than himself and Lila. It just felt wrong. But it was where they were at right now. And it was what they had.

So he walked back with her, holding hands, walked her to her car and gave her a kiss on the top of her head. "I'll see you tomorrow."

"Yeah," she said. "See you tomorrow."

He turned and went in the house, and he felt a restless ache inside of him. Then he opened the computer that was sitting on the table and searched for the name of the shelter that Fia had mentioned the dog Sunday had gone to. There was a contact form. And he wrote in it, trying to explain the situation. That he knew it had been a year, but if they could trace the whereabouts of Sunday, and if they could give him the info, that Lila, the dog's former owner, just wanted to know she was okay and happy. And that if she was still looking for a home, she would have one with them.

He sent it and closed the computer.

He heard footsteps on the stairs. "Hey, Landry," she said.

"Yeah?"

"I can't sleep."

"Something wrong?"

"I just think… I think it's weird to not live with both you and Fia."

He gritted his teeth. "Yeah. It is."

"Listen, I know that you aren't a couple, but it seems to me like this house or her house are big enough for us to all be together."

She had no idea how complicated that was. The truth was, she was thirteen. They were getting a limited experience of parenting. And there were plenty of divorced couples who actually continued to live together, he did know that. People who kept intact households for their kids. "Well, maybe that's something we can talk about."

There was little more important to the Kings than King's Crest. But he knew that the first thing he would have to do was offer to move to Sullivan's Point. Because family names and all that… They didn't matter. Hell, it hadn't even been a conversation, as far as changing Lila's name. Unless she asked to have a different last name, it was important to both him and Fia that they honored her parents. If they could be a family while including that. He could still be a King somewhere else. And he might just have to be.

"We will definitely talk about that tomorrow."

## CHAPTER EIGHTEEN

FIA FELT TENDER and weepy the next day. She knew that Landry was going to come by with Lila because he wanted to talk about something, and part of her wanted to tell him no. To stay away. To give her some time to convalesce.

But she knew she had to be more mature than that. Because this was a decision that she'd made. To revisit the attraction between them. To indulge it. It had been incredible. Everything that she could've possibly wanted. Everything. He was so sexy. And he was still absolutely it for her. He fit her body in exquisite fashion. The way that he moved his hands over her skin, the way that he had licked her, tasted her.

Nothing could ever compare.

But there was no way they could come together like that without feelings. The feelings had been very, very potent. A little bit over the top, in fact. But when Landry pulled up, she did her best to pull herself together.

And when he and Lila walked up the steps, she flung the door open and plastered a wide smile on her face. "Hi, there," she said.

"Hey," he said. "Good to see you."

"You too."

Lila went into the house. She had a favorite spot in

the farmhouse, and had a crochet project going, so she was obviously ready to get down to that. It thrilled Fia that Lila was now as obsessed with crochet as she was. They worked on projects together while watching TV in the evenings sometimes.

"I wanted to talk to you," he said.

She was ready for it to be some strange conversation about last night. She really needed him to not say that he regretted it. Because that was going to make her feral.

And maybe homicidal. And nobody wanted that.

"What about?"

"Lila said that she thought it was weird that we were living apart. And I agree. Us doing things together in Portland… It was great."

"Yes…"

"Fia, what would you think about me taking a room here at the farmhouse?"

She felt her eyes go wide. "You want us to live together?"

"Yeah. As co-parents, still. I'm not suggesting… I'm not suggesting we jump into anything. But this is a big house, and you're here by yourself now."

"You're a King. You're working on that barn building project."

"Most people have a way longer commute than that. Yeah. I am a King. And… We've got, what, five years before she moves out? Five years to have this. To make the best we can? Christmas is coming up, Fia. We're going to, what…have our first Christmas with Lila in separate houses? Or we can get a tree here. Make our Christmas morning here. We can do it all together. If you want to move over to King's Crest, I'm happy to do that, but that would leave nobody here and…"

"No," she said. "It would have to be you coming here."

"Only if you want," he said. "Or like I said, you can come out to King's Crest. But we need to do this for her."

Five years. They only had five years. Not eighteen. They'd missed so much already. Could they afford to continue to be a family separated like this?

He was right. There were divorced couples that were able to do this for their kids.

"I… Yes. Okay. Let's do it."

"Where?"

"Here," said Fia. "Let's live here."

THE NEXT FEW days were a blur. Landry broke it to his siblings that he was planning on leaving the ranch, and they were more than a little bit confused.

"You're a King," said Arizona. "You can't live at Sullivan's Point."

"I sure as hell can," he said. "Because it's where my child's going to be."

"That's kind of why I live at King's Crest," said Micah.

Arizona frowned. "It's legacy."

"Yeah, and Elsie Garrett lives at McCloud's Landing, and so does Alaina Sullivan."

"You're not *married* to Fia," Arizona pointed out.

"Yes. Thanks," he said, his teeth gritted. "I'm aware."

"Are you going to be?" Denver asked.

He realized that actually that would be good. He

would like it. But he knew that Fia would absolutely freak out. The truth was, his feelings for Fia were deep. And they were independent of Lila. And as much as he wanted to broach that subject in the name of making a family, he also knew he had to resist the urge to do anything that looked like manipulation. Or anything that looked like he wanted to have more control in parenting Lila, and whatever else.

If he made a move like that with Fia, it had to be about her.

"No plans to."

"Are you sleeping with her?" Justice asked.

"I don't see how that's any of your business."

"Well, that means yes," said Daughtry. "Because if it's no, you'd just say that."

"I'm not currently sleeping with her now."

That was true. Just because they'd had sex the one time in the last thirteen years didn't mean they were actively sleeping together.

"Something happened," Denver said.

"None of your business. Also, since when do we do this sharing bullshit? I don't like it. Cut it out."

"As it turns out, you had a secret child that you didn't tell us about. You're on probation," said Denver.

"I'm not on probation, you dick. I'm more grown-up than you. Than any of you. Not you," he said to Arizona. "I've got responsibilities other than myself and this land. So I'm going to move in with Fia. So that I can spend the five years that I've got Lila at home actually in a home with her. We're going to have family dinners and…" He realized he didn't actually know what a functional family did. The Kings had done a pretty good job of assembling something that looked a little bit like one. It was what they tried to do every time they got together. Tried to make some new shape of a family. Because God knew they hadn't had one growing up. But as he tried to reach for an image of all the things he wanted...

Well, they had something. They really did. And it was... It was good. They had the gecko, and they had stuffed animals. They had dinner together. Sometimes with his family, and sometimes with just Fia. They played card games. They were family. It was strange, the shift inside of him that felt a lot like inadequacy. It was strange to think you were doing well, and then feel like maybe you weren't good enough. He wondered if that was fatherhood. Parenthood in general. The whole state of it.

Trying. Feeling like you were trying hard enough, even though you were giving all of yourself.

"Well, I guess we're going to help you move then," said Denver.

"No more objections?" Landry growled.

"I guess we have to let you fly from the nest," said Justice.

"There's no *letting* me do anything," he said.

"I'm proud of you," said Denver. "Because you're a better man than Dad ever was. And you're sure as hell a better dad. Having Lila around has given all of us a chance to be better too. We can be good uncles. Even if we're never going to be dads ourselves. You and Arizona are breaking the curse for us."

"You never know," said Landry. "You might find love yourselves yet."

And he realized he let it slip. The way that he felt.

But it was true.

Always had been.

"Yeah," said Denver, not looking convinced, but also clearly choosing to not dig out what Landry had just said. "Who knows. Maybe we'll figure out how to hold it too."

## CHAPTER NINETEEN

BEING NEAR FIA without touching her was torture. But at least it was familiar. That was what he told himself as he brought another box up the front steps and into the farmhouse at Sullivan's Point.

If his dad could see him now. Changing his whole life for a woman.

Two females, in fact. His daughter and Fia.

His dad would think he was weak.

That made Landry all the more confident in his decision.

King's Crest had been home his entire life. But it had begun to feel fractured these past few weeks. Because it wasn't complete. Because he and Lila weren't complete when Fia wasn't there.

Lila had been thrilled about the move, which had been a huge relief to Landry. He knew that it might have added to that anxiety she had about instability in foster care, and that was the last thing he wanted. But the idea of having her parents together...

He had been quick to make sure she knew they weren't together. Not like that.

Though, the memory of their last time together, of kissing her, touching her, played out in his mind without his permission frequently. At all hours of the day, in fact.

"Moving is boring," said Lila, hefting her own box into the house and setting it down on the ground before dramatically sinking into one of the bright turquoise chairs at the kitchen table.

Landry had to wonder if moving was more than boring for a girl who had been taken out of her home after losing her parents, and then shuffled around the system before having to make another big move out of the city she had grown up in.

Right at that moment, Fia appeared in the doorway and looked at him. He had a feeling they were thinking the exact same thing. They often were. As long as the topic was Lila.

It was refreshing to be on the same page as her at least.

"Let's take a break," said Fia.

"Really?" Lila asked.

"Yes. I think that we should pack up a picnic and go get a Christmas tree. Because this is going to be our first Christmas in the house together, and I want to get started with it as soon as possible."

She shot Landry a questioning look. Holidays had been complicated so far. Birthday, Thanksgiving, because while Lila enjoyed them, they were also tangled around a lot of grief.

He moved over to where she sat in the chair and squeezed her on the shoulder. "I have an idea," he said. "We can do things exactly the way your parents used to do them, or we can do something totally new. And that's up to you. Whatever you want. Whatever feels right."

"Something new," Lila said. "Something different."

"Okay," said Landry.

"We can get a Christmas tree from our own property. Would you like that?"

"That sounds fun. We always used to go to a tree lot."

With that decided, Landry and Lila helped Fia pack lunches. He made a note of where everything in the kitchen was so that he could be of help after he moved in. They might not be in a romantic relationship, but they were blending their lives together as a function of this new living arrangement. Roommates. They were roommates.

He felt his mouth flatten into a grim line.

But even if it was a strange way to find himself cohabitating with his ex-girlfriend, he intended to be a good...partner. They might not be partners in the romantic sense, but they were partners in parenting. And they would be partners in the day-to-day running of the household too.

He helped Lila get bundled up, and then they got into his truck and took a drive deep into the property. There were mountains on the back side of McCloud's Landing, and he knew that they might find some snow there, which would make it both festive and fun.

"This is all still the ranch?" Lila asked, sounding dumbfounded.

"Yeah," he said. "It's the size of a town. I mean, technically it's four different ranches, but only technically."

"How did you get started again?"

"Well," said Landry, "Fia is the best to tell that story. I'm the youngest in the King family. I didn't have anything to do with establishing all of this."

"And I was the youngest to be part of forming the

board," said Fia. "And the only woman. I was eighteen. It all happened not long after you were born. My mom was still around, but my dad had left, and she didn't have any interest in running the place. So I…"

"You were seventeen?"

"Yeah. Still in high school. Trying to figure everything out. But I had already been through so many big changes in my life…"

"You could never have done all that if you had me, I guess," said Lila.

He watched Fia's face crumple, then it went smooth. "I worried about that. I had no idea how profoundly I was going to have to show up to represent Sullivan's Point at that stage. But I did know that I had to take care of my sisters. My mom got better after my dad left, but even then, she was struggling. The responsibility was daunting."

He wanted to touch her. Wanted to comfort her.

"Gus McCloud and Sawyer Garrett had been running McCloud's Landing and Garrett's Watch for a while. Denver had taken control of King's Crest right before then too. But really it was… It was my dad vacating that kind of opened everything up. For us to try to reimagine it. I think we realized at that point we couldn't really do it alone. Our parents had left things in a bad state. We had to figure out how to make it better. We all got together in the barn that we needed now on Sullivan's Point. Sawyer led the discussion— it's why he leads all the meetings now. Our families always had agreements, we always had certain things that we shared, but not on the level that Sawyer wanted us to try. He wanted us to share our finances. To support each other. And that's how the official collective was born. We all chose which strengths we wanted to focus on."

"I hope I'm like you," said Lila.

Fia looked at him, her eyes wide, wild.

"Because you're pretty badass. To be able to figure all those things out. I had it really easy for a long time, but things have been really hard the last couple of years. It makes me feel better. Knowing that I'm related to somebody who knew how to solve her problems. Even as young as you were."

Fia's gaze was watery now. "Thank you," she said.

They reached the top of the mountain, where the trees had started to get substantial enough. They parked the truck and got out. He and Lila explored around the snowy area, looking for trees, while Fia hung back and set up the picnic in the bed of the truck. Though he had a feeling she was working to get her emotions straight. Hell, he was feeling a little wobbly himself. Lila had really seen Fia for what she was. Strong. Determined. Resilient. And that Lila saw those traits as things to emulate made him feel…proud of them both.

"What about this one?" Lila asked, standing in front of a bushy, misshapen beast that looked like the patriarch of the Charlie Brown Christmas tree.

"It's lopsided," he said.

"It's imperfect, and I like it. It's weird and unique, and I think it will be beautiful." She leaned forward and gripped his arm, shaking it. "It's us, Landry."

She said it silly, but it still touched him. Deep in his soul. "Yes. It is."

Fia came over just then. "What is it?"

"It's the Gates-Sullivan-King tree," said Landry, gesturing to the tree.

"Well, I love it," said Fia. "Why don't we eat first."

They trundled back to the truck and got into the bed, where Fia had set out a blanket, hot chocolate and sandwiches.

They sat there in relative silence, with the cold air pressing in all around them and the snow making a cocoon around them.

The pine trees were capped with white, the mountains down below green.

"'Have yourself a merry little Christmas,'" Fia started to sing.

He felt the corners of his mouth lift up. "'Let your heart be light.'"

The three of them started singing together, their voices echoing around them. It was the most simple, glorious song he'd ever heard. The most perfect moment.

Landry had never given much thought to Christmas one way or the other, though Denver made a pretty big deal out of it because he had always tried to make life at King's Crest better and more normal in the absence of their father. But nothing had ever been like this.

This simple carol, sung with his family.

His family.

After they finished, they got out of the truck and walked back over to the tree. Landry brandished his ax. "Get it, Landry!" Lila shouted.

Landry rolled his eyes, then started to cut down the tree.

"Very lumberjack," said Fia.

"Stop objectifying me," he said.

He turned around to look at her, and their eyes clashed. Heat flared between them, and he turned away again. Because this was supposed to be a wholesome family outing. Dammit. They were singing carols.

They got the tree chopped down and loaed into the back of the truck.

And began their journey down the mountain, singing "Jingle Bells," and he tried to ignore all of the conflicting feelings in his chest. The deep emotion and the intensity, the heat that he felt when Fia looked at him.

They made it down to the house and carried the tree into the house and put it into its stand.

Fia got out all of her ornaments, and they began stringing lights and decorating, with Christmas music playing in the background. The music eventually got changed to Taylor Swift, which he insisted on singing, and loudly, because it horrified Lila.

They finished the tree, and Lila stood back, looking conflicted. "There is something I want to do," she said.

"What's that?" Fia asked.

"We had stars on the tree. With our names on them. They were made out of paper. I want… I want paper stars."

He and Fia looked at each other, and the lump in his throat was so intense he was afraid to move. He didn't want to go crying. In front of anybody. Not even himself. But this whole experience with Lila had been an exercise in getting in touch with emotions he liked to pretend he didn't have. Turned out he had them.

Fia got down her kit filled with craft items. He really wasn't surprised to find out she had that. She was handy, and made all kinds of decorations for the farm store. She knitted, she crocheted, she baked. Basically, if you could make it yourself, Fia did it. So she got down beautiful paper, scissors and glue. They sat at the kitchen table, which was brightly painted.

He touched its top. "You did this, didn't you?"

He looked around the kitchen at the cheerful yellow cabinets. Red accents, bright everywhere.

"Yeah," she said. "I couldn't stand it being so dark anymore. I needed it to be different. I needed it to be ours."

Yes. If Fia could make it, she would. She did.

They assembled 3D stars using ribbon and paper, putting patterned paper in certain sections of the stars, while leaving the other sections bright red. And on each one they wrote their names. Fia. Lila. Landry.

They hung them on the tree, just like that. With Lila between them.

Lila wrinkled her nose, and he could see that she was holding back tears.

"It feels like Christmas," she said.

Landry put one hand on her shoulder. Fia put her hand on Lila's other shoulder. "Yes," said Landry. "Yes, it does."

When Lila went up to bed, Landry and Fia sat in the kitchen for a while, saying nothing.

"Landry," Fia said, looking up at him. "We need to get her a dog."

# CHAPTER TWENTY

FIA COULDN'T BELIEVE when her phone rang and it was the animal shelter with news. Both she and Landry had contacted them and left information, and they were calling to tell them that they'd found Sunday.

Fia was still raw from the Christmas tree experience a couple days ago, but it was a good raw, and this just about made her burst into tears.

Sunday had been adopted, but she'd been brought back when the family had to move. "I need to put a hold on her," said Fia.

"We can do that. Until the end of the day."

"Please. It's my daughter's dog. My… I just adopted her. But she's my daughter. She had to give up the dog when her parents died…the parents who had adopted her before. And she got put into foster care so she couldn't take the dog with her. They took so much from her and I just… I really need the dog."

The person on the other end of the phone was clearly a little bit confused.

"What?"

"Can you look at the dog's file?"

She did. "It says here that she was surrendered because her owners died, yes."

"They had a daughter. My daughter. And she couldn't have the dog. But now she can. It would mean the world to her to have the dog back. Please. I don't think we can make it by closing time, but we can drive up there and come first thing tomorrow."

"Okay. We can definitely hold her for you."

"Thank you."

She went to Landry's house without delay. He was still packing. "Landry, I found Sunday."

"What?"

"Lila's dog. They… The shelter called. They found her."

"You're serious?"

"Yes. They said they'll hold on to the dog for us, but I'd need to leave now, and I'd have to stay overnight. I'll just go and…"

"I want to go with you."

"What's she going to do overnight without both of us?"

"We can find out if she wants to have a sleepover at the King house. Maybe Rue will hang out and show her how to make bread."

"She better not. I want to show Lila how to make bread."

"Then maybe she can teach Rue to crochet."

He arranged it, and if Lila thought it was strange, she didn't say. And before they could really make plans, Landry and Fia were on the road to go and fetch Sunday.

"This is like… Well, it's like finding Lila in the first place," she said.

"Yeah. It is. Amazing."

"I realize that we probably have some talking to do about the move," said Landry.

"What about it?" Fia asked.

"Just the… You know, we're planning on making it. And I suppose we need some ground rules."

"Like having separate bedrooms?"

"Yep," he said.

"Right. Well. We've got to make sure that we keep everything centered on Lila," said Fia.

"Of course," he said. "Absolutely."

"She's the most important thing."

"Yeah."

They got all the way up to Portland, and decided to stay in the same hotel that they had when they were with Lila.

"Two rooms?"

Tension wound through her. Knotting in her stomach.

"No," she said.

Because when they got back home, when they moved into the farmhouse, they were going to have separate rooms. They were going to be good.

They were going to make it about Lila. But she wasn't here.

She wasn't here.

He looked at her, his jaw going tense. "Right."

"One room," he said. "King bed."

They were given a key card and a room number. And they took the elevator up to the sixth floor. They walked down the hall, and Landry put the card in the reader. Her stomach got even tighter.

They went into the room, and he closed it behind them. Locked it.

"Fia…"

He didn't need to say it.

She knew.

She rushed over to him and stretched up on her toes. She kissed him. She kissed him like she was dying. Because she felt like she was. She was so happy to have this moment. This separate moment. Just with him. Nobody was here. And this was in a cabin in the woods. It was a hotel room. It wasn't part of their past. And no, it wasn't part of their future. But it was them. Right now, it was them.

"Landry," she whispered.

"I've got you, baby," he whispered against her mouth.

It was the exact right thing to say. Because she felt like she was flailing. Floundering. Losing herself in the need that was threatening to swamp her. But he had her. In his strong arms. Because he was Landry, and he was everything. Just like he always had been.

But Lila had to be everything.

She didn't know how to be with him, and be a mother. She didn't know how to be everything. But right now all she had to be was his.

He stripped her clothes off her body and looked at her like she was a delicacy.

"Take your clothes off," she said, her voice husky like a stranger's.

There was nothing more she loved than Landry King's body. He made her feel giddy. He made her feel sixteen. But even better he made her feel twenty-nine. Because she would rather be twenty-nine. A woman who knew exactly what she wanted. She would rather be herself right now, in this moment, than anyone else or anywhere else, and in her life, that was the singular realization.

"It's been too long," he growled as he stripped his shirt off. "Way too long."

"It's been a week," she said.

He grabbed her and wrapped his arm around her waist, pulling her against his chest, her nipples scraping against the hair there, sending a spark of pleasure through her body. "You're right," she whispered. "Way too long."

He kissed her. Devoured her. Sent shock waves of need arcing through her.

There had never been anyone like Landry.

She knew, because she felt this electricity when she looked at him across the room.

"That bastard Landry King," she whispered.

"What?"

"That's how I refer to you. In my head. Every time I would see a hot man and I didn't want him. Every time you would walk in and make an earthquake inside of me. That bastard Landry King. Because you ruined me. For everyone and everything. And I made it about my fear, Landry, but the truth is I just didn't want anyone else."

"Neither did I," he said. "And I tried. But it was empty. And it wasn't you, Fia. Nothing has ever been you. You're the most significant person in my life."

"Mine too."

He kissed her. Deeper this time, harder. And she felt all of these things rising up inside of her. Feelings and promises and words. She wanted to say that she loved him, and that terrified her. Like there was a hook in her stomach, holding her tense, and it had just been twisted. It was nearly painful. She couldn't say that she loved him. She couldn't love him.

Except… Had there ever been a moment where she hadn't loved him? Really? The issue had never been love. It had been the shape it had taken.

Unfortunately.

So she didn't say it, because it would only be confusing. So she didn't say it, because it would only hurt them both.

But she felt it. As his hand skimmed over her skin. She moved her own hands to his belt buckle and undid it. Exposed his glorious cock to her vision.

She knelt down in front of him, moved her hand over his length and took him in her mouth. He was bigger now. He was a man. He was everything that she needed.

Salty, masculine. And most of all, him.

There had never been anyone like him.

There never would be.

Landry King was her forever. And that was difficult. Because even if that was true, it didn't mean she could have him. Even if that was true, it didn't mean they could be together.

But they could have now. Now. And then they would move in together. And they would make a perfect life. They would be perfect parents, and they would orient themselves around Lila. Not around each other. Not around their own pain. Not around their own passion.

She sucked him until he was groaning, until he was pulling her hair. And she liked that. That pain counterbalanced the pleasure. Did something to ground her. Rooted her in the moment. Did something to remind her that pleasure had a cost.

That these feelings had a cost.

And there was no amount of wishing that would make that not true.

But not here. Not tonight. Tonight was just for them.

He lifted her up and held her against him, kissing her deeply. Then he pushed her onto the bed, stepping out of his jeans, his boots. His socks.

He looked like a predator, staring at her like she was the most beautiful thing he'd ever seen. Like he was going to devour her. And he did.

Landry King made a feast of her, and she reveled in it. She clung to his shoulders, her thighs up over them, and let him carry her away.

And then when he returned to her mouth, she kissed him deep, as he thrust home, joining them.

She wanted to cry. She always did. Because every time felt like it might be the last time. And that made her feel like she might die. She reached her peak as he thrust into her, over and over again. He held back, teasing them both. Tortured them.

In the aftermath, he held her, shaking and shuddering.

He held her beneath those soft sheets. In a bed they'd get to sleep in together all night. They'd never done that before.

They'd never been able to.

And that made her want to weep too, but she couldn't do that. This was right. This was the proper send-off for what they were. A real, grown-up night together. In a bed. When one of them didn't have to leave in the morning. She lay there, holding on to his forearm, which he had wrapped around her, rested over her breasts. Her head was leaning against his chest.

"It's always too good," he said. "I don't know how I'm going to go back to not having you."

His words terrified her. Because the stakes were just too high. Didn't he understand that?

"I don't want to talk about that," she said. "Tonight is just ours. Tonight it's just us. I don't want to think about anything else."

"Okay."

They lay there for a long moment. "What are your dreams?"

She closed her eyes. "That's not a less painful subject."

"I don't mean those dreams. Yeah. My dream was to marry you. That was all I wanted when I was sixteen. I was going to marry Fia Sullivan. There. I said it. You don't have to. But before that. What was your dream?"

She felt torn up. It didn't help that he'd been the one to say it. Not when it was the clearest dream she could recall.

"I guess… I wanted to be a pastry chef. I loved watching baking shows on TV. And I wanted to do something like that. Or maybe have my own cooking show. You know, those really reasonable dreams that you have when you're a kid. My mom said that people from nowhere don't get to do things like that. She's right. I was just a girl from nowhere. It was never going to happen. Having a store where I sell my baked goods is close enough. I get to do what I love. And I found a way to make the family business sustainable for all of my sisters. So…that's living the dream, isn't it?"

And there were other things unspoken there too. They might not be married, but they had their child now. They had a family, in a fashion. What was that if not a version of a dream. The same as that TV chef dream. You grew up, and you realized you couldn't have everything. You realized that there was a practical version of the thing, and it was probably better anyway.

"I wanted to be just like my dad," he said. "A cowboy. Who ran the ranch. I wanted to be so cool, like him. Smoke Marlboros and rope calves. It's all I ever wanted. And I never could measure up to him. I couldn't measure up to my brothers. And I quit having dreams. Until you."

"What a shit," said Fia. "Really. Your dad deserves to rot in the seventh circle of hell."

"Why the seventh?"

"I don't know. I was being dramatic. A little inferno reference goes a long way. But I can't actually be expected to remember what all the levels were."

"Yeah. Sounds boring."

She laughed. "But seriously, what a dick."

"Yeah. Well, your mom too. Like, I get it. I get wanting to maybe get your kid to focus on something that feels a little more realistic. But there's a way to do that without implying that they aren't special. There's a way to guide without… At least I think there is? I wouldn't really know."

She touched him. "You do a good job at that."

They looked at each other, and she knew a moment of pure regret. That this wasn't her life. That they weren't lying together in a bedroom in *their* house. That they hadn't raised their daughter from the cradle. Because maybe it would've been this? Maybe? That they could never know.

She felt tears threatening, and she shoved them back.

"You did better than your dad," she said. "You're

a cowboy, you're expanding King's Crest and you're a good father. So I guess you have your dream too."

"In a fashion," he said. Then she knew he was thinking the same thing. It was on the tip of her tongue to say maybe they wouldn't be so toxic now. To say maybe they should try. But it felt so high stakes. If they tried and they failed, then Lila would be wrapped up in that failure. And she knew how awful that was.

Landry went and bought snacks and drinks down in the lobby, like they might need fuel. And they did. They didn't talk much for the rest of the night. Instead, they seemed desperate to burn impressions of themselves into each other's skin. As if they hadn't done that already. As if that wasn't so much of who they were.

And why they hurt so damned bad. But being together was good. It made her want to ignore the ways they were dangerous.

Tonight, in this hotel, maybe she could just embrace the flames.

## CHAPTER TWENTY-ONE

THE NEXT MORNING they ordered room service—or what passed for room service at that particular hotel, which was basically a bundled-up version of the continental breakfast—and ate in bed together.

It was a luxury. Being together like this.

Landry had never spent the whole night with a woman. He had never wanted to—other than Fia, that was. He had dreamed of it when they were younger. When he'd held her after they'd made love, and he'd stroked her hair, he'd imagine waking up in the morning with her, the sunlight streaming in and making that red gold hair light up.

And this morning he had it. And her. She was naked, with the sheets around her waist, clutching the cup of coffee in her hand.

She was the most beautiful thing he'd ever seen.

"The shelter opens at nine," she said sleepily.

They hadn't slept very much. He didn't regret it. Not a single hour they'd spent clinging to each other.

"So we have a little time." He leaned in and kissed her. She put her coffee down, and he proceeded to push the limit of the time they had left before they had to leave.

They both dressed slowly. He got them both some

coffee to go from the little dining room before they headed out to the shelter.

When they got there, they walked through the front door. "I'm Fia," she said to the person sitting at the front desk. "I called yesterday."

"We spoke on the phone," said the girl with piercings sitting at the front desk. "You're the ones who are here for Sunday."

"Yes," said Fia. "We're here for Sunday."

Sunday was the most beautiful dog he'd ever seen. She was big and happy, her tail wagging wildly the minute she saw Fia.

"I think you look like someone she knows," he said.

"Stop," she said. When she looked up at him, her eyes were full of tears. And he was pretty sure that he loved her.

Yeah. He was pretty sure he had. All this time.

They took Sunday out to the car after they filled out all of the paperwork, and hit the road.

There was a celebratory feel to the drive back, and yet, he couldn't quite shake the feeling that they were leaving something else behind, even as they brought the dog back.

He couldn't quite shake the feeling that they were supposed to leave all of their need for each other back in that hotel.

And it just wasn't going to work that way. Not for him.

But he sensed a whole lot of hesitance in Fia. Deep, intense walls that she still had up around her heart.

He had earned those. He knew that. He was trying to figure out all the ways that he could atone. It wasn't, apparently, agreeing to move in with her. It wasn't, apparently, being a decent enough dad. It wasn't multiple orgasms, either.

He would keep apologizing until his throat was sore. He could never stop being sorry for the way that he'd failed her.

But he didn't especially know what else to do.

He would let it sit for now. Because if there was one thing he'd learned over thirteen years of not having the woman he loved in his bed, in his arms, it was that he could endure a whole hell of a lot.

So he could wait. He could wait until he could figure it all out.

And in the meantime, he would try. He would try to keep challenging himself. He would try to keep changing. And most of all, he needed to keep on listening to her.

Because that was what she'd said he hadn't done. And he knew it to be true. He hadn't been able to listen because he'd been so caught up in his own bullshit. In his own issues.

And he didn't want it to be about him. It needed to be about her. What she wanted too.

And it needed to be about him being able to give her what she needed.

And maybe that was the thing. He wasn't quite sure what all she needed yet. So until then did, he needed to move slowly. He needed to not spook her.

That was the main thing.

They finally arrived back at Four Corners, and they decided to go straight to the King residence.

"We're going to have to give her a little heads-up," Fia said.

"I'll wait out here with Sunday," he said. "You go in."

"Really?"

"You're the one who found her."

Fia got out of the car, and he watched her the whole way.

He looked down at the dog. "You have no idea," he said to her. "But that woman over there just made your life. She really did."

A minute later the door opened, and Fia came out with a stunned-looking Lila.

And that was when he chose to open the door.

"Sunday!"

The dog raced across the grass. Right toward Lila.

And he had never seen a single thing that matched the joy on his daughter's face right then.

They couldn't work miracles. They couldn't bring back the parents who had loved her and raised her from the time she was a baby. But if Sunday could be one thing, it was evidence that they would move mountains to give her what they could.

That they would always listen, and always care.

And right there, something shifted within him. And he realized he could love Fia independently of Lila. He couldn't want her independently of wanting to make a family for Lila. Yes, that would be great. But it wasn't why he wanted Fia. He always had.

Because she was everything to him. And she had been for a long damned time. Thoughtful and beautiful and funny, and his whole soul.

This utterly beautiful person who had bewitched him from way back when.

He loved them both separately. He loved them both together. He loved Fia as Lila's mother. But he loved her as a woman.

And there was something about this that just secured it all. Cemented it in his head, and his heart.

And it made him not so afraid. Not so afraid to trust his love.

Not so afraid he was his dad. Because he would go through hell and back for those women. They were his.

But not his to manipulate. His to care for. His to love.

Lila was crying, holding on to Sunday. And the dog was whimpering too. Her own version of crying, he thought. In pure joy. Happiness. He knew there was something bittersweet in it too.

But life, in his experience, was like that. Where there was love, there was always loss. And where there was restoration, there were always cracks.

Right now, though, he could say with confidence that they made love all the sweeter.

That maybe the bitter had to be there for the sweet to matter.

"Fia… Landry. You found her."

"We both contacted the shelter trying to find out what became of her. It just so happened that the family who had been taking care of her for the last year had to move. And they couldn't bring her with them. So she was there. Waiting for you."

"She was just like me," said Lila. "Waiting for the two of you to find her."

"I think it's about time we headed home," said Landry. "All of us. Don't you?"

"Yeah," said Lila. "Let's go home."

So they all loaded up in the car. Father, mother, dog and girl. And they headed back toward Sullivan's Point.

Because that was their home now. And they were family.

And Landry knew that he wouldn't let anything shake that.

Not a damn thing.

# CHAPTER TWENTY-TWO

SUNDAY WAS RAMBUNCTIOUS. Galloping around the house in her excitement. And Landry and Lila had decided to use one of the crochet animals as a toy for her. So a whole lot of rollicking around the Christmas tree was happening while Fia was trying to make dinner.

She didn't mind.

There was a comfort to their presence.

To Lila's laughter and Landry's encouragement of shenanigans.

But there was a pressure building behind her heart. And every time she felt joyful, it pushed. It pushed and pushed, and she wasn't sure what it was, or why it was trying to break through this moment of happiness.

She focused on finishing dinner. And when she brought the enchiladas and beans to the table, Lila and Landry were already sitting there eating chips. And Landry was feeding some to Sunday.

She slapped at his hand. "Don't make the dog fat," she said.

"I, personally, like a fat animal," said Landry, scratching Sunday behind her ears. "Lends them a stately quality."

Lila giggled.

Fia rolled her eyes and sat down at the table.

"You're incorrigible, Landry King."

"That is so much nicer than what you usually call me."

"I suppose it is."

He put his elbows on the table and smiled at her.

And that was when it cracked on through.

It was like she was looking at an alternative reality. At another life. One that she could have had. One that she didn't have.

Not really. One where they'd had Lila all these thirteen years. Where she and Landry had gotten married back then. And decided they loved each other.

That they could make it work no matter what.

It was painful. It was just so damned painful. The reality of all of this.

Of the fact that Lila had been hurt. Hurt by the choice that Fia had made when she had been trying to spare her any pain.

She had ended up in foster care.

Maybe they should have just stayed together. Maybe they should've weathered it. Maybe making her love those people who had been her parents had actually been a cruelty because they were only with her for such a short time.

Maybe the trauma that Lila felt from that would've paled in comparison to the trauma that Fia would have dumped on her as a teenage mother.

She held it together. She sat there at the table and she pretended to eat. Landry and Lila didn't notice, since they were still busy entertaining Sunday and making jokes while they ate.

"We should introduce Sunday to Gort," said Lila.

"Now," said Landry, "I think that might cause some issues."

"Why?"

"You don't want Gort to eat Sunday."

Lila found that hysterically funny.

"He's a predator," she said sagely. "It's the circle of life."

Fia quietly slipped from the table and went over to the sink. She started doing dishes. And then...stopped.

She walked quietly to the front door and slipped out to the front porch. Then she leaned against the wall of the farmhouse and let her tears begin to fall.

And let herself grieve. Deeply. Properly. For the beauty of this life. For what might've been. For what she could never know.

For the good in the lost years. And the loss in those same years. For the certainty that she could never actually claim.

For everything. Everything and anything, all at once.

And a moment later, she heard the door close. And strong arms came around her. "What's the matter, baby?"

"Landry..."

"Did I make you cry again?"

"No. Not you."

"What is it?"

"When I see you with her, I can't help but wonder if you're right. If you would've been a great dad. From the beginning. And I tell myself... I tell myself it was you. And us. And my family. And your father. But in the end... I was scared that I was going to fail. I couldn't handle that. I was so scared of being the one to fail her, because my relationship with my own mother was just so bad, and I…I wonder if I really wasn't strong enough to give her to you. To have her here, to have you take care of her. What if that's what it was? What if I was being selfish? Because look, here we are together, and everything is beautiful. But look at all she's been through, this poor little girl. She lost her parents, and just seeing her face when she saw Sunday…"

"Hey," he said. "Maybe it would've been fine. Us trying. We would've made mistakes. We would've been poor as shit. But maybe it would've been okay. Or maybe it would've been the destruction of us. Because some people overcome and some people don't. The thing is, Fia, we can't know. And we can grieve for what might've been. God knows I did. Not well. Not fairly. But I did. We can grieve for what might've been. But all that really exists is what it is. That girl is who she is because of what you gave her. And she's awesome. You didn't take her parents from her. You gave her a chance. You're a fucking great mom, Fia. From conception to now, you are a fucking great mom. You're right. You made the hard choice. The complicated one."

Fia drew a shaky breath. "You know what's funny, having you angry at me across the ranch made it easier for me to not be angry at myself. You were so unfair to me. Just so damned unfair, and then I never had to attack myself, because I knew you were doing it. I felt so justified. And when you forgave me, all this other shit just sort of started to bubble up. I think it's because there's no balance now, and now I'm free to question myself. To ask honestly how I might've hurt you. And to care about it. You being fair really messed things up. Because when you made me the villain, I got to be more secure in my heroism. It gave me something to fight against. And now I'm just fighting against myself. My own sadness. My own grief. I love her so much, and I feel so aware of the time that I've missed with her because she ended up with us now. And it makes me wonder what the point is in a way that I never would have if…"

"I know. I get it. I think we can feel both. Happy that we have this now. Wistful about what we didn't get. But it would've had to be another life, Fia. Another time. And we didn't get another life. We got this one. But we have her now. Maybe it's fate. Maybe it's not. Maybe it's life. In all of its great and glorious messiness. Maybe it's not as simple as right and wrong. It's just making choices. The best ones that you can. The best ones that you can at the time. Because none of us can see the future. And we can only see the past through our own perspective. But goddammit, nobody tried harder than you. To make the best choice. To be the best mother. Nobody tried harder."

She dissolved then, right there in his arms, because they were safe. Because he was Landry. And she felt sort of undone by the strangeness of this. That he was one of the people who meant the very most to her, and that he was here in the house. After being lost to her for so much time. Much in the same way that Lila was. And it all felt so fragile. And so important. So essential.

She was so scared of breathing and breaking it all.

She didn't know how to make that feeling go away.

"We already have too much to hold without holding guilt too," he whispered. "You're not my enemy, Fia. You're my partner."

"You're not my enemy either."

As declarations went, it was kind of a weird one. But it suited them. It was necessary.

And there were other words that crowded her throat. Things she wanted to say, but they were far too scary in this moment. Because everything was too scary. High stakes.

When they were kids, they'd been playing with things that were too big for them, but it hadn't gotten any smaller. They were going to have to find a way to expand to accommodate all this. They were parenting a child, but one with full consciousness. One who was watching them. Learn and fail and succeed, and she would always remember it. At least babies didn't know if you were terrible at parenting.

At least they didn't remember your every error as you tried.

But a thirteen-year-old always would.

She had her own lumps and scars; she had her own baggage.

Dammit. This was just so hard.

"I'm with you," he said.

"I'm with you too."

It was like getting married. Out there on that porch. These were promises that were deeper than any piece of paper.

It was spiritual. And it was real.

He held her. She held him back.

"Thank you for taking care of me."

"It's my pleasure. It damn well is."

"You're a great dad."

She felt his chest hitch. "It's one of the only things I ever wanted," he said, the words husky. "To know that

I could be that. To know that I could love somebody. That it wasn't broken from all of that. But there was a reason for me to be here."

"There are so many reasons." She had trouble speaking after that. Because she was all feelings and deep, wordless need.

Because they lived in this house and it wasn't on fire. But she still somehow felt...distant.

Like she was in a place where he couldn't quite reach her. And she didn't know what wall to tear down, what door to open, what window to crack.

And she hated her mother again. For never showing her. For never being there for her.

"I just want to be different," she said.

"You will be."

He meant than her mother when her father left. He didn't understand. She also wanted to be different than herself.

Because she just didn't feel adequate. She didn't feel worthy. She couldn't get to the bottom of why. And it made her want to scream. "Do people just feel like this? When they're raising another person. When that person is their responsibility, they just feel like this all the time?"

"Only if they're good parents. I'm pretty sure parents never thought this much about what we were feeling."

And that was the sliver of hope she needed. In this small moment of hopelessness. Of weakness. This permission to be uncertain. And to see it as a strength. To see it as love. She put her hand on his face. "Thank you. That was what I needed to hear."

He took her hand and moved her fingers to his lips.

She was frozen with the desire for more. And she had the feeling, the sense, that maybe this was the door she was holding firmly closed. But she was too damned afraid to open it.

"Landry," she said softly. "I need this."

She meant this family. This living situation. This life. It was a plea. A desperate one. To not push her further than she could go, because she was afraid of what she might do.

"I understand."

He dropped her hand. "You gonna be okay?"

"It's so silly. I've really never been better. In so many ways. But this is challenging. And it's…"

"Growing us up?"

"Yeah. I pretty much thought I was done. But there's a lot of stuff we never really turned over."

"We didn't have to. Now we do."

She nodded. "Yeah."

"Let Lila and I do the dishes. Why don't you go… Well, you can sit out here. You could go visit your sister."

"Thanks. I think… Yeah. I'll sit out here for a bit."

She sat there, on the front steps. And finally, she picked up her phone and called her mother.

"Hi, Mom," she said.

"Finally," her mom said. "I've been trying to get a hold of you. Alaina told me that I needed to give you some space."

"She was right. I needed space. Thank you for respecting that."

"You can say what you need to say," said her mom. "There's nothing you can say to me that I haven't said to myself already. I failed you, Fia. Pretty profoundly.

And I'm aware of that. Finding out that you were pregnant back then... Well, it's given me a lot to think about. That's what I do here. I think."

Fia chewed her thumbnail. "I was given to believe that what you did was take new lovers of an evening."

That was a bit mean. But oh well.

"Sometimes that too. You know you can think and have lovers."

It was so strange, to talk to her mom like this. Her mom who had joined a commune life, and who had clearly let go of needing to be attached one person and pour all of her feelings into that person.

Her mom, who had traded in the intense marriage that she'd had with their father for casual polyamory and breezy pansexuality.

"It's important to be able to tell people that you wronged them. I wronged you. You girls needed something from me that I couldn't give you. Not at the time. I had to go away and I had to get away from your father, and that was when I realized that I could feel different things. Prioritize things differently. That I could be a whole different person."

"You still haven't come back here."

"No. And maybe it's because I'm afraid. I'm afraid that coming back there will make me more like I used to be. I'm sorry that you're all caught up in that. In that part of my life that was so difficult. I don't know what to do about the mess that I made there. I've done a lot of therapy. A lot of thinking. I know that doesn't help you. It doesn't make me a better mother. I said things to you that were unforgivable, Fia, and from my own hurt."

"Do you remember. Do you remember when you

told me that you were trying your hardest? And that I would be a terrible mother?"

"Yes," she said. "I thought about that often, especially when you ended up staying single. But I did not realize that you were actually pregnant at the time. I was in a bubble. I was being selfish. The most important thing to me was my relationship with your father, and when it wasn't going well, nothing was going well."

"But you feel like you're a different person now than you were then."

"Yes."

She realized then that this was actually the more important thing. It wasn't coming to terms with her mother. She had a feeling that for her, coming to terms with her mother would always look a little bit differently than it did to her sisters. She had a feeling that for her, there would always be some resentment. She would never ache for a closer relationship to her. But she did want to learn something. As she was, steeped in regret.

"Do you think you would've been a better mother if you would've waited longer? If you would have maybe been with someone else?"

"Yes," she said without hesitating. "Some people can learn on the job. I didn't learn fast enough. And so you were all caught up in my mistakes. I shouldn't have been mothering in my twenties. I should have been dating. I should've been finding out all the things about myself that I didn't actually find out until I was in my forties. If I would've known that I could be happy by myself, if I would've known that I could be happy with other partners. With men. With women. If I would've known that, I wouldn't have clung to him so hard. I wouldn't have made him my entire identity. I would've given you different advice. I would have treated you better. I would've had more patience."

"I'm struggling. Because I really do believe that I did the right thing by giving Lila up for adoption. I do. It's hard because now Landry and I are both so good at it."

"But you don't know who you would've been. How long it would've taken you to get to this point if you'd been struggling through that whole time. I'm evidence that a person can change. But also evidence that a person could just be a bad mother."

There was something about that that was balm for Fia's soul. An honesty that she hadn't really expected.

"It's tempting to believe that love covers all that stuff," Fia whispered.

"I loved you, Fia. I always have. But I couldn't prioritize acting on that love when I felt so miserable about myself. I couldn't put your needs before mine because I felt like I was going to fall apart if I couldn't fix my relationship with him. And then I just sat in that farmhouse, and that life that he wanted, and I felt myself getting smaller and smaller. It was the worst when I envied you."

"You envied me?"

"Yes," her mom said, broken. "I knew you had a boyfriend—you weren't that sneaky. I knew you were in love. You were radiant with it. So young and with your whole life ahead and I was stuck. It made me jealous. Of my own daughter. After your dad left it was a slow process, but I realized my life was only fixed if I stayed in one place. It was only too late for me to live if I decided not to live. I knew I needed to change everything in order to find myself. I was going to just continue. I know you were angry that I left. But having me there was only ever going to get worse and worse. We didn't get along…"

"Yeah."

It was right then that she realized in her way, her mother had made that decision for her. Because Fia loved the ranch and she didn't. Because back then being near each other was only toxic. It hadn't been wholly selfish. It had been a gift in its way. And she'd never been able to see it that way. Because once their mother was gone they been able to paint the farmhouse in bright colors. And find new life and new focus. Because sometimes you had to cut ties to change things for real.

And that didn't mean you couldn't circle back. But she could see it. Clearly. And she could see the truth of all this in her own life.

"I do want to come visit. I need to come see Alaina's baby. And yours."

"Well, it so happens that Landry has been renovating some guest quarters. You can come visit, and you wouldn't have to stay in the farmhouse. You wouldn't have to be at Sullivan's Point. Maybe that would be easier for you."

"Maybe," she said. "You've changed a lot, Fia."

"I have," she said.

That was the other best thing she could've heard.

Because she had so much worry about old patterns, old feelings and old failings. But she had changed. Because in some ways, she'd figured out that she was okay without Landry King. She sure liked having him around, though. But she hadn't died when they'd broken up. She'd been strong, and they'd made a new life for themselves. Even if a commune and multiple lovers hadn't been her answer.

She would never be the same kind of jealous that she used to be.

It wasn't actually because she would be okay without him. It was mostly that she could see the clear differences between him and her father. When at the time it had been too easy to decide that her father made a case for men being all one thing.

Landry wasn't her father any more than he was his.

"Thank you. For the conversation. I appreciate it. I had some things to work out."

"I'd like to try," said her mother, "to have some kind of relationship. I'm learning. That you girls are growing. I'm learning more and more what I need to do to be there for you."

And for them, for their mother, the answer hadn't actually been for her to be there. It was complicated. But it was true. For them, it was true. For them, distance had mattered. For them, that had been important.

"I love you," said Fia.

Because even with everything, that was true.

"I love you too."

And she believed it. She just believed that it was shown in ways that sometimes she couldn't see.

Hadn't been able to see.

She hung up and walked back into the house. Back to her family. And she knew that Landry was right.

What if it didn't matter? Not in the face of what they had.

## CHAPTER TWENTY-THREE

IT WAS A whole week of living with Fia and sleeping in the bedroom down the hall. It was hard. Damned hard. Because he wanted that woman. With all of himself. With everything.

More than that. He loved her.

That Monday, they took Lila to the one-room schoolhouse for the first time. There were only three days until Christmas break, but still, she was ready to start. She already had a couple of friends there, plus Daniel. And they felt good about leaving her. But Fia was still emotional like it was Lila's first day of kindergarten. And afterward he drove Fia to Becky's diner and got her a hamburger.

"This is so silly," said Fia, wiping her cheeks.

"No, it's not," he said.

They still made a spectacle about town, going around together. But everybody knew now. Everybody had seen their little family. He took pride in it, and he knew for a while it had embarrassed Fia a little bit. He also knew that it didn't now.

That it was a little different. But things felt more... positive for now.

And he felt like he was getting close. To the right moment.

"How are you feeling? I mean, other than all this. You still liking living with me?"

"Yes," she said, eating a french fry.

They breakfasted together every morning. Had dinner together every night. He really was never quite so happy as he was with her.

They were beginning to have more of a relationship independent of Lila. And independent of sex. They sat and talked about their days, just because they wanted to.

They were filling in all these gaps. They had done things so out of order. All sex. Then all parenting. And now it was like their connection was coming through, kneading them together into something stronger. He still wanted her, though. And he felt like it was getting close to the right moment to bring their romance back into play.

"I am… I'm happy."

"Good. That's all I've ever wanted. To make you happy."

It was true. She seemed like she didn't know what to say to that, so she turned her head to the side. He didn't push. They stayed busy, him working on the barn, and Fia back at the farm store until it was time for them to pick up Lila. And when they did, she was chatty and filled with stories about the day. They had Sunday in the car, and she was wildly excited to see her girl.

They drove back to the farmhouse, and he offered to make dinner.

That meant it would be steak and vegetables, but nobody complained. Lila and Fia sat together working on crocheted animals. They ate dinner, and Lila went up to her room.

Because she was a teenager. So as much as she enjoyed spending time with them, she of course enjoyed spending a good portion of her time by herself, in her own space. He often thought that her bedroom was perhaps the thing she appreciated the most that they'd given her.

Fia lingered downstairs for a bit while he did cleanup from dinner. And then she went upstairs too.

He looked around the house. It was a hell of a thing. To be living about three-quarters of what he wanted most. To have his daughter. To live with Fia. To love Fia.

But he didn't really have her.

He sighed and headed up the stairs.

He turned and headed down the hall, and the door to Fia's room opened.

He stood there. Looking down the dimly lit hall as she appeared. He found himself walking toward her. And he could see a kind of helpless expression on her face. Not sure whether she wanted to tell him to fall back or tell him to come near.

But he needed her. He really did. Because the truth was, he had everything else. And so he knew that if something was missing, it was her. In his arms. In his bed.

She was in his heart. Just like she had been from day one.

But that heart hadn't been mature enough to hold her in the way it needed to. He hoped it was now. He hoped to God that it was now.

"Baby," he said.

Because it was what he'd called her then. It wasn't the most personal. It wasn't the most special. But it had been the most passionate thing. From the depths of his soul. Just like it was now.

She moved away, making room for him to walk through the door.

She threw her arms around his neck, and she was trembling. And he just held her. And memorized the feel of her. The press of her breasts against his chest. Her smile. The way she was familiar. The way she was different.

The way she was his. He would've said that he wasn't an emotional man. He would've said that prior to the last few months. And now it felt like they were always so close to the surface. It felt like they were all of him. Everything. And he didn't even hate it.

The chance to hurt for these women who were everything to him, it felt like a gift.

It made him feel like he ought to be here. He wished that he could go back and tell that boy it would all be okay. Not the way he imagined it, but better. That love meant more when you gave it the right way, at the right time, when you had the right stuff to give.

He tilted her chin up to his and he kissed her.

It was slow and aching. Because he didn't need a whirlwind. Because they weren't racing anything. Their better judgment, their parents, the clock.

They had time. They had this room. They had a bed.

In their house. Their house.

So he took his sweet-ass time undressing her. Revealing that glorious body to him.

He took his time, because she was worth all the time. All the years, all the waiting. All the wanting.

Because she was worth it. Because God knew that pain. But they deserved pleasure.

He couldn't give her back all those years. But maybe he had needed to be away from her. Maybe he had needed to become a different man, a better man.

He wished to God he could go back and be better then. But in the absence of that he would take this. He laid her on the bed, and he worshipped her. His Aphrodite. His everything.

His woman. His woman whom he'd loved since she'd been his girl. And he'd never been anything as young and simple as a boyfriend.

Now he wanted to be her husband. Her protector. Her man. The father of her child. God, he wanted to have more children with her. That was a plea. A prayer.

And every kiss was a supplication. A request, not a demand.

And when he entered her, he felt that same rush. Like the first time. Like every time. Over and over again.

Because she was beautiful. And she was his. Fia Sullivan and that bastard Landry King. She clung to him. To his shoulders. Wrapped her legs around his waist. He wanted to be closer than inside her. He wanted to drown in her. In this.

He wanted to lie beside her. Every night. Forever. He wanted be with her always.

"I love you," he whispered against her mouth. He'd said it to her before. It had been a long time ago. A lot of years. What they had meant then was: *I love your body. I love to have sex with you. I love the pleasure that you give me.*

And now it meant… *What can I give you? How can I be there for you? How can I build my life around yours?*

Because the same two people could have the same passion, and find something more. Because the same two people could say the same words, and mean something different. Because the same two people, who had once been too young, too immature, could make a family. They could. With time. And healing. With a willingness to look at where they had gone wrong, and to change.

"I love you so much, Fia. I love you."

She cried out, her internal muscles convulsing around him. And he kissed her. On her nose, her cheeks. Her mouth.

"I love you," he said again.

She shuddered and shook, and he held her after.

And it was okay that she didn't say the words back. Because his feelings weren't tied to them.

Finally, he knew that it was love. That he wanted to give it without expectation. Without a need for a response, because it wasn't about tricking her into doing something or feeling something or being something. It was just about him loving her. And yes, he wanted to be in her bed.

Yes, he wanted.

But it wasn't a trade.

He had been hoping for the baby to hold them together. And when that had been removed, it had knocked the wind out of him. Taken the power out of what he had professed as love.

He wasn't looking for glue now. Love was enough as it was.

He fell asleep holding her. And when he woke in the gray light of dawn, Fia was gone.

FIA SAT AT the top of the hill, out by the cabin. Waiting for the sun to rise. Waiting for something to undo the oppressive darkness winding through her soul. Waiting to feel whole. He loved her.

Landry King loved her. She knew for a fact it was the last wall she couldn't demolish, the last door she couldn't beat down.

She knew for a fact that it was the thing she was afraid of.

And so she sat there, in that place where they had run underneath the stars holding hands, when they were sixteen, and thirty. When they were younger, and older. And she cried. For the girl she'd been and the woman she was, who still didn't quite know how to have all this.

How to feel it all.

She knew what she wanted. It was clear.

It was right there. And yet she had felt safer these last few weeks with a portion. It felt manageable. It felt like something the world wouldn't take away.

And just as the sun rose, there in the distance, she saw him walking up the hill. The bastard Landry King. His hat on his head, the gold lining his body. He looked like an angel. Except Landry had never been her angel.

"Hey, baby," he said. "What are you doing up here?"

"Running away," she said, wiping at tears on her cheeks.

"Why are you running from me?"

"Because it can't be real. I can't be. Because I gave you everything I had once. Just you. And if I give it all again, then what's going to be left? I don't know if I know how to love you and keep my sanity. I'm afraid. Because what's going to happen if I do something that breaks us again? And this time I was in the middle of it. It's not fair, because you've apologized to me. Over and over again, but I cannot forget what it felt like to look at you and see that you didn't love me anymore. I will never forget that, Landry. And the worst thing is that not only did I see the love leave your eyes, I couldn't even fight for it. Because I didn't think I was worth it anymore. And I fixed that. I found better for myself. I trusted myself and I believed myself. But I just…"

"What is it?" he asked. "What is it that you need, and I will give it to you. I'm listening. It matters to me."

"I know it does. I know."

"What do you need from me? I will love you with no expectations, Fia. I will never leave you. You don't have to love me back. You don't have to agree to marry me. We don't have to have sex. I just love you."

"Why?" she asked. "I don't understand why, and if I don't understand why, how the hell am I ever gonna trust that you're not going to take it away? Everyone has left me. My father left because he found another woman. My mother left because she had to go find herself. And you left me when I did the only thing that I knew to do. I have had to keep it together, to hold it together for everybody around me… But everybody leaves me."

"I am sorry. I will never forgive myself for that. Because you deserved better."

She breathed in deep, her chest feeling like there were shards of glass in it. And she knew it wasn't fair. She knew it wasn't fair. She was holding seventeen-year-old Landry to the same standards that she held her parents. The people who were supposed to parent her. And she knew what being a parent was. She knew that her parents bore the weight of this pain. Of the doubt. Because it wasn't up to Landry to be an adult when he wasn't one. They had both grown and they had both changed.

And she realized that it wasn't anger. Not anymore. It wasn't anger.

It was fear. It had always been fear. She had looked at Landry then and she had seen exactly what she wanted to see. Something unfixable. Because she had known that she was the one who had to make the break with him. That she was the one who had to break it off, so that he wouldn't. That she couldn't endure another loss. And that was all she was doing now.

She was protecting herself.

"I did what I had to. But I came back empty. In a baggy sweatshirt, with no baby and a broken heart. Because whether or not I thought it was the right thing, whether or not I knew it was the only choice, it broke something in me. And I have spent all these years working to fix it. To become whole. Knowing that a part of my heart was out there. I did a pretty good job. But I'm so scared of something breaking me again. And the minute I came back the first thing I did was break up with you. You made it so easy. Because you were cruel. And that was actually a blessing. Because then I could just hate you. For what you did to me. For what you promised me. And it let me not be heartbroken. I'm afraid. I'm afraid of what would happen to me if I lost you. If I lost this."

"I need you to trust me," he said. "Trust my love. Because it is real. And it is deep. It is the sum total of who I am as a man. I realized weeks ago life would've brought me here even if Lila hadn't come to us. She was a damned good catalyst, because damn, did it mean we had to get it together. We had to figure out how to talk to each other. How to be together. We had to. There was no other option. But I love you. If that wasn't true, the house, the family, that would be enough. But I love you like a man loves a woman. Not just as the mother of my child. I have loved you this whole time. I just wouldn't let myself. Because like you, I was freaked the fuck out. About what it would mean to want you and to not have you again." He sat down next to her on the hill. "We loved each other too early. It was too big for us. We couldn't catch up to it. It was never the love that was wrong, though. It was just the time. And maybe we would've been fine if the people around us had helped us. Had taught us anything. Had given us any support, but we were kind of just out there giving it to each other. And we didn't know what we were doing."

"The scary thing is that I still don't. I don't feel grown enough to handle all of this."

"That's why we have to go together. We've done a damn fine job of it. If you don't love me, Fia, then I'll drop this. I'll let it go. But if you do…"

"Of course I do," she said. "Landry, there's not another person for me. Not in this whole world. I just tried to tell myself that being Lila's mother was enough. That I didn't need to be yours too. I can't stay away from you. You asked what my dream was. And I didn't want to say it. It was to marry Landry King. It was to be Fia King."

"Does any part of you still want that?"

"Yes. Of course if I do that, then I'm not going to be able to pass on Sullivan's Point. Because the name is going to end…"

"Names don't matter. Be Fia Sullivan, or be Fia King. You know that's not what it takes to be family. Look at us. Family with three different names. Honoring all the places that we come from."

"The name is the least of my worries. Landry, I love you so much it could shatter me."

"But I'll never shatter you. Because love means something different to me now. Because all these years taught me something better. Because I looked at myself and I didn't like what I saw, and I decided to change it. I loved you from the beginning. But I couldn't say it to you until I was confident that I could without demanding a thing in return. Because of the way that my dad used those words to manipulate, and I…I don't want to do that. My love back then was selfish. I'm not saying that on a given day my love's not going to be a little selfish. But I hope that it's better. I hope that mostly it's about what I can give you."

"These last thirteen years were nothing," she whispered. "They were just us learning how to love each other. Better. Different."

"It was probably a good thing. To take the sex away for a while. Because we're so good at that."

She felt herself blushing. "Yes. We are very good at that."

"You had to get to know me. As the man that I am. This wasn't something we just fell into. Not like the first time. We are making choices. I choose you. The woman that you are now. The mother that you are now."

"I choose you," she whispered. "The man that you are."

"We might fight sometimes," he said. "That won't make us toxic. We might hurt each other sometimes.

But that won't mean we should quit. Anytime you feel yourself on the edge with me, I want you to look at me and tell me where I'm failing you, and I'm gonna listen."

She realized then that there were other true things that she still needed to learn. That yes, love didn't cover everything. That sometimes distance and time and growth were necessary. But also that not only could she not know for sure how things would have gone if they'd made a different choice, she also could never know for sure what the future would hold.

And all of it required trust. In who they were, and who they'd become. And in their love. To make better choices. To make the right choices, because they were loving from a place that was different than the one they'd had before.

"I love you," she said. "And I trust you. With all my past hurt. And my insecurities. And the things that still scare me. I love you. And maybe…maybe it's easy now, because we both know we're never gonna leave each other for anybody else. There's no one else. We've proven that."

He chuckled. "Well. That is true. But you know, the last thirteen years have been the making of us. We went our separate ways and we discovered something."

"What's that?"

"We can live without each other. But it's just not as good."

"No. And I would never choose to."

"Me neither." He leaned in and kissed her. "I can't love anyone but you. I just can't. It's you. And there were a lot of things about that love back then that weren't right. But it was real. And it was only you."

"Only you."

He picked her up off the hillside, and they stood in front of the cabin, where they'd built their family, for better or worse. The foundation of them, right there.

And she had so much compassion for those kids that they were. Who had wanted this, but couldn't get there.

And so much gratitude for the adults they were now. Adults who could make this life together.

Because the clearest thing right then was that they lived through that so they could arrive here. And she did agree. Even without Lila, even if it had been ten years from now. Eventually, they would reach this place. She wasn't sure about the particulars of fate. What all was meant to be, and what all was random. She knew for a fact that choices mattered. But one thing she knew for sure, beyond a shadow of a doubt, was that it wasn't so much that Landry King had worn grooves into her heart as it was that she'd been created with a heart that loved him. And nothing, not time, not pain, not separation, had ever done anything to change that. He was her one and only. She was his.

The love had always been there.

They just had to grow enough to be able to hold it.

And now that she did, she finally felt whole.

When they walked back to the farmhouse and opened up the front door, it felt like that last door had finally been beaten down.

Like there was nothing inside her separate or distant.

It had been loving Landry all along.

The final thing. The only thing.

Lila came down the stairs then. She looked at them, and at their hands.

"What's going on, guys?"

"I feel like we had a lot of parties lately," said Landry. "But what do you think about a wedding?"

Lila ran toward them both and wrapped her arms around their necks. And she felt the three of them, held together. By love. And she knew right then that everything was going to be okay. She let out a breath that she'd been holding for thirteen years.

She'd been home the whole time. But somehow, this was the first time she'd really felt it. She looked around the living room. At this house she'd painted in bright colors when her mother had left. Now Landry's boots were by the door. Lila's crocheted animals were everywhere. Sunday was chewing the stuffing out of a pillow.

They had a Christmas tree, with presents for all of them.

This was the home she'd always dreamed of. Finally, it was time. Finally, they could have it. Finally, they could have each other.

She looked at the stars they'd put there. Those stars that marked traditions in Lila's life before them, and showed their family now. The traditions they would build. The life they would have.

*Fia. Lila. Landry.*

"I love us," whispered Fia.

"Me too."

## *EPILOGUE*

As LANDRY PREPPED for his wedding with his daughter, who was also the best man, the flower girl, the ring bearer and the maid of honor, he knew a particular kind of joy that actually made him feel sorry for other people. The family might not be conventional. But he didn't regret a thing. Because how many other people could appreciate what they'd found in the way that he did? In the way that Fia did. They knew loss. And they knew love.

"You look great," said Lila.

"Thanks, kid."

They were having the wedding in the town hall barn, not at the lake, because Fia had not wanted to get married in the same place her sisters did. It was their long-awaited wedding, after all, and the whole barn was decked out beautifully. Lila had led the charge on decorations, and she had done a fantastic job.

Everybody was there already, and Lila, in her tulle skirt and tuxedo jacket, took her position with him up at the front.

And when Fia Sullivan walked through the door, dressed in a white gown, he knew for a fact that all his dreams had come true. And he was damned glad he was here to see it.

"She looks great," said Lila.

"Yes, she does."

And he didn't feel any shame in letting a tear fall down his cheek. Because he had loved this woman for so many years. She was finally going to be his.

She took his hand, and they said their vows. Though he'd said them to her over and over again in a thousand different ways over the last year.

And then it was Lila's turn to read something to them.

"'I didn't know how much I needed you both,'" she said. "'Landry, when you first came to get me at the CPS office, I was afraid that you weren't real. And when I met Fia for the first time, I couldn't believe that I was finally seeing someone who looked so much like me. I couldn't believe that this was really going to be my home. But you've done everything to build a life for me that helps remind me I can forget things. What you gave me is a miracle. And I love you both. And I would've loved you even if you didn't marry each other, but I'm pretty happy that you are. I know you've talked a lot about names and such. Because of legacy. And Fia deciding to take Landry's name made me think of a few things. You aren't abandoning your family just because you're choosing to take a new name. It's about honoring where you are now. Because it feels right to you. I want to be Lila King. Because I want to be part of this. And I want to... I want to call you Mom and Dad. Because it doesn't mean that my mom and dad didn't matter. And it doesn't mean I don't love them. But you're my family now. And you taught me that where you come from matters. We can remember it and honor it. But now is what we have. So that's what I want now.'"

He and Fia both gathered Lila into their arms and did their best to hold it together, since they had an audience.

"That sounds like a good idea, kid," he said.

"Thanks, Dad," she whispered. He was done after that. But hell, there wasn't a dry eye in the house.

When he and Fia kissed, when they were presented as a family, it really meant something.

When they went out to the bonfire to dance their first dance together, Fia leaned in and whispered in his ear. "She's pretty great."

"Yeah."

"I'm her mom. You're her dad."

"Yeah," he said. "Did you know she was going to do that?"

"She warned me. She thought that I would cry too much if she surprised me. She was okay with you crying a little bit."

He chuckled. "Yeah. Thanks, kid."

"How do you like being called 'Dad'?"

"I like it," he said. "A lot."

"That's good. Because I think you're gonna have to get used to it."

He felt stunned. "What?"

"Landry, I'm having your baby."

He couldn't dance then. He couldn't speak. He couldn't do anything but gather her up into his arms. "I love you so much, Fia King." It would never be lost on him, the ways that love had found him. Persistently. Regardless of whether or not he deserved it.

But love, he realized, was the most resilient force on the planet. Wasn't that another thing they said at church?

The greatest is love.

Well, in his life, it certainly was.

Landry King had never believed in love at first sight. He did now. He believed in love at first sight, and love after long years apart. He believed in love that gripped your soul and never let you go. He believed in love that made the foundation of what you were. Love that lasted no matter what. Through trial and tribulation. Through indignity and heartbreak. He believed that love was the most enduring force in the world.

If only you were brave enough to grab hold of it, and hold on tight.

\* \* \* \* \*